Symphony X

'Hey, babe, welcome back. Have a good break? Or should I ask, how many people did you help to have a good break?'

I hit him playfully on the arm and murmured, 'A few.'

Then Ryan dumped the news on me. Right there, with two minutes before the rehearsal started, with no time to seek revenge or to cry.

'He's got pictures of what he says is you.'

I swallowed hard. Surely it wasn't the sex club. But then, how did an estranged husband get those photos?

Other titles by the author

STRIPPED TO THE BONE

Symphony X

JASMINE STONE

BLACK
lace

Black Lace novels contain sexual fantasies.
In real life, make sure you practise safe sex.

First published in 2001 by
Black Lace
Thames Wharf Studios,
Rainville Road, London W6 9HA

Copyright © Jasmine Stone 2001

The right of Jasmine Stone to be identified as the
Author of this Work has been asserted by her in
accordance with the Copyright, Designs and Patents Act
1988.

Typeset by SetSystems Ltd, Saffron Walden, Essex
Printed and bound by Mackays of Chatham PLC

ISBN 0 352 33629 3

Prologue

Final Diary Entry:

> Music is a moral law
> It gives wings to the mind
> A soul to the universe
> Flight to the imagination
> A charm to sadness
> A life to everything
>
> > Plato

*A*nd is a great backdrop for loads of juicy sex!
Ran out of space. Can't leave this book like that.
So full of good tidings – an overflowing of joy. Oh, so
comfortably wrapped in S's throw, watching him
work on another masterpiece, made with me in mind.
Lovely. Waves are crashing outside. Fire burning,
illuminating these octagon walls. Wait! I believe I hear
the strains of violins. Wouldn't that be terrible? Thank
God S hears another instrument, one closer to the
human voice and heart.

All worth it, every single tribulation if it meant
arriving here. Btw, according to ex, D is furious, says

that I will have a happy time in court. Hopes I get my money's worth. Oh, I intend to, you creep. The anti-stalking laws are going to put your face on a poster as proof of their necessity. The blessed tour – fun while it lasted but . . . so nice to be rested safely in the arms of the most thoughtful, giving, uninhibited, scrumptious lover I've ever had. I'll always be grateful to SX for that.

New Word: cantillate.
Example: exactly what S did to my netherworld of pleasure – chanting in monotone chorus. Newly nice.

Need to call Ryan, make him jealous of last night. Yes, Ryan and I are still in touch. L R. Going to see him and his love next month (they're still together and have organised a two-man show).

Can't stop thinking about how fine, fine, fine S is. Him lowering the bottom half of my silk PJs last night, saying, 'I want to have all of you, my sweet music.' Slowly easing his tip in from behind, rubbing me with those gentle fingers, playing me like a delicate lute. He pulled out slowly and then dropped to my crotch, where he put his tongue on my clit and hummed a favourite piece of ours (you can imagine who wrote it). Singing into my crotch a new pastime SX tour uncovered (though it was acquired info I had to pass along – somethings one is not born knowing how to do). The buzzing and his fingers, the mood like a monastery disrupted by sexual riffs of an electric guitar. Those are the buzzes which set my clit spiral-ling about my brain. That perfect half-demonic, purely Slavic chant set my hair tingling. S hummed louder, vibrating my clit until the music, his tongue, massaged themselves deep inside. When I began coming, S pulled his fingers out and substituted his cock, with-

2

out missing a beat. Still singing. Ornamented minor key melodies flitted about our stone walls. So ritualistic and tribal, feeling like a deeply repressed fantasy from another life with S seducing my primordial genes. Filled and continuing to come to a beat started in the ancient past. It's as if we've always been lovers and I don't mean in that monotonous Saturday-morning-obligation-sex way. S is in perfect sync with my being – his breath my breath, his thrusts mine. I yearn to cup, caress and hold him. Never tire of hearing my name on his lips and seeing his love and devotion for me in those fantastic green eyes. When he gazes upon me and penetrates my very soul, I feel all time fall away and I see that we were destined to be. Sappy to write but so happily consuming to live.

Who could have imagined this pleasure six months ago? Even after all those orgasms (thanks SX!!) – I never thought they'd be permanent. Never thought they'd be there for the asking, anytime, anywhere. That they'd be mine. And S is mine, mine, mine!

Out of room. Don't take this as any indication of a lack of trust but ... this book is being safely tucked away because, as I learned, you can never be too careful.

THE END

Chapter One

New Word: tonsured
Definition: the opposite of untonsured.
Example: if my cunt were tonsured, perhaps D
would find it more inviting.

Oh, who am I kidding? Better resign myself to
having a boring sex life. This honeymoon is *way*
over. Just need to learn to cool passions. Get used to
the wake-up ho-hum of routine and the occasional
extra-glass-of-wine frolic. Decided to improve vocab-
ulary instead of stewing over loss of romance. Everyone goes through this – why did I think we'd be
special? Does seem our cooling of romance, though,
started a few months after the marriage. Doesn't
seem normal. I'm a vibrant, sexual creature brimming
with needs – not sure even know what they are but I
know it can't be this. Daniel can't be happy with
things the way they are either. Oh, if only I could
make him touch me like he used to – just do it more
slowly and for longer. Perhaps it's our age difference

5

– I'm growing into my sexuality and D is declining from his.

Or mine, more likely. God! Have turned into a sexual cripple unable to articulate – to be other than this passive mouse in our monthly sack meeting. Not even turned on by cheese. But I am alive inside – Daniel, know this. I'm alive. It does not have to be like this, of that I'm certain.

Oh, take this day and change it, Katie. But how? And who? Me or him?

Btw, if our house were not so untonsured, perhaps I could locate my old diary. I feel a bit out of sorts starting a new one when the old was only half full. Or half empty.

Or I have half a life for thinking things like that. Katie, wake up. You need a life.

Am starting *Ulysses*, which I believe will do something for my soul. It's hard to read anyway and that should at least feed the mind, which has gone numb from playing with the petunias and wondering what's happened to my career, my sexuality, my life! Would've never used hands like I'm using them now had I made a different decision. Can it really be true that I've confined my life to digging in dirt and my raptures to witnessing little shoots finally take hold?

April 5

New Word: osteoid.
Why: I like that it rhymes with haemorrhoid and asteroid, toyed and deployed, Freud!
Example: when I look into D's eyes lately, their osteoid presence bores into my soul and I feel like the one turning to bone.

Lately, Daniel has been making me feel hard and not in a pretty way but more like I'm OD-ing on calcium tablets. He muddles my mind somehow so I never feel that I say what I mean. Think a better vocab might help – I mean, he uses lawyerly words I don't know all the time and then baits me to ask what they mean. I don't ask – seems a sign of weakness. And I do *not* instinctively desire to be weak around D.

Does love have to be this difficult? I long, long, long for a new beginning. What went wrong? Difficult to imagine this is all my fault, the way D tries to paint our lacklustre love life. How I do nothing for him, especially give head at five in the morning. 'I haven't had morning head since our first year together,' he screams at me.

'Perhaps if I got morning head, you'd be getting some too,' I think but never say. He still gets it in the afternoon but things are hollow now. Want to say, 'I've never had morning head from you or afternoon head or even evening head without begging and pleading and then you pretend to be doing me a great favour. Rodent!'

You want the truth, D? I don't come *because of you*. That's all. I'm not a body with convenient buttons that you push and bingo – you've got a writhing wife. I need affection, attention, involvement, warmth, creativity – in short, passions and feeling. When was the last time you really cared about anything I did?

April 13

Days upon days of fighting and now the truth. Horrid, fuck-me truth.

Blinding eye of mad wolf, searing anger, seething, writhing, smashing, bludgeoning, cannot see in front of me, furious. Tired of pounding pillow, grinding up wedding vases in garbage disposal, kicking the wall until toe bleeds. Tired, angry, tired, tired!

Well, finally caught him. In bed with something that resembled half spider, half woman. Daniel thought he was so smart, too sneaky for me to ever notice. Guess I *am* a dunce. Clues everywhere and me buying the excuses: 'Honey, this case is making me work extra hours'; 'Honey, one of my colleagues grazed my collar with lipstick when she greeted me'; 'Honey, I've got to take a shower right away, *because love juice is clinging all over my scrotum.*'

To future biographers: you may notice some time lagging between this book and the previous one – if you ever find my previous journal. Goddamn Daniel stole it. Suppose hoping to find that *I* had had an affair to justify *his* own adultery. Said, 'It just fell open and there was my name.' Didn't know Daniel was able to read my handwriting – or that he really does possess an interest in things I do, unless they involve making him dinner. The D-rat burrowed diary away in his office – should introduce ferrets and moles there. They'd thrive. No, wait, they might be confused that a bigger one of their kind was taking up more than his allotted space.

Just have to accept it's gone. Looked everywhere. Damn D, damn D! Missing diary pissing me off more than D's affair. Like he took my arm or something and is going to slap me in the face with it later.

Surprised I'm still writing? Like living in a bad neighbourhood, got used to it, I suppose. Can't live without it really. I've got few people to talk to. And too much going on inside, proving April is the cruellest month. Two days before taxes and Daniel says, 'I want you to move out.' I said, in a few more words, 'Why me?' He hates me, he moves out. But money (his money – I'm flat broke) wins once again. The same old argument, same old guilt – damn, he's good

– even works when I am seeing red, Serbian-angry, ready-to-kill mode. (I agree with Grandad – don't get a Serb mad ... he should know, Mr Gun-for-Hire.) Die, Daniel, die, die, Daniel die, die, Daniel, die. (Note to investigators: if Daniel Ungerbedorfen is actually dead shortly after this entry, I didn't do it. It's just a matter of speech, you fucking legal heads!)

Note to myself: never marry an attorney again. The horror, the horror (the tedium, the tedium) – did we ever once get to the bottom of anything except his skilful debating? Sci-fi fans: the truth is *not* out there – it's within ourselves ... sort of. For me, a normal human being, truth is a question begging an open mind and a long perspective. For Daniel, who is not a normal nor decent form of protoplasm, it lies in a list of points which are black/white and non-negotiable.

Daniel's Argument 356 (I know there is little difference from 298 – but notice the subtleties. The goddamn is in the details):

1. He found me on stage and brought me home.
2. He bought me that $20,000 viola.
3. He has supported me throughout my musical career.
4. He pays for everything in the house – even my goddamn phone bill.
5. I'm a goddamn, lousy, no good cook.
6. I don't play enough (implied *well* enough) to warrant a $20,000 viola.
7. I don't appreciate a goddamn thing he's ever done for me.

Ah – and now, Katie, would you care for your five seconds of a screaming rebuttal to, 'When did you stop beating your husband and stealing his money?'
Ready, set, go!

1. I paid for that viola with the money I got from my grandmother.
2. OK, he paid for the viola but I had paid for his grad school with that money.
3. I thought he was paying me back – I don't owe anybody anything.
4. My musical career is only allowed a 30-mile radius in upperstate New York – thanks to hubby's untrusting and non-understanding attitude about what musicians need (good orchestras, other good musicians) ... and thanks a lot for the insipid gigs with farmers' wives caking up the stage with mud on their black boots.
4a. I don't care if he does pay for everything in the house – he earns over $300,000 a year. So pay!
5. That's what restaurants are for.
6. He doesn't even know the difference between a viola and a violin, so how dare he judge me? I was subbing in the New York Phil when he met me. Asked if he could carry my cello.
7. True, now that I found Spiderwoman in our queen-sized bed. Amazing how certain incidents can colour our version of the past forever.

Isn't it tedious? I'm tired of it all. Long and short, I'm crashing at Polly's, trying to figure out the next course of action. Mr Tax Attorney has supposedly filed our taxes but yesterday, as I was packing up, he says, 'Would you mind signing this? I didn't get a chance to file yet.'

It was a blank tax form. He just must think I am stupid, stupid, stupid. Today, I left a blank divorce form at his office with a sticky yellow note which read, 'Sign here.' Let's see how that goes over. Meanwhile, I've filed the legally separated papers. I'm doing my own taxes and hoping he forges my signature so I can have a field day in the fraudulent court. (Is there such a division or am I just being redundant?)

Yes, OK, damn it. I do have tears in my eyes. This was my first marriage, you know. Six years. Now I'm all used up. He took everything from me and then spat it out. How could he have an affair with me around? Me, Katie, wonder violist. Despite that Daniel has tried to convince me otherwise: I'm not boring, I'm not predictable, I'm not ugly or even the slightest overweight.

Which proves I'm too good for that son of a bitch.

I've got to get a job and fast. Feeling uncertain that I can still play said viola. Haven't spent much time on the finger chops (unless beating the pillow over D's affair counts). Spent all free time 'working' on marriage with Daniel and planting petunias – what a lousy investment that proved to be.

April 27

Would you believe it! Polly knows someone who knows someone. I'm touring with Symphony X. Actually, the real name is Xevertes but who the hell could pronounce that? Turns out Jason, my old stand partner from the Yard days, used to play principal. He won't be on tour though. Won assistant principal in Houston. Damn.

I have always wanted to sleep with him. Or somebody like him, or, well, anyone really. Well . . . I need to sleep with someone again fast to erase Daniel's touch. Why did I mistake alcohol, cigarettes and swaggering for experience? I married too young. Daniel, eight years older, just smelled like he would be successful, so I married him. Smelled like he would be good in bed. I should have slept with more people before marrying – or even during marriage. I know in my heart of hearts there is more to sex than pools of sperm flowing out on to my thighs. More to love than a lonely young woman masturbating herself to sleep, wishing the hand on her mound weren't her own but attached to the husband in her bed. Then thinking: *Well, he wouldn't get it right anyway.*

Wish *that* had been in the diary Daniel confiscated. All I remember writing is how my entire career was slipping away and how Daniel didn't love me. How I needed him to love me. How I wished he understood our age difference better. How I wished he cared more about the dishes in the sink. Blah blah blah.

Humiliating. Afraid I was writing then too about sexual desires – how I needed him to be tender, gentle, to take his time, to look into my eyes. In short – to love me! What could I do to make him know that I needed him to look at me, see me, and love me!

Pitiful.

May 5

D phoned. Wants me back. Says it was all a big mistake. He's finished reading my diary (oh, if you could see my face now – bastard) and he understands me better. Understands *my* problem. *My* needs. Understands how he made a terrible mistake (got that right – don't take my diary and don't take comic-book woman into my sheets). D wants me to come home. He'll be more loving from now on, more concerned with my needs. Faithful. Attentive. Gentle. Etc. Excuse me while I wretch. Wish D were nearby . . . on his nice pink silk shirt and favourite paisley tie is where I'd aim. Come closer, Daniel. I've got something to tell you. Bleeeuch!! (Barfing ensues.)

No indication at all that taking my diary, reading my diary, *keeping* my diary was wrong. It'll all work out in that attorney head of his. Possession is nine-tenths or something. Want to put the diary in a blender and make him eat my words. Did I say 'bastard' already?

Later . . .

Daniel stopped by Polly's dressed in his attorney power-suit. I'm a sucker. I actually kissed him. Said I'd think about things. When I don't hate him, he's cute. Knows how to dress those broad shoulders and tight ass. Downright handsome with that jawline that commands people to obey him. Get a grip, Katie. And not on him. He's a habit, not a love. Hard to undo body saying that it's used to D. I even think my body still wants him. Why? you ask. My body is an idiot!

Damn, the devil is in the confusion. Don't go back, Katie. He can't change. Remember the bed? The arguments? The tedious arguments full of malicious intent? Ms Tarantula? He wants to break you. Eight years at the quarry and he still keeps hammering away. In bed and out. It's not to love you but to break you. Takes your most intimate things – viola, diary, sex – to use against you. As if your pleasure were a commodity he could trade if he didn't experience too much of it first-hand – or know of second-hand. Like he could give me a little pleasure here and there and that entitled him to seek his own pleasure somewhere else. A pleasure debt.

To be fair, D could be sweet. Maybe some of this is my fault. The dupe believes he's given me lots of orgasms, poor thing. I've been the one lying. Only two in six years. Ouch, to actually write it. Ouch, ouch, ouch. And then I was stoned both times. He was too. Helped get the panic out of his touch and made me feel I could ask for anything. Maybe I still could. If only, if only, if only . . .

Yeah, if only he were someone else. Can't teach an old dog new tricks. I'm sure I gave him pleasure but did he ever know my body? Did I ever let him? Did he ever want to know it? Seems that leggy thing was pleased. Daniel said, upon discovery, 'Oh, didn't know you'd be home so soon.'

That was it. No it's-not-what-it-appears-to-be excuse, no 'Forgive me for my one transgression'. Just, 'Oops'.

Why didn't you just get stoned more often? you ask. Daniel didn't like it. Said it was too risky. Implied I had a drug problem for even wanting more. Seemed to think I got enough satisfying sex as it was. Want to drop rock quarry on D's beautiful, Apollo head. Wish he were ugly so I'd have not an ounce of regret. Wish he were poor or emotional or something so that my leaving him would hurt. He's still proposing our reunion like it were some business deal waiting for my signature. He'd have better luck if he cried.

But sharks can't, can they?

Chapter Two

I'm going. Got the letter today. I'm last stand, last chair and I don't recognise a single person on the roster but I'm going.

Symph X tour music doesn't look too difficult, and the headlining act's intriguing: Angelika, the drag queen, and Kristine, a dominatrix diva. Add a Renaissance guitarist named Salvadore and the world's lowest bass, Serik. I've heard of him. Polly says he is affectionately referred to as 'the three-legger'. (She says if you hug him while he speaks, it justifies the other name: the Human Vibrator.)

The group call themselves A Mission Impossible, and are known for staging semi-impromptu musical immorality plays. Interesting how Symph X landed the gig playing for them. Polly says that all are a rather motley crew and I'd best leave those connections to the concert organisers and promoters. It's supposed to be a big hit. They've got Europe booked and have the possibility of extending the tour if things go well. I checked the box that said I would be interested in continuing the tour if it went beyond the allotted time. Why not run away indefinitely?

Polly is a real pal. I am so lucky to have such a friend. I've known her since music camp days – though she's now happily married with two kids and has hung up her cello for good. I find that disappointing but it's not my life. And, truth be told, she wasn't ever cutting edges with her G-string. But . . . relief to be out from under Polly's roof just because I feel like such a loser. I should be staying with Rick, who never seems to have any relationship work out. Staying with a happily married couple while you yourself are filing for divorce – well, it's like an atheist offering wafers and wine to the Mormons knocking on the door.

June 12

I'm on the airplane. Packed one big black bag, brought viola. Problems + Distance = Profound Relief.

Love that first feeling when the plane leaves the ground and I think again how great mankind is to have accomplished that. Fly closer to the sun. Freedom, freedom. Plus, it seems to pull clit down with G-force. Nice, if you squirm the right way.

Freedom. Or is it disaster, disaster? Anyway, it is exciting, to say the least. And better than sitting around my old home in a comfort-zone flannel nightgown dreaming about putting all that practising to use. Come to think of it, what did I use to do all day? No wonder Daniel thought me useless.

Stop it. Remember . . . distance.

Symph X's tour plan is to fly from New York to Germany, play a few concerts to the fringe crowds there, then proceed south playing in France, Spain, Italy, and perhaps beyond. Eavesdropping on the other musicians, seems they have heard those 'perhapses' before and don't bank on the tour lasting more than a few months. Sounds like we're picking up Cirque de Soleil's leftovers.

We're on the way to Germany now. Besides an annoying oboe player I've seen in Albany, I don't recognise a single face. That's good. I can pretend I'm not married, though the white is still showing on my ring finger. The ring is safely sequestered at Polly's. Wondering if I should keep it. Could probably buy two really good Hill bows for it. Always thought it gaudy, the ring. One of those huge, 'I'm so successful my wife gets this' diamonds in platinum setting. I know, I know. Earlier entries are about its praise. It's a bit like a mistaken belief in the gold standard. We give value to what we deem valuable, right? Thought it a representation of Daniel's love. Unfortunately, it was. Ostentatious and a big interference with playing the viola.

Funny, though. It's off and I feel naked and vulnerable. Why do I feel less sexy now that I am on the path towards divorce? I bet it's the uncertainty. I don't know if I'm still good at IT. I've got to sleep with someone soon just to get some confidence back. I do not want Daniel's to be the last hands I remember on my body. Don't want to think of Daniel trying to tell me I was not good enough for him in bed. Miles and miles between us and now I finally understand: I hate him!

Not to change subject, but did I mention that *Ulysses* is my travelling companion? I've been trying for five years to finish it. This tour will be perfect if I have nice, comforting sex, learn to play the viola again and finish Joyce. James Joyce – though God knows, I'm in the mood to try anything.

17

Later . . .

Must've dozed off over Iceland. Woke to large hairy hand shaking my shoulder.

'Katie, do you want your dinner?'

Groggily, I stared into the sweetest green eyes I thought I'd ever seen. God, am I horny? Not sure I responded to the dinner question but a plate of some nearly edible goodies was placed in front of me. Felt uneasy talking to Green Eyes, since teeth felt as if they'd grown fur. Politely covered my mouth and said, 'I'm sorry. I forgot your name.'

'Dave. Went to high school with you.'

Ran the name and the face past the memory banks that were struggling to awaken. Turned up nothing.

Dave continued. 'Played trumpet in the orchestra. Had a crush on you and used to tape your hair to the front of my stand.' Seeing me frown, he added, 'Your loose hair. Ones that had fallen out.'

Then the ball fell into its roulette wheel. Dave, the creep who made me never want to come to orchestra class because he used to blow his trumpet in my ear, pull my hair and generally try to touch me in uncomfortable ways. Plus, he was a pimply, geeky, social dumb-ass who would never have been thoughtful enough to get a dinner for a lady. Must be another Dave.

'Tell me you're not Dave Muller,' said I with hand over mouth, certain now that the bad breath of sleep was out and about. What happens when we drift off into dreamland – I mean, does our body just start decaying?

'Yeah, that's me. Listen, always hoped to meet up with you and apologise for my insanity.'

I started to warm to the new Dave. I like a man who can admit he's done wrong. Even might like Daniel again, if he could admit it without ulterior motives.

Dave is cute, with a shock of black hair falling over a chiselled, mischievous face. Hard to believe so much could happen in ten years to change a rejection into an acceptance. Maybe he'll be the first guy . . .

I know most musicians view tours as a sure way to get laid. That's why Daniel was dead set against them. For me, anyway. Probably knew from first-hand business trips the likelihood of the faithful. Very few married, with or without children, stay that way, and those with girlfriends or boyfriends are out of their knickers in no time and into a hotel bed with the first available 'willing and able' – referred to henceforth as 'WAA'. Even female tuba players have someone to shack up with as the many bodies trade places.

Anyway, I said to him (with turtleneck pulled up quite high over mouth) 'You know, Dave, I'd nearly forgotten it. God, you were a dumb prick in high school.'

The guy actually asked to sit down next to me – which gave me a bit of a panic. I pulled legs up on to chair rather than stand up because – well, clothing is uncomfortable. I couldn't remember if my pants were on under the blanket I'd thrown over me. They weren't. Jeans had been rubbing the little one between my legs and it had grown a bit raw. Not used to clothing staying on more than eight hours.

Wasn't the jeans that gave a shock.

'Ow!' said Dave as he sat down. He pulled a bra out from between the seat cushions.

Shit, shit, shit. Vaguely remembered wiggling out of it just before nodding off. Too much wine.

Dave – fatal error, Dave – looked directly at my boobs. 'Nice.'

Cleared up one thing: he is still a creep.

Crossed my arms over chest and breathed a cloud into his face, saying 'So, don't mind me while I eat.' He did seem to lean back a bit. Appears that I'd gotten

19

that peculiar smell in the mouth dogs have after they've eaten a piece of roadkill. Not pretty.

The entrée looked all right. Something vegetarian, which I'd requested. I'm not a vegetarian but learned from Daniel that one nearly always eats better food on planes if you say you are. God, just like Daniel to lie to gain an advantage. Oh well. Sometimes he did things right – I mean, do people lie for other reasons? What was absolutely missing was a stiff drink.

Thought best to make new friend work – give time to wriggle back into pants. 'David, dear, do be a good boy and get me some booze.'

'Like . . .?' was his reply from the far corner of the seat. He nearly sprawled into the tray of the man two seats over.

'It's a test,' said I. 'Let's see what you've learned since high school and Boone's Farm Apple Wine.'

And then – shudder, shudder – I involuntarily winked. Daniel is not right. I do *not* flirt with every man I meet. I'm just friendly. And fuck those lesbian friends of mine who say that I flirt with everyone, including their partners.

Reading that, I can say it didn't come out right. I'm not, you know, though if all men disappeared, or if just Daniel disappeared or if some really nice – no, anyway, I'm not. Not that I'm aware of. Have some very cute female friends but, well, I'm pretty sure I'm not. You know what I mean. Just wanted to get that clear.

Dammit! If I don't watch out, Dave's going to be the bane around my neck. Or is that the bone of my existence? Anyway, I'll finish the story but you do have to be careful who or whom you sleep with. It could be that I'll be spending the entire latter half of the tour trying to throw off those I cohorted with the first half of the tour. So tawdry. Reminds me of high school.

Unfortunately, something about men makes me seek their approval. I should drop them once I get it. Wouldn't have been married to Daniel. Oh, who'll ever really know why it didn't work out? 'It's not you, honey, it's me.' Isn't that the standard line used in confusion? Well, want to say to Daniel something with more reverb, like 'No, honey. It's you. And, remember how, when your parents divorced and they told you it wasn't your fault? They were lying!! Remember all that great sex? I was faking it!'

Evil laugh – ha ha ha!

Now, what is wrong with a lifetime of one- and two-night stands? My unpleasant marriage might never have happened had I formed the habit of sleeping and dropping.

Anyway ... ate food quickly, barely tasting it. Nothing plastic or rancid and that's enough for me with airplane food. Good to know where to lower expectations so one won't get frustrated. For yours truly, it's good to always add two or three hours to when they say we'll arrive and treat things running on time as a special miracle to be taken advantage of. Back in the Yard days, Jason had always been amazed at how many massages or swims I got in before a rehearsal. I know how to maximise stolen time – or things simply running on schedule. At least once I'm out from under the House God.

So, Dave returns with a bottle of white wine and a gin and tonic. For some reason unbeknownst to my conscious state, the camera around his neck gave me the creeps.

Thanked him for the service, drank both and then fell asleep in the middle of his telling of the second year after high school.

June 14(?)

New Word: jejune
Example: I feel as jejune as a corroded penny and
absolutely disorientated.

Where am I? When is it? What is happening? Give up
control, Katie. It'll be all right. Those earlier tours
worked out all right – ten years ago and counting –
because I didn't have an agenda. Good to remember.

Shoved bra back on under airplane blanket (no
mean feat) then jostled with everyone else to catch a
glimpse of the little man with the red cap: our tour co-
ordinator. Forgot his name – better learn it soon.

He went off the plane really fast without seeming to
care if we followed or not. Can't you hear it now?
'Sorry, Maestro. Lost them in Munich.' 'Oh – the pity,'
says Maestro. 'Well, we'll just pick up another ad hoc
from the farmlands.'

Easy come, easy go. They could you know ...
should see the music. Aunt Bertha the accordion
player could snooze through the viola part on these.
We've been assured, though, that this is only the
preliminary music. When the composer hears how we
sound, he'll write something different.

Bizarre, *n'est pas*?

Then, there was Dave again, willing to help me.
Took a picture. 'Recording the first day of trip.' I'm
surprised I didn't break the camera. Seven hours plus
gave my curly blonde a special left-side mat look. And
the Milky Way decided to make itself seen in a zit
cluster on my forehead. Well, the good thing about
oily skin is I do look younger than my 31 years. Like I
still get carded. Like some of the 19-year-olds on the
tour seem to be eyeing me.

Wish they weren't laughing.

Dave introduces me to Slava. Slava and I pose as Dave videotapes us. Then Slava takes a picture of me and Dave. What is going on here? In our seventies, do we pull out all the old pictures and videos and finally enjoy all those moments we lost while posing and filming?

I'm not sure I hate the idea. At least I could edit. 'Why does the tall man in the attorney power-suit have a big condom over his head?' might be a topic at the nightly drool hall in the nursing home.

Anyway, greasy-headed Slava likes to hold his drumsticks. A lot. Wouldn't shake hands because he had to keep his hand on those sticks – nearly poked my eye out in the picture moments. And Slava's main way of expressing himself seems to be through mangled proverbs. For example, 'Up with this I will not put' referred to, I think, the waiting in the airplane terminal.

Dave left us, moving backwards with camcorder in hand, saying, 'Wave bye-bye.' He thought he'd go see why we were all waiting in line. Thought we should have some diplomatic pass. What an idiot. Usually, musicians get the drug-sniffing dogs treatment. Since when are we diplomats? Except Rastafarison – and he's such a womaniser it seems unfair he be allowed to wander the world with cello in hand playing on broken-up walls and against warring tribes. You know, there are a good many women who would sue his ass had they been in the right country at the right time. No woman appreciates having her boobs groped by a stranger in public, never mind how famous he is. And no girl appreciates being told that sleeping with her cello teacher will make her a better player. Polly experienced his 'charm' in a masterclass. No, she didn't succumb or suck come or whatever. Jerk. Him.

Maybe Rasta and Daniel should hang out together.

Slava said, 'Dave thinks all life is a movie. But, a

23

friend in need is friend indeed! Your famous saying, no?'

I replied, 'Yes. Well, it's something like that. Where are you from, Slava?'

'I, me –' he gestured emphatically at his chest with the drumsticks, 'I from a place. Maybe you know? It's called –'

Just then a male voice shouted over the PA system for all those with hearing to do something. Tried to listen with fingers in ears but then understood it was in German. Suddenly the red cap was bobbing up and down and then moving forward. I left Slava and hurried after it. Just in time to see viola loaded on to a cart with other instruments on top. Heart stopped. I did have insurance, right? But Daniel had possession of the policy. In a panic, I grabbed my viola off the cart, telling Red Cap I was sorry.

He seemed relieved not to be responsible for one more instrument. I mean, in general he seemed relieved whenever he had to do less. Slava caught up, sort of, and said, 'Time to follow our fearful leader, Katie.'

Thought it best to ditch Slava in a way to avoid Dave – who was fast becoming an unwanted new best friend.

The bus arrangements are spacious and courteous, each taking a maximum of seventeen players. Magnificent. Heard from Jason that last year's Symph X tour forced the entire orchestra on to one large school bus. There was nearly a riot after the beer party and no bathroom.

These 'coaches' have refrigerators, showers, bathrooms, sleeping quarters, a living room, TV, stereo and other homey stuff, which made me relax considerably. Thought it best to get on quickly and hide before Dave found out where I was and sat himself next to me for the remainder of the tour. That really could be the worst of it. A stand partner you could not stand and annoying people travelling with you that made time move backwards. Not that I'm entirely against Dave but am entirely convinced he doesn't carry enough weight to spend hours away from *Ulysses*.

It worked! I'm writing right now from the top bunk where I stashed myself earlier behind a flimsy curtain. None of the voices boarding were Dave's. Bus engine is now going and I'm going to poke head out.

Yikes! Heart did one of those pancake flip-flops. Saw a whip, a guitar in the corner, and several wigs scattered about like ashtrays. I'm on A Mission Impossible's bus. Thought they were travelling separately. Usually, the main performers are less talented but more egotistic than their fellow musicians in the pit. Hence, it is an unwritten, sometimes written code that the twain shall never meet. Had an idea just to hide away in that top bunk and finish Joyce by the end of the tour. James Joyce.

Later . . .

Bus door opened and I went into hyperstealth mode. Sucked in air but afraid to let it out. Must have gained 10 pounds in oxygen.

'One of you men, undo me, will you?' said a sweet female voice.

'Oh, we'd all like to see you come undone, doll,' replied a very low male voice. The Human Vibrator?

'I think Salvadore should do it. He's got those amazing hands,' said the female voice. I made mental note to investigate Salvadore's hands.

'I'm sorry. I can't. I'm not risking my nails on a bustier,' said a rich, melodic male voice.

'Come here. I'll do it. I've had much more experience than any of you lowlifes,' said another male voice, giggling.

I debated if I should announce myself up front and give them the opportunity to kick me off, or should I chance it and wait to be discovered? Opted for the latter, enjoying being the fly in the bunk overhearing the conversations of the stage gods.

'Oh, yes. Free at last, free at last. Thank God Almighty, I'm free at last.' The female voice, which must have belonged to the dominatrix diva, sounded fuller. Bustier must be a regular pain in the boobs and a major source of the diva's breathiness.

'Your people were set free a long time ago. What about my people?' It was the last male voice. Probably Angelika, or her male counterpart. But he wasn't black. Must have been an inside joke.

A laugh that sounded like a very excited cow shook the entire coach. Then the unmistakable voice of the three-legged vibrator began singing. 'Old Man Tour, he just keeps touring, he just keeps plodding along.' My bunk mattress vibrated with every note. Man, someone could get off just on the guy's reverberations.

In came the soprano. 'Old Man Liver, he just keeps giving, he just keeps pushing us out along.'

A guitar started. Was this improvisation? Orchestra people wouldn't or couldn't do this. I was dying, trying to record it all.

The voice – Salvadore's, I discovered – began singing along to his guitar-playing. He was doing a great fake tenor voice. 'Old Man Diesel, he just keeps fuming, he just keeps farting along.'

The guitar stopped. 'I don't think I can take the smell anymore.'

'What smell?' asked Angelika.

'You don't smell the fumes?' asked Salvadore.

'It's John's hairspray,' said the dominatrix diva. 'I told you to not go aerosol. You'll kill all of us.'

The bus pulled away and off we went. *Sans* Dave! Yippee! I decided to wait a few minutes and then pretend to wake up startled. Wanted the gang of four to think I'd gotten on the wrong bus, which was partly true. Nobody had said it was off limits but I was feeling I'd clearly violated the unspoken code of separation of the pit from the stars.

Yawned and let arm slip out from under the bunk's curtain. Then pulled arm back in and yanked the curtains open.

'Where am I?' I tried to ask in what I hoped was a sincerely surprised tone.

'Hey, guys, look. A stowaway,' said Angelika, who now looked just like your average handsome Italian stud. He giggled.

'No, I'm a violist.' Can you believe I said that? Kept waiting for the onslaught of viola jokes I unintentionally let myself in for. Nothing. These guys were truly not orchestra musicians. Thank God!

Salvadore, a white-haired man with beautiful and unusually wide-set green eyes, stared at me and asked, 'Isn't there a web page with viola jokes?'

Serik (equally cute – perfect olive skin, big black moustache) said, 'Just a minute. I'll see if I can call it up.' He was already seated, typing away furiously at a laptop. 'Yep. Here it is. First one: what's the difference between a violin and a viola?'

Well, you know the drill. Replied, 'Viola burns longer.'

'Ah, very good,' replied Serik. 'So you *are* a violist.'

'I think she's cute. Let's keep her,' replied Angelika. 'What's your name?'

Told them. Asked if I could stay.

'Sure,' said the dominatrix, who didn't look very scary now in sweats and a turtleneck. Her skin was still as white as snow, hair black as ebony and lips red as rubies. Were the rest on board her dwarves? 'My name is Kristine. I need the female company. John/

Angelika tries the best he can but, well . . .' She arched her left eyebrow.

They laughed.

Serik, still at the computer, asked, 'But why does the viola burn longer?'

'Because it's still in the case.' Smart one – I.

'She's good,' said Serik.

Told them, 'You're only on page one. The real difference between a violin and a viola is that a viola holds more beer.'

The entire company was now seated around the table where Serik had set up the laptop. Drinks were offered, accepted and I began to feel quite comfortable with this crowd.

Another impromptu song broke out between the soprano, Kristine, and the guitarist, Salvadore. It had a Mexican theme since the entire crew had switched to tequila, supplied by Serik (who swore he almost exclusively drank wine). Soprano swore that she wanted a *burrito con queso, por favor* while Salvadore swore that all he had was Hyundais. An attempted Flamenco dance ensued with Serik and John/Angelika on the table. They kept from falling down with all the swerves the bus was taking by keeping their hands up on the ceiling. Unfortunately, the table broke around the third chorus.

'Ms Katie Stowaway, you can't tell anyone,' said Serik, his waxed moustache going up and his brow going down.

Everyone looked at me, realising, I guess, that I was the only unconfirmed secret-keeper. Swore on my mother's dead cat that I wouldn't tell.

'That seals it,' said John. 'She stays with us.'

So, now I'm resting in the bunk, writing it all down. Gang thinks I'm recovering from jet-lag. Know I should sleep but this is too perfect. Me with the stars. Not a bad escape.

Bus stopped shortly after last entry and I limped to hotel room. The corner of the table had slammed down on my foot.

It's been a long time but, after a long plane and then bus ride, good to be in a German hotel. Remember it from the conservatory days when we toured. Everything so clean, efficient and orderly. Love French rooms even more because they aren't. But late at night, a German room is much better. No need to think about where the light switch might be and all that.

Stripped off jeans, T-shirt and tennis shoes, and stood in front of the mirror. Not a bad body. Butt round, breasts small but normal. Short dirty-blonde hair makes my neck look long. Nothing extraneous about me, if I'm beautiful, in a no-nonsense way. Squeezed breasts together, trying to imagine them in a bustier.

Got excited imagining I had an alter ego. Like the one Kristine has. Leather, sunglasses, high-heels – throwing pouty kisses to all the admirers. That's what she was doing when we boarded the plane.

Yawn. No more fantasies for now. About to call it a night. Itinerary on the pillow, strategically placed so that no one can say tomorrow, 'I didn't get it.'

Rehearsal at 10. Bus picks us up at 9:30. Another rehearsal at 2. Then dinner and an evening rehearsal?! Isn't that against union rules? Three rehearsals? The wind players are going to be furious if their music is at all demanding. Usually with these pop shows, the brass has to blast out at least one number to pep up the act.

Oh well, it's beginning. Seems I've been here before. The complaints, the tiredness from too much booze and/or screwing, the relentless music, the hurry up and waits, the three-quarters of an idea being executed: in short, an orchestra tour. Remember to just follow the schedule, give up having your own plans or ideas for excellence and everything will be fine.

Much the same as playing in an orchestra. Too many frustrated soloists always sorry they didn't make it to the big time – either losing a few competitions or never entering them or having the wrong agent. The result's the same: prima donnas with no work. So they audition and win an orchestra seat and then spend the rest of life complaining how unfair it is that so-and-so famous musician is where he is today.

Never wanted to be a soloist. Just love the huge sound of the orchestra around me. Daniel thinks I'm lacking ambition. He never got it. Not that he really understood what it would've taken to be a star. (Lots of time away from him, coachings, recitals, practising! – and it's lonely.) When an orchestra plays together and really makes music, it's better than sex. Much better than sex with Daniel. Maybe he's good at the tarantella. But playing in an orchestra can be like sex with eighty-five people all at once with the sound pulsing through you. The ecstasy of synergy is sublime. One Brahms Four Symphony performance a few years ago had brought me to the brink of an orgasm onstage, so sweet and intense was the passion and the overwhelming mixture of melodies and harmonies. All of the players seemed to be breathing together, gasping towards the last climactic moment of the piece as if they would die in bliss when they reached it.

But ... more often than not, it leans closer to the Fellini film where the orchestra is really just collected chaos with everyone and his own petty needs ruining the greater whole. Pray the tour won't be like that.

Later . . .

Can't sleep. Have decided to do the old masturbating trick which always helps me sleep afterwards. Going to focus on green eyes: Dave's and Salvadore's. Ooo, and Serik's moustache. How many women has that tickled? Have to try them all. Why not?

Chapter Three

June 17

Ryan is my stand partner. Like Ryan. He said immediately upon our meeting, 'I'm not too awake today. I met a fireman in the lobby and had a long night – if you know what I mean.'

Rest of violas look like a cross-section of liposuction and hair implants. Pretty, pretty, all too pretty. Hope they're nice but don't expect it. Girl with the well-hennaed hair and nose-ring turned around and smiled, mouthing, 'I know you.'

No clue what that was about.

After tuning up, concert organiser got on the podium. A short man who looked like an ex-flyweight boxer. Red baseball cap was still perched on his head.

'Everyone, I just wanted to introduce myself. I'm Leo. Don't complain to the conductor, to your section leader, to the hotel, to the bus driver. Come to me with your problems, OK?'

Ryan leaned over and said, 'He's such a moron. Complain to me if you have problems. I know how to get free air miles, free room service, free food.' Glancing at me sideways, he added in a false whisper, 'Plus, he has the world's smallest . . .'

Wanted to laugh but knew better. It was too early on in the tour to figure out how the enemy lines were being drawn up. For now, I'll take Leo at his word and complain to him if there's something to complain about. Yet, must admit – am intrigued by the air miles.

Ryan is cute. Too bad he's on the other team. After fourteen hours of travel, he wants to make IT with a fireman. Stamina. He has one of those slippery-eye bedroom looks that oozes sexuality. Relieved that stand partner thing is OK. And I liked my bus ride with the stars. Things are turning out well!

The orchestra sounded horrible for the first hour as we all got used to each other's sound. Ryan tends to play a bit sharp but I adjusted. Like his playing. He's confident, relaxed and has a big, gorgeous sound. You can tell a lot about a person by how they play. (Hmm, wonder what impression I'm making right now. Probably sound like a has-been.) Marked music with appropriate bowings and to keep from falling asleep.

Second rehearsal sounded better, especially for the violas. Well, why shouldn't it? All the parts are easy, the viola part inane. Why do pop music people treat that particular instrument as if it were handicapped? (Orchestra musicians, don't answer that one.) As usual, the violas mostly play the 'pah' of the 'oom-pahs' – and then only with another instrument, usually the bassoon. Out of boredom, most of us begin practising a kind of Zen during the music. Made up a game – sort of – trying to remember the biggest dick I'd ever had. But, just as I was remembering a certain water polo player in high school, the violas had a section solo. I wasn't even on the right string. Suddenly, forty eyes stared at us, smirking, giggling – the trombones guffawing. Oh, you'll get yours, you little bones, you. Like their instrument carries any dignity.

Unfortunately, the reason the viola has become the laughing stock of the orchestra is that every once in a while, we're handed a solo. With everyone zoned out in one form or another, if and when the orchestra drops out for the viola section solo (a fairly rare occurrence), violists drop out too – save a few lone players who are past the point of caring how they sound or how the orchestra sounds. Past the point of hearing, really, or knowing if they're holding a bow or a baseball bat. It is always a horrible sobering up to realise that one resembles the freak in the children's choir who's been left out of the joke not to sing a particular word during the concert.

'OK, uh, violas. Don't cry in your beer, huh?' the conductor sneered down at our section. Ryan turned to me behind the music stand, feigning to write something in the music but, in fact, making a pig face and imitating the conductor. I tried hard not to laugh and succeeded – something all professional players learn their first year in college: don't laugh, don't sneeze, don't cough, don't yawn. Can think of a few times in early career when I was sure I'd lose an eyeball from the pressure but managed to keep up a calm front.

We got it right the second time and the rehearsal progressed. Went back to dreaming of dicks. Let eyes drift around the few players I could see, trying to imagine what occupied their jeans. Thought the conductor acted like a cocksure prick, but that was probably it – a bit of blustering. Concertmaster looked like he might be well endowed. So did the third stand, outside player in the first violins.

Yikes! The guy caught me eyeing him. Came straight over to me at break. 'So, I'm Ted.'

Introduced myself.

'So why are violas bigger?'

Can you see the eye-rolling? So tired of that joke.

Turned punch-line around, feigning to ask, 'Isn't it an optical illusion since most violinists' heads are so big?'

Ted might not be all bad. He laughed. I continued. 'What's the difference between a violist and a proctologist?'

Ted laughed harder. 'Tell me.'

'A proctologist only has to deal with one asshole at a time.' I am funny. Proud of witty retort, turned on heel and went over to relay the story to Ryan.

Dave caught up with me just as I was taking viola out of case, getting ready for the next half of the rehearsal.

'Haven't seen you around. What bus did you end up on?'

He is cute, I have to admit. But something in those green eyes seems a bit empty. Or a bit off. And there's that camera around his neck. Can't say why, but it reminds me of the hair he used to tape to his stand. Some type of new fetish, no doubt.

Said casually, like I'd rehearsed, 'Oh, would you believe it? I ended up on the Mission's bus.'

'That freaky group? How could you desert us for them?'

'I don't know. I sort of like them. Plus, there's only five of us on the whole bus.'

'Unfair.' Dave sounded quite hurt.

I replied that that was just the way the tour ball bounces and went onstage.

'What are you thinking about?' Ryan whispered to me during the new set of 'oompahs'.

Hoping to shock, I explained my newest short-term attention-keeper: Spot the Biggest Penis.

Love Ryan. Said, 'Ooo. Can I play?'

Why can't straight men jump right in and play such a harmless game? They do anyway, but on no-brainers: sizing up women's breasts. What kind of imagination does that take? Plus, most guys seem clueless as to how bras can really alter a woman's physique. I bet even Daniel fell for Spiderwoman's Wonderbra. He often complained my boobs would be perfect if they were just a little bigger. Started wearing wire push-ups to please him but he already knew the real truth.

Anyway . . . the game: I look at someone and Ryan points his thumb up or down. Sometimes he makes a disgusted face. It makes playing the 'pah' part a bit harder and is keeping us awake for any sudden solos.

Conductor got a zero. Concertmaster a thumbs up.

'I know it's true for a fact,' said Ryan slyly, with a wink. 'The concertmaster is one nice piece of monster meat.'

June 18, morning

Forgot how much I like the first moment of sex with a near stranger. God, it has been a *long* time. Can be so good but depends on how willing the other party is to let go and do an all-out body/soul merge as to how fabulous it can be. But like those many years before, just as the guy is warming up, I feel a cooling down. Remember Polly saying that for any good relationship to last, there must be distance. Maybe it's a respect thing – maybe after they want me, I think there is something wrong with them. Question is: is it me not respecting them or not respecting myself? What's wrong with a guy clearly wanting you? And then continuing to want you after that initial conquest? My fatal error: fell in love with Daniel's coldness. I thought we'd make it because of the distance between us – or something like that.

Anway . . . I did IT. IT, IT, IT! Broke the D thing. Ted came to room last night with some flowers. Said he wanted to apologise but I knew he was there to see if I wanted a romp in the hay. Teddy, boy, you are as lucky as a mosquito in a blood bank!

After pretending to look for a movie we could watch together on TV, Ted leaned over to kiss me. It was a nice kiss. Polite, a little provocative but no tongue jammed down the throat.

Decided to practise new belief: patience is not always a virtue. I asked, 'Want to have sex, Ted?'

Clothes flew off. Was amazed at how long and slender Ted's cock was. A bit like a stiff long-john hot dog. Very different from D's. Got down on knees for a taste but, here's the weird thing: he pulled me up.

'So, you won't believe this but . . .' he hesitated, his face turning red. 'I don't like oral sex.'

Who ever heard of that? Was stunned and vastly disappointed, for I love oral . . . especially when performed on me, me, me. Not by D (aka Nervous Rat Mouth aka Cunt Unappreciator).

Thankfully, Ted added, 'I mean on me. I'll go down on you if you like.'

Oh, OK, thought I. I mean, I've been having a shitty life and I deserve an orgasm for the trouble, right? Was flushed and primed and thought it might just happen if I didn't think about how long it had been since it had happened with another. Let Ted pull my legs over his back while he kneeled by the side of the bed.

Ode to Ted's Tongue: it moves like butter through and through! A million different cocks flashed through my mind, some I knew, some I invented. They all wanted to pump into me, split me open. There were no men attached, only cocks. I was a juicy fruit they pierced and licked. (I know cocks don't lick but they should – and *do* in *my* fantasy world.)

At first I thought it was Ted's finger that slid in and out slowly. It was his cock. It really is slender, but he pushed it to the top of my hole, which made me

37

twitch with pleasure. Ted continued slipping in next to the underside of my clit.

Felt his hands on my ass, picking it up and moving it as if it were a bucket of dirt – no, wait, honey. I want to get this exact. Ted rocked me back and forth so he slid in and out of me, jamming my clit up against his pelvic bone. Never worked with Daniel but I came with a feeling of utter release. I was primed, ready and utterly out of my mind with desire and the previous eloquent waxing of Ted's tongue. Whole body sighed contentedly and the feeling of boneless-ness was upon me.

Though I kept silently repeating, 'I came! I came! I came!' could not stay awake. Too much masturbating myself to sleep. Bet Ted is furious – he didn't come, poor thing. Oh well. I know it's not fair but I'd like to even the score a bit – I mean, didn't come with D but he came all the time. Know Ted isn't D but body won't accept it. Likes the turnabout.

Later . . .

Love Ryan. We looked at each other in the rehearsal, *both* sporting slippery bedroom eyes.

'Third stand firsts, outside,' I began.

'Ted?' Ryan asked.

I was surprised and a little wary they knew each other.

'We were in the Con together. Not much, though.' Ryan said it all, but not very nicely. It's *not* the only thing that matters – unless you're not in love with the guy.

Told Ryan I didn't want to know how he knew about Ted.

'Concertmaster,' he replied.

'Did you fall asleep on him?'

'Hell no. Not until we were both exhausted. You didn't?'

Ummm.

'That wasn't very nice,' said Ryan. Touché.

This is so perfect. From now on, can tell Ryan about all future sexploits and vice versa. Oompahs are going to a new level.

Tonight's concert: fun, though could see neither the audience nor most of the Mission from the pit. Every once in a while, Angelika or the dominatrix got to the edge of the stage and I winked at them.

It's not a bad show and music-wise is getting better. Salvadore has a good feeling for orchestration – he's the composer, performer, singer, guitarist. Did I mention the green eyes? *Stunning*. The three-legger sang a little-known Rodgers and Hammerstein piece, 'I Enjoy Being a Girl', which had the Deutschlanders howling. I'm dying from not being able to see it. We all feel Serik's low notes in the pit rumbling the snare drum and vibrating our strings. Wonder how big he is – need to ask Ryan's opinion. No. We both know: Serik wins! Be fun to confirm the depths of the Human Vibrator.

Kristine also sang, with exaggeration and great emphasis on certain words, 'I came on two buses and a train. Can you imagine that? Can you imagine that? Two buses and one train.'

Know the piece. Certain that was not the composer's intention with that sweet song. Howls from the pit made it difficult to hear what else she did to the piece. What fun they must be having up there. Dying to see it!

June 20

We've moved to another city. I don't know. In Germany somewhere. Every cute town looks like every other cute town. Feels cold for summer. Last time I was in Germany I was 19 and a vegan. Idiot – no bratwurst, no beer ... didn't even do butter (no strudel) or eggs, so no mayonnaise for the *pommes frites*, which was about the only thing I ate. Came back looking like the Pillsbury doughgirl with yeast bubbles on the face from the grease. Here's to the current omnivorous Katie. Guzzling beer with the Mission and popping down as many weenies as I can. Convinced this is the way NOT to gain weight.

There's only a few standard numbers from other musicals left now, which have boring viola parts. Salvadore has been listening to what SX can do and adjusting accordingly. When does he have time to do it? He's out there on the snittzle binge with the rest of us.

It's soooo sweet. Salvadore keeps writing solos for the last stand violas. They're not overt but they are getting there. Wonder how the front stand feels. It's a girl and guy team up there, each one so pretty they could be a member of the opposite sex.

Truth be told, I wish he'd stop. It's not easy to pay attention when measuring up cocks during the musical rests, suddenly seeing: Solo, Chair 8. At this rate, I might be forced to practise.

What kind of tour would that be?

June 23

Tonight was the last show in Beerland. Ryan and I decided to do a few stints for the stars, to 'reward' them for the hard work they were throwing to the last stand violas.

Had a cucumber handy and each time Angelika or Kristine neared the edge of the stage during the final number, Ryan slowly peeled the thing. It brought both of the stars to laughing on stage, but they managed to control themselves. That is until the last time, when Ryan pushed the peeled cucumber into my face and I began to give it fellatio. Instead of looking at Angelika, I looked over at Ted, who seemed utterly aghast. Thank God the parties involved were all angled slightly behind the conductor, who went about making his famous 'taffy-pull' and 'wind machine' conducting motions in sheer oblivion.

When Angelika reached the edge of the stage, I looked straight up and bit the head of the cucumber clean off. Angelika, for a moment, snorted but Kristine covered, whipping the drag queen back into some solemnity. The audience loved it (too bad they couldn't see the cucumber in the pit) and broke out into wild applause. Angelika gave in and laughed heartily. Kristine pushed her down, planting a spiked heel on the trannie. The orchestra stopped playing (we'd run out of music, though the conductor didn't seem to notice) but Salvadore and Serik came over and sang a quick version of 'God Save the Queen', apparently a German favourite. The applause went on and on.

'Look what you did,' said Ryan. 'We could have been out of here ten minutes earlier but now we have a goddamn encore.'

We both quickly glanced around the audience when asked to stand for the orchestra bow.

'Guy, third in front row?' queried I.

'Nope, I say he's not in the game. Nothing in those leiderhosen.'

'You know, I always wondered,' I said through a

smile as the audience continued clapping, 'why it matters to you guys so much. I mean, in fact, wouldn't you want someone smaller? Less pain and all?'

'It's the aesthetics, babe. Come on. Do you think we all like to dress up like little girls and get butt-fucked?' Ryan's bright audience smile was killing me, face aching with pent-up laughter.

'Well, no, but even orally, I get worn out with a big one,' replied I with a big Hollywood smile.

'Sounds like you need some lessons.'

Did I say it before? Love Ryan. Promised to give some pointers. Him to me.

We sat down again to play the encore number – something a stagehand had hurriedly passed about. 'I'll make you the most popular fellatio girl around. Rule number one: no biting.'

Played the hot-off-the-press encore piece entitled 'It May Burn Longer in the Case than in my Heart'.

Later . . .

Ted came to room holding a cucumber.

'Was that little show for me?' he asked in a way that made me aware that tonight could end up being an angry fuck. Figured I owed the guy one. Apologised for falling asleep on him.

'And avoiding me.'

Got me there. Was too embarrassed to even say hi. Said, 'You'd think I was a guy or something.'

Ted sat on the bed with one leg up and an arm back – reclining Venus, I think. Assured me I was 100 per cent female. Ted had a bit of the air of an ascetic and his pronunciation of 'female' hissed with Adam and Eve overtones.

I liked it.

'What do you want me to do with the cucumber, Ted?'

'Oh, something later. Right now, I'm going to do something with it to you.'

He pulled out a knife from his back pocket and attempted a glare at me. I suppressed a smile, trying to let Ted think that he was giving a dangerous impression.

He ran the cucumber along on my cheek.

'You know, I was very hurt that you fell asleep.'

I liked this game. 'I am so sorry. What can I ever do? Forgive me?' I said in what I hoped didn't sound too melodramatic of a tone.

Ted cut into the cucumber right next to my ear. He took off a large peel and snaked it down through my robe, leaving it on my left breast. He peeled another strip off and repeated the gesture. Was trying hard not to laugh. Thought it fun if I could let go and pretend there was something dangerous in the moment. Weird the eroticism of it – have to mull over that one another time. Danger and sex do seem erotic.

Ted then laid the nearly peeled cucumber on the table and brought the knife up next to my neck. Didn't like that one.

'What are you doing, Ted?'

He looked to be suppressing a grin so I relaxed a bit, understanding it was part of the game – and maybe I was the only novice here.

Suddenly, Ted put the knife to the belt of my robe, jerked up and cut through. Was so stunned, I didn't move. Then he inserted the knife in between cleavage. He put his hand on my shoulder and used the knife to gently scrape the peelings off the breasts and on to the floor. The cool peelings had warmed but the knife blade was still icy. I trembled.

'Now, Katie, you are not going to come tonight until I have had my fill, understand?'

Was speechless. Who would have guessed that skinny, wiry Ted had this side to him?

He yanked off my robe and then cut my knickers off with the knife. Not too hard to do. They were the cotton, string-on-sides variety. Damn. I' ll have to buy more.

A heady burst of me, down under and excited, filled the air. Ted sniffed, commenting that he loved the smell. Was I interested in continuing?

I nodded my head. This was good and I didn't want to ruin it with a goofy comment, like 'Yeah, let's cut my knickers off again, shall we?'

'I was thinking all day today about making a Katie salad. Getting the dressing just right and, then, tossing it.'

He inserted the cucumber slowly into me while I stood. He was still in his full clothing and there I was, nude with a vegetable crammed up my cunt. Well, didn't bother me. The coolness felt delicious and I was sad when Ted pulled it out.

'Such a bad girl, Katie,' and with that, he bit the tip of the cucumber off.

He inserted it again, twisting it and pulling it out just so far that I couldn't get a firm hold on anything.

Ted pulled it out and took another bite.

'You are delicious, my dear. Who would have thought a violist could have so many subtleties?'

'Contrary to popular opinion, we violists do know more than one position.'

Started to laugh, then Ted grabbed my shoulders hard. 'I did not say you could laugh, did I?' Continued to laugh and Ted began to as well, although he was trying to keep a stern face.

'This is the tossing part.' Threw me on the bed, stomach first and then began spanking. Spanking seemed to be in earnest and I asked him to stop. If I need pain, I'm sure Daniel could provide enough of that. Ted stopped spanking (hard hand that violinist's) after I promised not to come. A very HARD promise, given that I was on fire now, aching to have something in me.

Shirt, pants, socks, shoes went flying past field of vision. Ted then climbed on, fucking hard.

To encourage this new twist, said, 'Harder baby.'

'I'll fuck you how I want to fuck you and that's all,' and spanked my now sore behind and continued a rhythmic thrusting.

Oh, yes. Even the spanking. Began to appreciate it, though earlier I'd been complaining in these pages of a lack of gentleness – consistency being the hobgoblin of little minds and all. It was nice and I had a lot of difficulty not coming – especially after all those years of not coming. But I didn't squeeze, didn't touch myself, didn't think of other cocks. Just imagined myself playing some of that music from the show and that took my mind off the pounding. Listening to Salvadore's music to unclench the Kegel muscles.

Pounding and pounding into me, yet Ted didn't come. After what seemed a very long time, he pulled out and roughly turned me over.

'So, I just thought you could show me what kind of fellatio you like giving. I do like to watch.'

Here he handed me another cucumber. My cunt was gasping to be filled again. Panting, saying, 'Fuck me, fuck me, fuck me.' It was. I thought it was screaming. Loud, voiceless cunt wishes. How could Ted resist?

Wasn't particularly keen on showing fellatio to a guy who didn't seem to really enjoy that stuff.

He grabbed my hair. 'I said, show me.'

I smiled, though this now was getting old. Knew I owed him but was tired and we had a long day ahead of us. Thought I better put on a good show to get Ted to leave.

Took the tip of the cucumber in mouth and began slowly circling the tip with tongue, gazing into Ted's

45

eyes. He had that painted eyeball look of the very aroused. Thought it might work after all.

With hand, stroked the cucumber from the bottom to the top, making sure to move hand over the tip.

Ted was playing with himself. Put the cucumber partly down throat and then pulled it up again. Ted did the same motion with his hand. Saw love juice glistening off the tip of his cock and knew I had him.

Pulled the cucumber into throat again and then played with the tip. Hands down, mouth down, up around. Ted's hands were matching mine so I moved faster.

'Whoa!' he exclaimed, shooting a stream of come directly on my face.

Now that pissed me off. Ted's sweet revenge. I really like everything about sex except *that*. It's disgusting, like having someone pee on you. Besides, in the eye, sperm burns. Wiped face on bedspread.

'Oops, sorry about that. You are just so exciting.' Ted panted. 'Maybe you could really help me learn to love head.'

Internally rolled eyes. Didn't sound like much fun to me, given that I was planning on throwing Ted out of the room any minute.

Ted offered to make me come but I'd lost the motivation in the sperm–eye transaction. Asked for a rain check.

'All right,' replied Ted in a dejected tone. 'Maybe in Paris. We leave at ten.'

'Maybe in Paris.' Knew it would be nice to offer more but after the semen hit the fan, didn't feel like being easy on the guy's feelings.

As I slid naked into bed, wide awake and unsatisfied, there was another knock at the door.

Half hoped it was Ted. Wondering if it wouldn't have been better to have him stay and finish the job. Was deeply unsatisfied.

Dave announced himself. I was too out of it to notice the room smelled of sex. Thinking couldn't keep postponing having a real conversation with the guy. Better to get it over with now.

Opened door after tying robe with the black belt from my jeans. Briefly entertained idea that Dave might just be the man of the hour.

He looked like the Cheshire cat. That's when I noticed the come-smeared bedspread in full view. Room looked like a tornado hit it and smelled – heavenly. However, love juice perfume is only intoxicating if you're involved. Dave made it seem squalid as his eyes snaked around the room with no comments coming from his lips.

Finally said, 'Got you off the Mission's bus and on to mine.'

Was immediately irritated. 'Why would you do something like that? I'm enjoying myself.'

Dave smirked at that. 'Well, management didn't think it was appropriate.'

'You talked to management?' My legs crossed hard over each other beneath the bathrobe (had decided to sit on come smear in case Dave missed it on his first room observation). Legs acting as if they were a cobra and Dave their prey. Body deeply unsatisfied.

'Came up in conversation,' Dave said as though speaking between bites of granola.

'Oh, I can only imagine.' Coolly answered his hot gaze with not so much as a hint that he was anything but vermin. Definitely not flirting. Very proud of self. 'Time for you to leave, Davey boy.' If he only knew how he'd ruined the moment – how close we had come to coming. I imagine that Dave somehow thought his act might actually get me into the sack with him. Creep.

Walked to the door and motioned for him to leave. His face folded like a card table and his eyes darted about, trying to decide what to do. Happy to have him off guard. He pulled up the camera from around his neck and said, 'Say *fromage*, Katie old girl.'

He got a shot off before I pushed him out of room yelling, 'With friends like you, who needs enemas?!'

A door across the hall opened up. It was Slava.

'Hi, Katie. I think you mean *enemies*, don't you? I think it well-known American phrase.'

Stared at poor Slava, wondering whether to laugh or cry, and then pulled the anger back inside myself, and slammed door shut.

Had to masturbate for a full hour before could come myself into sleeping. Dave's green eyes were never going to surface again. It was just one of the standard fantasies of faceless cocks and dark slithering walls. Typical had to succumb, had to be penetrated, no choice, no choice, no choice, until I broke into a million pieces and fell asleep.

Chapter Four

June 24, early, obscenely early morning – argh!

Called Leo with the old 'Houston, we've got a
problem' routine.

'Katie, isn't this a bit early for violists?'

Not up for sarcasm from some knuckle-grazing
administration person. Didn't answer.

'OK, well . . . let's hear it,' said Leo's tired voice at
the other end of the phone.

'I do *not* want off the Mission's bus.'

'I see. OK, you're not. This isn't youth orchestra you
know. There are no seating assignments.' Pause. 'Who
told you you'd have to get off?'

'Um, someone. Sorry to bother you.'

Hung up phone, swearing to kill Dave at next
opportunity. He's not going to ruin this tour for me
with some kind of psycho game-playing. Note to
investigators: if David Muller shows up dead, this is
just a figure of speech. I want him dead but am too
much of a coward to carry it out. But do let me see the
developed pictures.

Of his corpse.

Later . . .

Met John downstairs at the breakfast buffet, 8 a.m. –
we're two of the six people there.

'I never miss a meal on these things,' he says to me.
'It's free food. Who would pass up free food?'

'Looks like Kristine, Serik and Salvadore . . . and the
rest of Symphony X.'

'Or, if you look at it another way, the breakfast
buffet is a sure gauge of who didn't get any action,'
he giggled.

Hit him playfully (the only way I ever hit anybody),
asking 'What stopped you?'

'Hello. Look around. This is not your drag queen
crowd.'

'My stand partner?'

'Ryan? That boy is Mr Slut. Besides, I need something more than a three-minute tryst. And –' he leaned
forward conspiratorially '– he costs too much.'

Don't want to know what that means.

Slava saw us across the room and came lumbering
over with his breakfast tray.

'Mind if I sit down at this fine table? The early bird
gets warm, no?'

John shrugged, I shrugged, so Slava sat, pulling his
drumsticks out of his back pocket and putting them
on the table.

Slava said, 'I am trying theory. I think all work and
no play makes Slava a doll boy. So, I am ready to play
this tour. Like Plato said; all I know is that I don't
know nothing.'

Intrigued, or merely waiting for an opportunity to
poke fun, John asked, 'Play what, Slava? Do you
percussionists play together or do you play with
yourself?'

The pro – I didn't laugh! John, however, giggled
uncontrollably at his witticism.

'I, me, I, in general, I play with others. The more the merrier, no? That is one of your sayings, no?'

We vigorously nodded.

Wanting to show John I could play the game too, I asked, 'What do you call a drummer who just broke up with his girlfriend?'

'Sad?' offered Slava. 'Me, I, it is wrenching of the heart to lose the one you love.'

'Well, the answer is homeless,' mumbled I.

'Yeah. Well, Katie, it just doesn't work when you have to get out the crayons and drawing paper, does it?' replied John.

'Yes, well, speaking of drawing, it is back to the board for me. Like fitting round peg in square hole.'

Slava left.

John looked at me and giggled. 'I can see why you are so rested this morning. Mr Greasy was too busy with his idiom book to come over.'

'Fuck off.'

Later . . .

Late, late, still on bus. Are we going to Paris via Monte Carlo? Argh. Delays. Not sure which town we're resting in. Or eating in. Argh! Want to sleep on bunk but feel uncomfortable masturbating myself into oblivion while the stars are nearby.

Kristine and John began a game. They made a board with 'Sexual Encounters' taking up nearly every space on a ring and three 'Bad Musical Experiences' taking up the rest.

John giggled. 'OK, the object is to spin this bottle –' he pointed to our square tequila bottle '– and then spill your guts. Everyone in?'

All looked excited except Salvadore, whose eyes looked *very* neutral – not an easy expression, if you ask me. 'I'm not much of a storyteller,' he muttered.

51

Everyone ignored him. Seemed like old hat for them all – even the Salvadore abstention.

'Now,' John explained, most likely for my benefit alone, 'we roll these dice and see who asks the question.'

Serik won the dice roll. I was lowest so I spun first. The bottle rested on 'Bad Musical Experiences'.

Cries of 'Not fair' went all around. Newcomers HAD to land on the sex square. I wasn't budging. They made the game, they could lie in it. Or not. Whatever. Serik asked me what was the most mortifying time I recall happening on stage. Told Jason's story, pretending it happened to me. I mean, it *was* a story. At a kiddy concert, two people dressed up as popular cartoon characters were out dancing to the majestic sounds of Rachmaninov or Mozart – I don't remember the music most often used by Warner Brothers . . . maybe it was Rossini. Anyway, they got to playfully kicking each other and one of the characters, the dog, got a little too enthusiastic and kicked the other character, the cat, off the stage and down 12 feet into the open orchestra pit. Crash, thump, crash, thump. Then a weak little cry was heard from the still working body mike. 'Help me. Help me.' Paramedics came and the cat was strapped to a stretcher and lifted through the hall, children's faces broken with horror that classical music had been the demise of one of their favourite kitties in the whole world. My theory why music funding is so low in public schools.

'I heard that story too. But, didn't you say you live in New York?' Salvadore's eyes were locked on to mine and I felt him massage a confession out of me.

'Well, yeah. It happened to a friend of mine. A long time ago, I played in that orchestra.'

Kristine shouted, 'You have to tell a story that happened to *you*. That's the whole point.' The diva's lips did a quick sideways motion as if she were about to inhale from a hashish pipe. Caught, I told my true story about screwing a stagehand five minutes before the concert (OK, I had some sex before the marriage) and trying to hold the love juice in so it wouldn't seep through on to my black silk dress. Doing very well until we played Tchaikovsky's *1812*. Someone had programmed the midi the wrong way and when the poor guy went to hit the 'cannon' button, instead, chicken squawks came out. Then he hit another and a Chinese gong sounded. Those Russians will fight with anything.

Anyway, the laughing made the love juice spill out and I did not stand up with the orchestra for the final bow. Didn't really matter. It was one of those outside, 20,000-people picnic concerts so I was just a dot on the stage. Couldn't stand up if I wanted to anyway. My dress had glued itself to the seat in the hot evening air.

Kristine went next. The bottle, naturally, rested on a 'sexual' square.

I won the question this time with a double-6. Wanted dominatrix to tell a story. Pointed a mock accusing finger (à la Daniel mode – though the joke was just for me) at Kristine. 'Who had the biggest cock you've ever been with?'

'Now, I can't give away names,' replied Kristine without even batting an eye. 'But it wasn't too long ago. A certain conductor . . .'

Serik and I began hurling names at her – Wigglesworth, Essa-Pekka, Blume – to which she vigorously shook her head. 'You'll never guess in a million years and I'm not telling.'

'Stulberg!' I shouted.

'No . . . who is that anyway? Listen, can I continue?' Kristine's brown eyes flashed their little arched daggers at us interrupters and we immediately fell silent. 'Well, we began talking backstage about great singers we knew. I don't know how the subject shifted but we began talking about our biblical knowledge.'

'What a surprise,' said Salvadore, with a hint of irony.

'He said that sopranos were the best, although mezzos were meatier – more to hold on to.'

'What are you talking about? The fattest people I know are sopranos,' interrupted John.

'I'm repeating what he said, OK? Are you guys going to let me tell the story or not?' Kristine shifted on the bed – forgot to mention that we lost our table altogether and now the 'dining room' stays in its converted bedroom shape. Kristine's lips were still painted red and when she said certain words, like 'the' or 'thinking', her tongue darted over her lips making it seem the sexiest word in the English language. How does she do it?

'So,' Kristine continued, 'I asked him if he kept tabs on all the people he'd done. He said he had and then I said I did the same thing, but made my amount one more than his. Asked him if he'd like to catch up, give him something to write home about.'

'OK, we've narrowed it down. He's from the States,' said Serik.

'I'm not getting the math here,' chimed in Salvadore.

'Shut up, I'm not finished. So we begin to do it in his dressing room, only when he gets to putting it in, I begin screaming. I couldn't help myself. It was huge and like a square peg trying to fit into a round hole, if you know what I mean.' (Slava wouldn't.)

'You have a square peg?' asked Salvadore.

'Then he wasn't really the biggest dick you ever had?' said yours truly. 'I mean, isn't it supposed to be something you can actually get inside you?'

'Katie's right,' giggled John. 'Try again.'

'Oh, all right. But listen. This was the best lovemaking of my entire life. He did have a huge cock but not too huge. We lasted eight months.'

'That long?' Salvadore interrupted.

Kristine shot him a daggered look but continued. 'What can I say? Glorious. I'd tell you his name but you wouldn't know him. He wasn't a musician.'

'A plumber?' volunteered Serik.

'No, a grade school principal. But he understood that he had that cocksureness. You know what I'm talking about, Katie?'

I did know exactly what she was talking about. Suppose it's why I married an otherwise unpleasant guy. Something about the way Daniel was completely sure of himself in bed made him quite attractive – in the beginning at least. Got to admire someone who is so sure he's good – even if he isn't. Well, not for me anyway. The more you know, the more you know. Bummer, *n'est pas*?

'He was not beautiful. No, plain I'd say. But he had a way of touching me that mesmerised me to the very bone,' continued the dominatrix.

'His bone too, I bet,' chimed in Salvadore.

'In case you haven't noticed, I'm ignoring you. You never let me get through these stories,' Kristine growled at him, hitting Salvadore not so lightly on his white-haired head – which caused the guitarist to smile. Realised it was the first time I'd seen him do it. Wow! Babe material. His entire face lit up with the smile and cute little apple cheeks appeared – making him irresistible.

'So,' Kristine, yet again, continued (apparently, there's no stopping her stories once they start), 'the first time we were together, I had to ask him to kiss me. It was strange. I knew he liked me but was waiting for me to make the move. I did. We kissed on my roommate's couch, then ended up in my bedroom. When he put himself in me, I cried. I felt full, you

55

know what I mean?' She looked at me again. 'God, it is nice to tell these stories and have a woman around. These guys pretend they know what I'm talking about.'

'I hope you guys are learning stuff,' I said, though not entirely convinced Kristine's story was that instructive. Looked around to see what the others thought. Serik's moustache was not waxed and it drooped slightly, giving him a hounddog look. John still had eyeliner on, which he swore he couldn't get off. Salvadore seemed bored or absent – hard to say. Kristine looked like a sweet little girl, with her black hair up in ponytails and red liquorice lips. It's a sad day when a violist looks like the normal one in a crowd.

Wanted to change the subject. 'Look, you guys, what exactly is an immorality play?'

'That was Sal's idea,' said Kristine.

Looked at S quizzically and he seemed to perk up.

'Well,' he said, clearing his throat, 'you've heard of morality plays?'

'Just the tiniest.' Actually, hadn't a dog's hair what they were. Sounded like a Billy Graham revival.

'They are plays in which some concept plays itself out against another concept. Faith and Hope versus Greed and Lust, for example. These intangible characters battle it out, with the "good" concepts winning somehow – or at least proving that evil is really evil and not to be messed with.'

He looked at me to see if I got it. Hey, I'm a quick study. I was focused, obsessed, OK, on the sight of Salvadore's hands moving around as he spoke. He's got the hands of Michelangelo's God. S is really beautiful in a most unusual, otherworldly way. His green eyes are quite far apart and seem to look in you and into themselves at the same time. His white hair frames his face like a moon's halo. Interesting indeed.

56

Have no idea his age – could be twenty-five or fifty. Not a single line on the face.

'So, these were written and performed several hundred years ago – though some would say they are being performed right now in the area of wrestling mania. Hulk Hogan representing the white god of righteousness.'

Creative and smart to boot! The others looked a bit bored. More information than they wanted to hear, but I was intrigued. My eyes glittered (all right, I was flirting in an unspoken Zen type of way), encouraging Salvadore to tell all.

'So, I was thinking one day that it would be great to take the same concepts and make sure that no matter what happened, the "bad" concepts would win. That's why it's all impromptu. We go offstage, draw our concepts out of a hat and then perform.'

'But how do you do that? I mean, it isn't all impromptu. There's a written score.' I was having a hard time figuring out how this worked.

'No, it isn't impromptu exactly. There is a working backdrop. Do you think those jazz solos are really improvised? Those guys often play the same riffs over and over again, just placing them differently.'

'Don't let him kid you,' Kristine piped in. 'Sally's a genius. I don't know how he does it. He writes more music taking a shit than some people do in their entire life. I mean, he dissects those jazz solos as if they were some chopped Bologna.'

'They are,' said Salvadore.

Damn, now I really want to see them perform. In entirety. Now it's like I'm a third-dimensional creature getting a few views of the fourth dimension. Frustrating. And I was beginning to love the music. Told Salvadore that more or less. Didn't want to encourage more back-stand solos though.

'Thank you,' Salvadore said in a hushed, reverent tone.

'Why not watch us, Katie? Just pretend you're sick,' giggled John.

'Or that you play the viola,' laughed Serik. Hit him a little harder than I meant to. He responded with a very warm smile. That moustache brightening into a black sunset over his full lips. Bright dark eyes. Big feet. To repeat one of Serik's favourite mottoes: you know what they say? Big feet?

Big shoes.

June 26

Paris. City of borrowed and then finally honed cultures. Croissant from Turkey, bistros from Russia, grapes from the Roman Empire. The charm of the chaotic, mismatched pebbled streets winding like untied shoelaces next to cathedrals of perfect proportions. The avant-garde is old hat now but the titters of ripe and new things hum in the air. Have always believed that in Paris, I'd find the love of my life. (So then why did you marry a New York Attorney? Shut up, shut up, shut up. By the way, still amused that in Germany, that stupid little chain with the red roof is referred to as Pizza Hat.)

Anyway, in America, I've been, *we've* been – groomed to expect love with the perfume, the lingerie, the bedding. French milled soap to wash with, douches, ticklers, maid's outfit, bidets. Don't forget the champagne and Ravel's *Boléro* (which, by the way, was not so much intended to be a romantic piece as a representation of a factory ... perhaps driving it in is romantic, after all).

A Mission disembarked and we agreed to meet up at midnight at Aux Deux Magots, a suggestion of

Salvadore's. He seemed to relish mispronouncing 'magots' to make it sound particularly uninviting. I was a bit sorry to be going to a place where all the 'in' people thought they should be but, in all reality, 'in' people wouldn't go near the place. Yet, if I can recall it from ten-plus years ago, it's a charming café with statues of Chinese monks, not too surly waiters and a leftover air of intellectualism. Probably still has too many Americans there. Think it was Jim Morrison's hangout too . . . hey, was he American?

You, Katie, are a nerd.

Went to room, tired, looking for the light switch. Ah, Paris. The light to the room is in the bathroom, or entry hall, and you walked through the bathroom/entry hall to the bedroom. Nice. Confusing, but nice. The priorities here are right. The first thing one encounters is a bidet and fresh lavender flowers.

Later . . .

Have just wasted all my free time reading this. Can empathise with Daniel a very little bit. Other people's diaries *are* intriguing. And I have no idea whose this is. There is no Norton on tour – checked the roster. It was in my black carry-on bag and this diary looks surprisingly like mine. I'm keeping mine in my big shoulder bag from now on. Don't want to do the same thing.

At first I suspected I'd picked up the wrong bag in the hotel lobby, but no, it had my *Ulysses* and toiletries. Why do I have so many toiletries when I rarely wear more than a hint of make-up? Some annoying part of me has to hold on to anything I've purchased for at least five years. Free make-up samples can be thrown away, even the most luxurious ones. Makes me feel indulgent. Yet, a four-dollar purchase of eyeliner stays around for years.

The black book was stuffed among the Chanel foundation and the Princess of Monaco's facial cleanser (purchased with my own orchestra money and about five and two years old, respectively – how long does that stuff keep anyway?).

Creepy that someone had thrust an unknown object in my bag of private goods without consent. And a big person at that. The writer works in a huge scrawling hand.

I know years ago my own pages were filled with my big question of the early twenties: should I be a violist or a detective? Now, on this Symph X tour, I get to do both. Sort of. No one hired me for the detective work but, so far, I've been undercover (my little stupid joke . . . with Ted, get it?) and now . . . the mysterious author of the black diary, novel, memoir? Perhaps this is what happened to D – my curiosity has ridden over any morality I should have about people's privacy. And am going to copy down what I've read – double double bad. Naughty, Katie, naughty. Well, who'll ever know?

Chapter Five

Wolf Eyes

Question – do I dare write of her? Too real.

Cynthia, oh marvellous Cynthia, had the most statu-esque body ever beholden. Every woman on that tour envied her, mostly hated her and the men, they were falling over themselves to carry her violin, her luggage, her stand, perhaps her purse which might contain her toiletries.

That was at the beginning of the tour. Towards the end, poor thing, she couldn't even find a decent place to sit on the bus. Had to ride in the back next to the loo. With Jonathon and his spirulina concoction working horribly against him. What was he expecting? When you pour pond scum on *pomme frites*, the stomach is going to work up its own primordial soup.

Cynthia, as she often told everyone, was a prodigy. At age eight (or nine or ten – depending on what time of day you caught her story), she soloed with the LA Philhar-monic. She was a Curtis grad, which her dazzlingly adept technique belied. And so did her social skills – spending that many hours a day in an eight-by-ten practice room does not make for easy mingling. It's more like 'Thus

Spoke Zarathustra' – coming down the mountain with a proclamation except in Cynthia's case, it wasn't 'God is Dead,' but rather 'I am God'.

In certain situations, she was.

Oh Cynthia! Why did you have to be so complicated? Imagine a woman around thirty, tall and lean with well-defined arms particular to violinists. Beautiful, no? Now picture luxurious, thick, dark-brown hair falling to her waist in a timeless style. Perfect. Then there were the wolf eyes, a slice of pale blue which betrayed not an ounce of warmth. If scrutinised, not an easy act when dazzled by all the other charms, one could see the endless calculating going on behind their iciness. Oh, they need the poet here. I can only describe them with the hindsight of one who was their prey.

Not that she was a mean sort, just malformed. There is a difference, if only in the person's consciousness of the chaos she creates.

'Well, it was about the time that I was touring with the New York Phil and . . .' began Cynthia.

'Excuse me. Were you touring with them or just in the orchestra?' piped up a voice from the back of the bus. The new members, not familiar with the bassoonist's prior knowledge of Cynthia, thought him mean. His tone was certainly sarcastic.

'I thought you knew it was with the orchestra,' replied Cynthia, unfazed. She seemed not to notice the sarcasm at all, which won her an instant appreciation in some circles and horrified looks in others.

Again, the voice piped up. 'You were only in the orchestra, right? You didn't solo or anything, right?' His voice was garbled and a bit like a first-year law student's doing moot court.

'No, that time I didn't solo but you know, the man wanted me to.'

Another eager voice, young college girl fresh out of Julliard (the Yard) asked with wonder, 'You knew Be– Be– Be– Benny?'

'Of course. He was our conductor,' said Cynthia breezily.

The little crowd that had been listening to the tale on the bus began to go back to their reading, gossiping and homoeopathy tendering. Either they knew Benny or Cynthia or both and were not interested in the story.

The eager girl sat in the now empty seat behind Cynthia.

'So, what was he like?' she asked, brown eyes glittering a bit too much like a saint's.

Oh was Cynthia enthralled! Fresh meat. A new pair of ears for her stories. She told everything she knew about the late great conductor – mainly things she had learned through books. She had only substituted for the orchestra once, sitting in the back of the second violins, and then it was a guest conductor. But, I'm getting ahead of myself. If one didn't care about the truth, Cynthia did have a fascinating way of telling a good tale.

Let's call the eager girl Ked. Well, Ked sat there salivating at the information being poured into her ear. The longer she sat next to Cynthia, the more likely it was that soon Cynthia would be the only person she'd be able to sit nearby. Musicians are not big on clueing each other in on the pecking order. In fact, it seemed a part of the tour ritual to watch the newcomers either sink or swim. A bit like prison I'd say. Except the conjugal visits were much more frequent and consensual (all puns intended).

Ked was another violinist who came out of the Yard violin factory of Dorothy D's just a little too underdone. Sure, she had the technique to play anything but she was still underdone. Nothing had come to a rollicking boil – like an uncrisp chicken pot pie – a bit floury and cool in the centre. She meant well – chicken pot pies always do. Just, she valued the flashy and was terribly shortsighted. I suppose that is why Cynthia appealed to her. Why Cynthia appealed to most men, too. She seemed made for a quick fix.

Not that Cynthia viewed herself that way. In our first

interview, after she revealed that she was a child prodigy and still prodigious in her musical career, she spoke about her soul in music.

'It's like this amazing blend of the higher chakras culminating on an E flat. Whenever I hear that note, which is my head pitch, I just feel grand.' Eyes fluttering as she said this, then looking side to side when I asked what she meant by chakras.

'You don't know what chakras are?' she asked, laughing a bit too hollowly to make me think she found it at all amusing. But then her long fingers rested on the back of my hand and a wave of something, maybe it was energy, rushed over me. I was helpless. I'd overheard the other musicians describe the phenomena as being 'Cyndied'. In her clutches without minding one bit. She had a way of swallowing up the space around her so there seemed to be only you two – and, at the end, only one.

Oh, that night in Germany, looking out over . . . well it was Germany anyway. I think there were a few rat-cellars out our window. Things on a tour get so blurry. One minute you're surrounded by elephants, the next, kings. One moment beer, the next, a fine Sauternes. Then you wonder, 'Which was which?'

But Germany. That night, in the hotel, in the arms of Cynthia. Those sinewy arms that, if truth be told, held one a little too tightly for it to be considered affection. She was glorious. Not a trick she didn't know. I had more head in one night than I'd received in the previous year. Her hands moved up and down my cock with a fluidity that still boggles my mind. Around and up and around then suddenly a tongue, then the hands again, around, up, pulling then sliding down. One could not help but come within a few minutes, which seemed to only encourage her to reapply her fingers after a short interval. The intervals in between, though, were a bit disturbing, with her asking all the time how it was and did I find it the best head I'd ever had. Well, it was the best but then to have that forced out of you deflated some of the intensity. A bit like playing a rather difficult musical passage and then, instead of going on with the piece, stopping and asking the audience if it was good for them. Some things deserve their applause at the end – not like some careening sporting event.

But when her hands started again, all went numb. In the mind, I mean. Another portion of my body was pulsing with an uncontrollable heat. Soon, sure enough, I came again. This time, she caught me in her mouth at the last minute as I heaved out my happy-to-be-released sperm. She acted as if she were tasting wine and then said, 'You are having a bit of a problem with your spleen. Too much acidic food. You should cut out the whiskey altogether.'

Well, can't say it was my spleen but I am one of excess: drink till you're drunk, smoke till you puke, fuck till you have used every muscle in your body and will regret it in the morning. So, instead of answering Wolf Eyes, I pulled myself on top of her and put myself in before I shrunk too much. Her breath smelled like lemon and carob – not an unpleasant combination.

How can I describe the sensation? Her inner muscles soon pulled another boner out of me – which frightened me a bit, to confess. I was used to having control of my body and here was someone who was so completely its master. She clenched and unclenched, pulling the tip of me up into that delicious warmness. Her teeth sank into my shoulder, causing goose pimples to sprout on the back of my calves.

When she flipped me over, I remembered being dazzled yet afraid of her strength. She stared at me while sliding herself up and down.

'Look at me,' she whispered urgently. 'I said to look.'

My eyes shot open, not in response to the command but to the pain of the slap which accompanied it.

Those slices of pale blue were brimming with icy tears. 'You don't love me.'

And she jumped off me before I could foster any false proclamations. Or real ones, for I did love her at the moment. Who wouldn't? But try as I might to say a thing, my tongue seemed to be lodged in the back of my mouth.

Then, saying something which is unfathomable for we sad males, 'You're all the same – that's the only thing you want,' she pushed me out of the hotel room, butt naked into the German summer night.

Humiliated? Yes. But she got me thinking – is that the *only* thing we want? I think having a woman worship you on top of that is really the *crème de la crème*. 'Companionship?' you ask. Don't forget, I know, unlike the rest of all of you romantics, that we are essentially alone. We're born that way, die that way. Of course, with the birth, there is a mother's heaving to consider. Jonathon would say that is why all women are latent lesbians – because of the mother factor. Doesn't explain why Jonathon is a latent homosexual, though. Never met a man who had less fascination for boobs. Told me he was trying to appreciate each person for his/her own 'uniqueness' and 'energy quotient'. Bullshit. The boy's confused.

So, I tried to forget Cynthia, until she enticed me the very next day.

'Sit here,' she purred, pointing to the vacant seat next to her in the restaurant.

I sat obediently, wanting to show I'm good to my master – dog that I was becoming. She stroked my hair to complete the illusion that all was forgiven and I was indeed a 'good boy'. How my tail wagged!

Oh, the hands of that woman. She pressed those dexterous, nubile tips and joints into all the resistant lumps of my skull. I was a frog at the dissection lab with a pin in its brain, twitching to the jolts received by unexpected but stimulated synapses. Here she pushed and I remembered the warmth of my mother, the sour milk smell of her skin that pleased me. Another rub and a cloud of my first love and the heartache swooned over me. I even think I saw my birth. Cyndied indeed.

Recalled old times of penile arousal. Metre maid in tight skirt lifting up wipers and tucking slip under. Lifting, tucking – and the penalty. Adolescent by window touching himself while she lifted, lifting himself and tucking, lifting, tucking, and then Mother asking what I was doing and the penalty now made clear: no unconsensual looking. Or, more to the point, no masturbating in a room which possesses no locking doors.

Cynthia had me again, penis straining like a hound at a fox. The minx opened those willowy arms and beckoned me against her tight little bosom. Grateful, I hung my head there and sucked about without making complete contact.

'Shall we go to my room?' she suggested, perhaps more a command than a question. We both knew I was utterly lost. Under the spell. We silly men battling emotions too strong – we drink or fuck like the simple organisms we are when things are too overwhelming. And even when they're not. What being made woman out of such different clay?

Cynthia, you are again glorious. I climbed on you to break you in half but supple body, nebulous spirit, you broke me. You took from my hammering to find you, to see your eyes blur and your mind grow fuzzy – you took and you took and remained the same and I fucked you all the more for it. Cynthia, what touches you, let me touch you. I want you. I want you.

Well, at least until I came in a very mean torrent of spunk. Felt like a hose trying to put out the Cynthia fire but only sprinkling upon her flame.

'Not bad,' said she after a minute. 'You are really beginning to let go.' Hand through my thinning hair, somehow hand letting hair know it was thinning.

She pulled herself off me, stuck her middle finger inside herself and pulled it out. Sniffed then tasted. 'Yes,' she said, 'still an imbalanced spleen.'

Man, I don't care if my spleen were about to burst, I'd have given anything to see a woman do that again with so much relish. Lips upon a finger that was coated in my man's product, sucking, smelling, tasting, sucking.

The cock grew again, encouraged by its enthusiastic recipient. This cock surprising its owner with its own sureness. Aye, captain, ready again for the sailing. I was wood, I was stone, I was steel.

'You know,' she murmured in a catlike, throaty voice, 'Benny was a bit like you.'

What was she doing? Moving on top of my cock in a tight circular way, I ignored what her lips were actually saying and just concentrated on the lips. The 'B' gloriously made with her tight pursed lips and then the tongue touching the roof of her mouth and then falling down upon the 'n'. She said 'Benny' a few more times.

'Sasha, though, was more imaginative. He was more of a man.' The 'sh' made my little feline's mouth look like a cat's asshole. Sasha who? The cellist or that dancer? Oh, they're all named Sasha anyway. What did I care? Shut up, Cynthia. Shut up and dance.

'Fettucini, though. There's a man ready anytime, anywhere. He could sing, too, in very special places.'

The steel went back to stone.

'Tenors, you know. They're very creative. Good higher head chakras.'

The stone went to wood.

She continued her circular motion, pale-blue eyes challenging me to add a story of my own.

The wood went to pasta al dente.

Cynthia took me out like one would remove some apple peeling from the garbage disposal.

'Sorry I don't please you,' said the witch in a haughty tone.

I began to explain that it was in bad taste to discuss the other successful lovers one has had while making love. It was OK to discuss other meals one has had while dining, but making love was different.

'Were we making love?' she asked. 'I thought we were just fucking. Sorry for you.'

Laughing, she put on her clothes. Not a good laugh but the kind that reaches up and chokes your heart.

Said over her shoulder as she left her own room, 'You know, I really thought you might be THE ONE. My mistake. I always fall for the ones with the weak spleens. Oh well. Don't forget to take your evening primrose.'

I could see Ked out in the hall and hear Cynthia say to her, before the door closed, 'See, I told you.'

Lothario

They tell me there's one on every tour. I suppose there's one in every corporation. Jesus, there's probably one in every relationship. Mine that is. And it's not me.

Bass players. You know what they say ... big instrument?

Big case.

He was one, all right. Italian, tall, with glossy black hair that radiated sexuality. I mean, can hair do that? His did.

He started with the women at the back of the string sections and moved his way up. He never slept with the front stands. Something about their talent made the women up there not so appealing. Of course, it might have been the beards.

Sheila, a particularly vibrant violist with glasses that did nothing to obscure her piercing eyes, told me about her encounter with him.

They met the second day. Both married.

'You must be new on this circuit,' Lothario asked, throat swelling.

'I played for the large-nosed guy. Thought I saw you on that tour,' she replied.

'Nope, missed the nasal cavity.' Grinning, he played with his wedding band.

She found him disgusting, from the smoothness of his voice to the perfection of his face. He looked like a living suit to her – put on to impress and just as eager to take off to impress.

Yet, to her own horror, Sheila found her body in direct

disagreement with her mind. His slickness made her sick. Sure it was his sexual self-confidence that was striking a chord within her, she was determined even more to ignore the man. Sheila could do such things. Besides, she loved her husband and would never cheat on him. Interesting woman. And then there's those Wolf Eye connections.

Rumour has it that she and Cynthia were at one time friends. Years ago, they went to the same high school together. Studied with the same teacher. Dated the same boys. Went to the same conservatory. Something happened, though, that neither seem willing to confess – though there's nothing preventing my doing so. Any mention of their long-lost friendship and Cynthia's sky eyes grow to slits. Sheila's head jumps to and fro from her neck with the mere pronunciation of the ex-friend's name. She looks ready to vomit.

'Don't *ever* feel sorry for that woman,' warned Sheila. 'Whatever you do, don't feel sorry for her.'

Fairly certain a sorry feeling has never been extended to Cynthia – or myself, for that matter – I began to have some pity for the wolf. Add to that it was Cynthia who brought Sheila and Lothario together for one of the most memorable weeks of Sheila's life. Nothing intentionally mutual happening here.

The Arabs at the concert in Morocco seemed astounded by Sheila's blonde hair and many a smiling white-toothed stranger sought a way to detain her as she made her way to the bus from the concert hall. I think they even adored her framed 'veiled' eyes, disproving that Dorothy Parker remark about men seldom making passes at girls who wear glasses.

'Please, miss,' one man whispered urgently, shoving a pencil in her face and a small white writing tablet at her stomach. 'Could you just do this one thing for me? Please write your name.'

Sheila hurriedly took the tablet, scribbled, and returned it to the man who was dogging her at an uncomfortable proximity.

'Mike Hunt alias Petunia Peeg?! Ms Peeg, you are most beautiful,' he called after her.

Sheila ran towards the others from the orchestra, hoping to get within the safe little circle of men and women wearing black and carrying various cases which could be used as weapons if the young Arab deciphered her joke.

In front, suddenly, was a huge crowd. She saw the dazzling hair of Cynthia reigning above it and many Arab men were on their hands and knees, apparently obeying some whim of the violinist's.

'My feet, dear fool. I said to kiss the feet, not my calves,' Sheila overheard Cynthia saying. She seemed ready to kick the man who had done the transgression when suddenly a shout of 'Police!' rang through the air.

Scattering everywhere. Someone grabbed Sheila's hand and pulled her through the crowd. It was a warm, firm hand that pulsed an electricity into her.

Lothario.

'Some crowd,' he said, after they sat on the bus. 'Did you see the guy following you?'

'The one I wrote the autograph for?'

'The one yelling, "Who are you to call me a pig? American whore!" Being called a pig is especially harsh in this country.'

'I don't agree with you there,' mused Sheila. 'One of our guides today translated how a schoolchild was insulting his playmates. Politely, I imagine for us women, he tried to translate it as "fuck you" but I asked for the real translation.' Lothario nodded his head, impressed by the vivid green of the eyes behind those dark-rimmed glasses.

'The kid was screaming, "I fuck your mother while your father watches." Sweet, huh? Coming from a nine-year-old. Guide tried to explain this was a mere trifle on the insult scale – like saying "shut up".'

Lothario laughed in a way that suddenly comforted Sheila. She didn't protest when his arm gently slid around her shoulders. She sighed and rested her head on his shoulder and fell to sleep.

Nothing happened and both were glad. But they did feel that sweet bond which follows falling asleep in one another's arms.

Here's where the luck comes in. Our specially equipped, state of the art bus managed to obtain that first date sleight of hand: a flat tyre. A flat tyre, mind you, in the desert where things are hostile whether you remain inside or go out. I was having a bit of the old Camus problem, feeling it was so hot I might just kill a man for no reason at all. Jonathon's sweat smelled quite bad, buzzing around me, causing me to think, 'If it weren't for his evil smell, I never would've killed the man.'

Rocky, Schwarzenegger, Hulk Hogan and ... Lothario with those impressive arms seizes the day. Single-handedly, he jacks up the bus, locates the spare tyre, thrusts and turns lugnuts – I'm not sure the order of all this. I think mechanics are best left to those guys who can afford dirty fingernails. But Sheila ...

Oh, Sheila, she loves heroes. Twice he had saved her. And what could she offer in return, for it bothered her greatly to be in another's debt. Forget that sixty-five others were also in Lothario's care. Sheila knew he had done it for her. She had mentioned that she thought she saw the man who received the pig autograph trailing them. Lothario encouraged the story and soon the entire bus was up in arms. I suspect he made the tyre flat on purpose, though it would be mighty difficult to prove. Slick – and much better than his usual yawning and stretching routine to get an arm around a girl.

Poor Lothario. His muscles so tired, his back so aching. Sheila so nearby. But then came Wolf Eyes. Without asking, without noting who else had the same thing in mind, she slid behind Lothario and began giving him a bone-melting massage. She could do that. The sighs escaping from her hero's lips pushed the jealousy barometer over an acceptable level for husband-loving, faithful Sheila. This was survival and Cynthia was not going to be the one with the man of the hour on her arm.

Without much grace, Sheila shoved aside Cynthia, to the onlookers' comments of 'Go girl' and 'Oh my'. If truth be told (do you believe it ever can be?), I was of the 'Oh my' ilk. Interlopers are not my cup of tea but neither are catfights. These felines squared off.

But no fight. Cynthia licked her lips in a suggestive way and that was it. Sheila did nothing. Lothario knew an opportunity when he saw it and slid his arms around 'his' girl: Sheila.

She tells me he is hot in bed, with a prick that goes through every metal state there is until arriving at red-hot iron. He loves every inch of her body in a way that makes her understand how fleeting their time is together. His hands erase her children, her household duties, her husband, her life before Lothario. He deflowers her virgin arse while frigging her hole with his skilful middle finger. He licks and licks her fur muff until she is crying, once until she peed on him, she lost control that much. He videotaped their lovemaking and then fucked her while they watched it. He has toys and tongue technique that make Sheila look like she is creaming all the time, even while just playing in the orchestra.

She told me that he painted her back with violin-style f-holes and then bowed her. His bass bow felt slightly rough from the rosin. He held her up, swinging her back and forth to some internal jazz tune. He performed pizzicato on her pussy, light delicate tapping and then, every once in a while, a Bartok body pound that made her legs crumple. In went the frog of the bow – frigging her with the frog. Yes indeed he did. Made her go down on him while he played the 'Swan's Elegy' or whatever that Saint-Saëns piece is – coming when he reached the high B. That was a spectacular tape to review and it included Sheila taped to a hotel chair while Lothario went between her legs and she came so many times she was begging him to stop. He did, after he untaped her and threw her on the bed, pumping and pumping and pumping until her blood felt it was only part of his ever-moving shaft.

Too bad Wolf Eyes was watching that one. She told me herself, she and I being now 'just friends', which is the same as saying 'You're never getting any action in my cunt again.' The little spy. She had every good reason to watch her ex-lover get it on. And I'm not speaking of Lothario. She and Sheila in the Yard practice rooms, practising tonguing techniques in the wee dark hours. Feeling each other up on the piano keys, legs spread. Cynthia boasts that she's a good pussy-eater and I believe it. Sheila loved it. Didn't want anybody to know she loved it but she loved it. Husband doesn't know, children don't know, happy community might faint if they thought their neighbour is an ex-lesbian. OK, experimenter. But she inhaled, I'm sure. Sure Cynthia, anyway, sucked her dry.

OK, that's all of it. Hand hurts from copying and I'm frustrated. Want to read much more. Beats reading about funeral processions, damn bad cakes and a whole lot of Irish pubs, one serving gorgonzola sandwiches. Vaguely remember story about journalist riding around with the LA Philharmonic. The orchestra members, forgetting that he was not a co-conspirator but a writer, told him everything: their affairs, petty gossip and nasty comments about the conductor and other musicians. About their mistresses, lovers, fun in massage parlours. Then, to their amazement and their spouses' utter feeling of betrayal, he printed it.

Is this another one of those tours – an exposé for some aspiring media type? Have been debating for some time whether to turn the guy in or just to get rid of the thing. Can a spy rat on a spy? Maybe I've stumbled upon something that was never intended to be seen by anyone except the writer's eyes.

Decided to keep the book in my black bag and put bag where it had last been – in the hotel lobby. That's where I am right now. Don't want to be mentioned in the memoir as the snooping violist. Wonder who

Sheila is supposed to be? Oh, I know 'Cynthia' all right, though her name is Wendy. She's the assistant concertmaster on this tour – why didn't I recognise her before? We went to Julliard together. Nearly everything written was true. Can't vouch for the sex but the stories – everyone's heard of her in one form or another. To tell the truth, the description is disquieting – hope such a light will never be turned upon me. Have already done a few things that I'd like to keep out of the limelight. The divorce isn't in any way final.

However, my inner detective is working her way to the surface. I *am* going to find out whose book this is. Hence, why I'm in the stupid lobby behind a proverbial fern. The tour only has eighty people, including techies. Some of the members don't have members (ha ha I'm funny) and others don't want to have anything to do with vaginas. That leaves about thirty people – some who can't even write English. Easy.

A rush of Russian tourists have suddenly descended upon the lobby. Gotta go.

Shit, shit, shit! And a fuck. Missed it! Damn, damn, damn. Thank God I didn't give up my day job, if I had one, for undercover work.

None of the Russians seemed pleased with how their accommodation had turned out. Guide was moving rapidly between hotel clerk and the group of fifteen. They gave their passports with many vocal comments. Wondered if they really were angry or if it was just that I didn't understand. Why don't I speak another language besides my parents' gutter Serbian? Polyglot, bilingual, American. Not that I haven't tried. Have had about sixteen fucking years of foreign languages under belt. Even half a semester of Russian. Surprisingly, I could recognise, 'Da' and 'Nyet'. Those words are the same in Serbian, I think. I know 'to eat' is the same. Probably 'to fuck' also – you know taboo words rarely change. We'll be saying, in English, 'fuck' well into the next millennium.

Anyway ... the young women in the group looked a bit like American prostitutes. Thigh-high boots, tons of make-up, ratted hair and postures that would have made my mother slap me. I felt certain that every man there in his running suit and three-day growth, including the space between the eyebrows, gave 'Ivan Ivanovich' as his name. The older women looked as if they had loaves of bread for breasts and long spaghetti squash for legs.

Because of observations like that, I lost the forest for the various decorations on the trees. Couldn't make it through the Russian group to get to the bag left there. They would not part. They had found their place in line and I was not about to jump in. A lot of 'Nyets' were hurled towards me, forcing a run around the group. You can see this coming, can't you? Well, book was gone, bag was there. Tried to convince myself I saw a puff of white hair – maybe Salvadore saw whoever took it. Maybe it is Salvadore. How, though? The man is already rewriting entire shows each day.

Saw Dave. Yuck! Saw Slava speaking with the Russian tourists. Saw the male bassoonist, who looks like he hasn't quite digested a big piece of steak, loitering outside smoking.

There were at least half the orchestra downstairs, waiting to meet up with someone. Stupid, stupid plan. Sometimes Daniel is right – I don't know how to figure things out. More upset that it half-worked. Someone, after all, did take the book.

Chapter Six

June 28, afternoon

O rgasms galore! Nearly as many as in all the years of my life. Ouch – why remind myself? Still feeling a bit of the 'What have I done?' I need to hide. You'd think I had a Catholic upbringing.

Midnight (was that two days ago?) I went to the café. Music and garlic careened out of the windows. Could have eaten the night air. Yum, yum, yum! Had slipped into a simple leather miniskirt and cropped white top, wishing I could carry myself a bit more like the dominating Kristine – but since I was walking alone, felt safer sporting toned-down attire and gently sloping shoulders instead of the breast-leading type of walk of a woman on the prowl.

Think the catcall started the night. Was thinking how lovely it was to have had an orgasm with Ted that first night. Don't plan to have more with him but that I could do IT! Feeling sexy, alive. Surprised myself by going over to the catcall. At any rate, that is what it sounded like to me. Why not a little flirtation to begin the evening? I was in Paris, after all.

The man was in the shadows, so I sauntered over, staring where I imagined his eyes to be. He cut quite a figure in the streetlight's shadows. Tall, broad chested – maybe too strong for me to resist, which was both alarming *and* exciting. Instinctively knew he wouldn't hurt me. Stupid assumption but was in Paris and full of lust-love.

'Ay-yai-yai-yai-yai!' screeched the voice in the darkness, my heart doing the pancake flip-flop.

'Sally, you bastard!'

'Come on, you knew it was me.'

Did not want to tell him otherwise, for that half-minute's walk had my pantyhose soaked with the intrigue of the moment.

S put his arm over my shoulder and we walked down Boulevard St Germain to the café.

After the Mission's meeting at the café, Angelika – decked out to the nines in a Ross 'Crossdress for Less' velvet gown – left to pursue his/her own pleasures. Serik and the dominatrix seemed bent on finding a fetish club where they would be given permission to hurt French people. Kristine's French nearly perfect and she knew where to go anyway. She simply wanted the opportunity to tell some others where to go as well.

That left Salvadore and I sitting at the café, drinking black coffee and pretending to smoke cigarettes by inhaling them second-hand. Damn these European smokers – why don't they look like the cigarette hag who taught second grade: Ms Butts. They pollute my air and yet look so beautiful. Thinking that and other things, Sal and I watched people watching us from the Café Bonaparte, across that narrow little street. We had found a sport which suited us performers well: observing while being watched.

God – the colours of Paris! Red lips of women, lights around cafés, the highlight of white everywhere on the door frames. It has the best feelings of New York about it: the people walking everywhere to go someplace special, food and history every few feet. The women have charm here – no walking about in comfortable tennis shoes, no frumpy sweatpants and T-shirts. Why does their skin radiate so, those fucking smokers? OK, it was nothing like New York but I am a patriot at heart. Can't really admit that Paris is *better* – so much more better!

No alcohol but felt as if I'd been imbibing, so much visual and odiferous input. Even the strong body odour of the men seemed sexual. They were ready at any time, maybe had just come from a previous romp. You'd think America has sanitised the nose, the obvious conclusion being that BO is disgusting – but I'd forgotten that not disgusting if related to sex – weird.

A waiter with shiny black hair and a perfect handful of an ass kept coming up to me, to brush away crumbs, wave away a fly or ask if we would like something else.

'I'd heard that French service was pretty bad,' Salvadore commented. He said that it smelled that way at least.

'Not when you're with me,' said I, the sudden expert on witty repartee.

'You are so beautiful. Leave him for me,' the waiter whispered in my ear in heavily accented English. Probably one of the few phrases he knew.

Laughed but wondered if Salvadore had heard. Know that all foreigners think Americans are sluts. And this café had a special history with its ex-pats. Logic would seem that it had its special history with sluts too.

'Why disappoint anyone?' thought *moi*, and excused myself to go to the restroom.

Was washing hands in the tiny space when the waiter burst in and pinned me up against the wall, kissing my mouth with a wine taste in his. Didn't resist, pretty sure I hadn't flirted. It was my moment where anonymous cocks and strangers' hands actually spilled over into reality.

His hands flew under my skirt and I waited until a finger burst through the pantyhose and into my cunt before saying 'Non, non'. Such a tease. In truth, I was afraid of coming and falling asleep right there.

I was about to do a stepping-into-the-abyss night and didn't care. Lucid in mind, I tell you – the last abyss encounter (early, early conservatory times) had involved copious amounts of very good weed. In Paris, in that bathroom, with the waiter, I needed to stop thinking completely. My body was urging me to do this, breasts gasping to spring forth out of their blouse for the world to grab them. And my cunt . . .

Walked out, gave Salvadore a quick kiss and said I'd like to go back. Slipped the waiter my hotel room number, and key. It was a very impressive tip which he received with an aura of sexual dignity.

At four in the morning came the knock. Was waiting in a borrowed lingerie set from Kristine: a Merry Widow with black stockings and no knickers. I know men can never understand how females can borrow each other's clothing but it's a bit tantalising too. For a moment, you live in the microbes and all of another – until yours invade.

When I threw open the door, not only was the waiter there, but three of his friends. For a few moments I was afraid. But it was Paris, I was on tour, and had already abandoned myself to the fate of the moment. This was much better than the tryst in my late teens. I was sober, I was older, and my body was on fire from its own internal heat.

They took turns kissing me and fondling my breasts and themselves, watching my expression to see if I was ready to travel further down the carnal joyride.

No one touched the pussy yet, and I was aching in anticipation. The cocks, the many cocks.

A pair of hands pulled breasts out of the Merry Widow and lips fell upon them. Still standing, others kissed my forehead and my hair. Delicious. Someone grabbed ass hard. Clit was pulsing and straining and a thin string of pussy juice began dripping down my leg. Didn't embarrass me.

Excited them.

More hands on my hair, up and down my leg. Heard movement on the bed behind me. Then body was hoisted up by the other men and on to the bed and the cock that lay there. Two men pulled legs further apart while another man straddled the man below and put his arms around me from behind.

It was an interesting position. Had tried it before, of course, but without the help of others. Tried it with Daniel in fact. Almost came then but he gave up too soon – as did I. Now, the penetration was so deep and I, jumbled wetness of feeling cascading out of me, cried out like a wounded but happy wildebeest.

They sat me upright on the cock and then moved me up and down on it. Two hands threw my ass up to the tip of the cock and then lowered me again until I was resting on the man's groin. Then up again, while juices flowed over his pubic hair and on to the bed. My arms rested on the shoulders of the two men pulling me up and down. When the man beneath came in one long throb, they pulled me off.

Cried again, for I was needing to come. Thought it impossible to go up a notch on the desire ladder but was even more aching with a need to be filled. Was positioned with legs on the floor and stomach on bed and a thought circled briefly. 'What am I doing here? This isn't me.'

Yet, in another moment, it was completely me with no morals pulling me this way and that with 'shoulds'.

This was just happening and I was along for the ride. A bit passive, I know. But so deliciously passive. The moment of that encounter, when I was nothing more than somebody's desire to spill seed into, to come – there was an out-of-body feeling to it. Like I was air being fucked. Very substantial air that hummed and quivered and loved being part of men's overwhelming need to seize and penetrate. Unbelievable glass-fragmented moments of ecstasy and animal joy.

The men began taking turns entering from behind.

Each made four of five thrusts into me and then a new man would enter and do the same. They traded off for about twenty minutes – couldn't really say because, with the aid of their talented fingers, I came after a few rounds. These men were good, cock hitting high in just the right way with clit pressing into the bed. Somniatically (just made up that word) delicious. Six years of self-induced orgasms and sleep are not easy to erase overnight. I'm working on it though.

When I awoke, found myself sandwiched between two men. Disorientated and fuzzy from the nap, at first, I couldn't understand how both seemed to be thrusting into me but realised one of the men was in my ass. Wasn't something I had tried lately – only once before in fact, with that first bisexual boyfriend of mine. OK, we're probably all bisexual but he was a fifty-fifty split. Had this talk with John. He said that if I were going to say no one is 100 per cent gay then I would also have to say no one is 100 per cent hetero either. Good point. But I know which end of the barometer I stand closest to: I LOVE MEN. More men, more men, more men.

Anyway ... Moron! How could I interrupt this re-creation of last night's (still don't quite know what day it is) poundings? In Paris, imagining myself a different version of the diva, I wasn't myself, just this new alter ego that couldn't have enough cocks. To be the meat or filling while two strangers fucked me seemed the most natural thing.

The men pulled in and out and then began thrusting together, saying 'Un, deux, un, deux,' the few words of French I could recognise (yippee). They called me beautiful (*belle*), stroked my back. Apparently, the other two had left. I think this is the way to learn a language! Je swee tray bone soosuz – did I mangle that? Waiter tried to teach me a useful phrase to say I was a good cocksucker.

Felt the wall separating my two holes being massaged by the two cocks. The waiter was at the front, with his arms completely wrapped around my body and the man behind me. They looked at each other while fucking my holes. Loved it – feeling a vessel, a conduit for these men. A conductor of their pleasure. A pulsing hot mediator, throbbing and being pulled – in, out, in, in. My head was on fire, eyes in the back of my skull. Bonelessness. Was floating and the cocks with hands were holding me, rubbing me, pushing me to something very hot . . .

Came, with a feeling like a thousand tiny pieces of sand were pouring into brain. Woke to find myself alone in bed with 30 minutes to get to the rehearsal. Semen was all about lower half, dried and flaking. Ass sore (certain now that I write it, all activity must have occurred two days ago, for it's OK now – my, how time does weird shifts in libido land), legs rubbery as I let the bidet do its freshening. Cool water took away the momentary feeling of 'What have I done?'

Threw on loosest pair of jeans and a big shirt which covered rump. Still smelled like sex and was hoping that might mask a bit of it.

The run to the hall helped me arrive five minutes before the rehearsal. How awful – no impossible – it was to be late to a rehearsal or performance. It's tantamount to saying one is a complete amateur. Corporate people can never understand this. Even Daniel, when he drove me to those two-bit gigs, relished watching me sweat as we narrowed the time cushion with traffic or his slow driving. Taking all surface streets because it looked closer on the map – like that saves any gas money. Just another exercising of D's power over me, that's what it was. Wonder what he would do if he only knew how I am getting fucked every which way and thanking people for it. I'm sure D is right now working on a way to do the same thing to me on paper – but I won't enjoy that transaction.

Ryan turned another slippery morning eye on me at the beginning of the rehearsal. 'I didn't catch his name. Mr Louvre, I think.'

'The gardens?' asked I. Ryan nodded. 'You *are* a slut,' I added, admiringly.

'So . . .' he raised his eyebrows that looked like upside-down butterfly wings.

'I didn't catch their name either.'

'Their?' he asked, while tuning his A string to the oboe's pitch.

Was already tuning the rest of my strings and used the excuse to correct myself. 'I said, "his".'

'Right,' replied Ryan, suspiciously. 'Sounds more like our Katie's becoming a heat-seeking bitch.'

I had made sure Ryan didn't see me walk out to my seat. Both holes (and I'm not talking about the two f-holes on the viola) felt worn out and I was afraid that sitting down might be uncomfortable. Yet, thinking back on the night, who cared if the morning carried a bit of pain? It was like a hangover after an outrageous party – the endorphins of the memory were taking away the soreness as I kept reflecting on the fucking of the night.

There it was, in the second piece. After ten minutes of 'oom-pahing', a solo for the inside last stand: me.

Sat up with a start and played it flawlessly, surprising myself.

Still a bit upset with Salvadore. We'd talked at the café about how I wanted to play less, not more. Hadn't mentioned to him that it's so I can continue to have a sex life on the tour. No sleep and solos are, usually, a bad combination. Do not want to be the one grinding the whole show to a halt because of my mistakes. And am not giving up the encounters – I can say that much regarding the priorities of what is going to be sacrificed.

To his credit, Salvadore is making everyone's parts more difficult. Was overjoyed to hear Dave gasping for breath as he triple-tongued a passage and then had to do it again for nearly an additional page. The music was wild and amusing. Things kept happening where they shouldn't. Slava would play the cymbal loudly in a quiet passage and then, when it was clear that the whole orchestra was leading up to the climactic cymbal crash, there instead would be silence.

The last of these, though, had Salvadore running up, not exactly screaming (that was not his style), but emphatically saying in his melodious voice, 'That's not it at all. Percussion, you *do* have a cymbal crash where the audience expects it the last three measures. If you mess it up, the whole joke is lost.'

Heads in the orchestra murmured to each other. What the hell did this composer want anyway? There was nothing funny about the music from that rehearsal – just chaotic. The cellist next to me leaned over and said, 'I just have one question: why?'

Rhythms out of control and melodies aborted and distorted made sense to me. Salvadore's music sounded hilariously, hysterically angry. Wonder why the rest of the orchestra has to be such conservatives when it comes to new music. They could play the same damn Beethoven symphonies their entire life and not realise what a museum they'd become. What was the fun in that? Except that one didn't have to practise. *That* was the fun. The *raison d'être* really. But, I love this music and think Sal a genius of the supreme and mighty sort.

It might be complete egotism or hubris, but am beginning to suspect that the orchestrations are being written for *moi*. Even that solo, which sounded hard, actually was playable upon first glance. All melodies have been shifted from the first violins to the violas. Maybe this too is one of Salvadore's jokes. Maybe I'm the only one who gets it. Well, it seems like Serik had a good laugh backstage when we began the intro music. His cattlecall shakes the timpani every time. Orchestra just doesn't know Sal in a way to get the inside jokes. I'm in the in. I'm in the in.

Chapter Seven

June 29

*T*he concert tonight made the audience hoot, titter, twitter, tinkle (they don't laugh the way the guffawing Germans did) with laughter. Was beside myself trying to see what happened on stage. The theatre was a smaller one, left over from the avant garde days. Thought that if I could only turn head a bit more to the right, might be able to catch a good portion of the show.

However, the bastard Salvadore had written a bitch of a piece for the entire viola section – with the two dueling bassoons accompanying. How he managed to churn out something, in the course of a day, which rivals Richard Strauss is beyond me. I suspect this was punishment for me alone. Had he seen W & co. entering my room late at night? They do keep coming back. Sal might be upset that our Paris evening together ended so early and hasn't been repeated since. I've been locked up in my room after each show with three men, bottles of wine and infinite hours of fucking and a few hours of sleeping. To tell the truth though, I'm tired of them. We've used each other's orifices in every way possible and I'm ready for something else. Not that the many (up to twenty-five) orgasms hasn't been worth it. But it's no more virgin territory – just fucking. Nice, but even with the three, the eroticism is gone. I'm going to give them the slip soon.

That book has also been on my mind. It feels like a snag in the carpet that, if not careful, I'll trip upon and break my wrist.

Could the book be Salvadore's? No one on the tour is as gifted as he – why not have him write too? Serik said that Sally was lucky if he got four hours of sleep a night. It has put me on guard. Maybe that is what has made Sal a bit upset – the distance. Well, too bad. I've got to take care of myself. It's one thing to have mindless fucks and quite another to end up in someone's memoir about it. Knowing these encounters aren't going to happen again is what makes them so intense. And probably I smell different. I think I did flirt with Salvadore a bit and now I probably don't. Still think he is very cute and sexy. Just far away. Like he's observing me all the time. Makes me self-conscious. Can't say he's given off any jealousy vibe. His music, though, is furious and full of churnings and confusion. Descending where one expects the opposite and then sudden bursts of absolute quiet accompanied by screams onstage.

Oh well. Waiter & co. soon to end. Often thought that was why soldiers going off to battle were most certainly guaranteed to be laid. The waiter is soon to never serve me again. I think last night's encounter with the uncorked wine bottle up the ass and the three men jerking off on me, then licking up their come (though one gave an awesome clit licking which I came to and then did NOT fall asleep – a breakthrough) . . . well, it's run its course.

88

July 1

Surprise, surprise. At breakfast today, John was there, scarfing his free meal. Why he isn't fat is beyond me. The guy even brings tupperware to the buffets. Saving money can't be that gratifying. Today, J looked awful, like he'd stayed up all night in a barn, eating spoonfuls of tapeworms.

I didn't look much better. Resisting trysts is tiring. W & co. keep pounding on door. Don't dare complain – Leo probably would find out and tell and then I'd be hounded by members of the orchestra who might feel that if I was good enough for a few French waiters then some American musicians would be good enough for me. Have managed this long to avoid the title 'Orchestra Slut'. Not that I'm the orchestra prude but want people to just think I like having a good time – that's it. Wish Salvadore's room wasn't across from mine. Sure he's seen the comings and goings on. Wait . . . maybe. Hmm.

Well, it's always safer to keep the image of total slut a bit of a mystery. Don't want to have to start sleeping with people for gigs. Or . . .

No, really don't want that. It's helped Cynthia, aka Wendy, but that was not a route I opt for. And first and foremost, once started, can't be undone.

Back to breakfast. 'So, Katie. What's up?' John asked with his nose in a Kleenex.

'Tell you later. What's up with you?'

'I think my allergy pills are past their expiration.'

'You bought them at a discount place?'

'No . . . why would I *buy* them? They give them out free in some of these countries. These are from the cache I've collected over the years.'

Unbelievable, *n'est pas*? It's said that John/Angelika does not need the money from these gigs. He comes

89

along just for fun. It's still a hoot to him to be famous, I guess. Certain he sublets his house while away saving up stacks of croissants and guzzling *au gratis* cappuccinos. John is probably one of those million-aires who still steal the little coffee spoons from Mc-Donald's. They say he's made millions from some website he designed which boasts downloadable greeting cards. When I see Serik, we'll do some surf-ing. Kowabunga.

Asked the obvious. 'Why is it that you are always here for breakfast?'

'Free food, Katie. I keep telling you guys, I bought a house saving the money they give for food on tours.'

'Hey,' I whispered. 'Check out Slava. Quite a camera collection he's got around his neck.'

Slava, indeed, had at least four heavy cameras slung in various ways about his body. He was having a particularly hard time with the one on his left arm. Every time he went to reach for fruit, it swung down and knocked some glasses over. As soon as he righted the glasses, down it would swoop again.

Something must have been wrong with me. For just a fraction of a second, I found Slava attractive. He had showered and was wearing a close-fitting T-shirt which showed off a fine physique. He destroyed the image as soon as it was formed by knocking over the entire pitcher of orange juice and then trying to clean it up with a white tablecloth.

Dave swooped by for a moment with a video cam-era. 'Say something for the folks at home, Katie.'

'How about, turn that fucking thing off?'

Instead, Dave impishly moved the camera to my face. In my mouth was still an unswallowed bite of banana. Put lips up to the camera and shoved the mushy mess out through the spaces in teeth and on to the lens of the recorder. Not going to be some monkey subject for that clown.

red hair and nose ring gave me a thumbs-up and Ryan grabbed his crotch in appreciation.

Now what? Thank Sally or kill him? I do not want to be working this hard – it's shaving years off my life. Turning me into a firefighter – never knowing when the next outbreak is going to be in the music. And making me want to jump down any slippery pole.

To the Queen of Transgressions – call me QT. One of the WAAs (female hornist) asked me if I would like to come back to her room and join her and a few others in a game. Seemed intriguing.

Was. This musical chairs fuck took my mind off the energy spent on the orchestral performance. And on Salvadore. Now, upon rethinking our last encounter – am sure was set-up. Got one of his buddies to fuck me on the sly. No, that doesn't quite fit. Insane but am mad at him for making me feel tawdry. Like he didn't enjoy himself, no matter what happened. And to think, I really was falling in love. Or something.

Anyway – about the 82 orgasms. The game worked like this: three women (myself included) hold arms (did I mention we're naked?) and bend over so our heads were nearly touching. Then we begin to move slowly in a circle. There's a clarinetist off in the corner. She's playing some kind of Klezmer music – ludicrous for the game we've embarked upon but still, somehow, appropriate.

Four men are stationed behind us. They move in a circle in the opposite direction. You can see this coming (pun intended), can't you? Music stops and they have to find the nearest hole to fuck. The one who can't get it into somewhere on the first try has to sit out. So does the woman whom he was fumbling. They can screw in the corner if they want to. One of the couples did, the other watched, as yours truly was down to two guys. My fantasy. Problem was, they both were getting in. I know, I can't believe I played it now. But time and time again, I had two guys in my twat. It felt fabulous. And once, one managed to get up there in my ass. (He had rubbed Vaseline over himself, I'm sure – though I guess things have loosened up at the backside due to W & co.) After three turns at 'Pop Goes the Weasel', the group decided that they both won and I went over to the bed to take the two men. As their prize. My prize. Whatever.

One of the men was a trombonist and boy did he love to slide in and out. The other was a guy who sits in the back of the bass section. Damn that Norton. I kept wondering if this was Lothario. He was extremely well hung and gave directions to us other two to flip this way or that while he moved to his optimal advantage. I knew he was moving us around for his own pleasure but it didn't bother me the way that did with Daniel. Let's just say it was Lothario – he bumped into me hard from behind while the trombonist's cock moved in and out of my throat. I thought of those Greek vases with the prostitutes immortally impaled upon two cocks like a barbecue brochette. Still wonder if, for those men, is this something more gay then hetero or vice versa? Lothario seemed to love just having a hot, wet, swollen place to ram into. The trombonist was looking at him with a bit of territorial breach – I don't think he liked getting so many directions: turn this way. Pump into her mouth as I shove this in. Hold on, I'm going to ram her up on to your cock with my cock. Let's switch – I need to come in her mouth. Let's switch again. I need to pound. Would you like some good pounding? To me. Hold her head, don't want to conk her out on the headboard. Fuck, baby, that's right. Nice ass. Great pussy. You are hot. I want to spew into you. I want to fuck and fuck you. Would you like that? Fuck you and fuck you while he holds your head. Suck his cock.

I'll keep going if you suck his cock. We won't stop until you drop.

I think I made a few of those lines up – but that was the gist. God, it made me hot. I wanted to be his good love slave – to be fucked and to please. So clearly domineering was he that I found it sexy. Don't ask – I'll call a biologist. Must be something deep within, because I don't think I'm the only woman to feel that way. When a man is good at it . . . watch out!

Then, I remembered where I'd seen the red-hair before. She wasn't there last night but something shook the memory loose: the conservatory. Anyway – the female hornist came over and began to go down on me. This was while L was fucking away. I was on my back by this time and he was yelling out that I had a super-cunt: it never went dry. That seemed to intrigue the female spit-valve player who came to suck on the clit while observing the seething wetness flowing out of me. She threaded my clit into her mouth and began giving it the most delicate head, like it were a very little precious penis. Men don't suck that way. Fought urge to clamp my legs around her neck and get her off me. Don't want to have it known that I do it with girls. And I don't really. Except that time in the conservatory.

This was fabulous. Soon, everyone focused on me. Me, me, me. Man inside, filling me up, woman outside giving sensitive pleasures that made my body twitch. The other two women came over and each took a breast to lick and nibble. Now all the women were occupied with me and I think the men started to think that they too should be hitting on whatever spaces I had left. The trombonist was the one who had so expertly slid into my ass when we were playing the musical fuck game, so he slid underneath me, lubed up, and inserted his cock. My back arched into the French hornist's mouth in a most delightful way.

Lothario continued to pump away – the man was a machine for he hadn't come yet and I was afraid. Thinking about the torrents of come swimming into me (he had on a condom but the thought . . .) sent me over the proverbial edge. I came into the French hornist's mouth. I mean, I really think I ejaculated something. God, it all felt so wonderful. Another man was in my mouth. Then Lothario came with a roar – a real ejaculation of sound and spirit. The 'oh baby, yeah' said with his deep voice was enchanting, stimulating – whatever . . . I came again with a little help from the French hornist's hand. L pulled out and another man inserted himself.

Once, at Daniel's parents' place by the lake, I witnessed a line of male ducks taking their turn with a female. All very polite and all patiently waddling forward to have their fill. But it was the female duck I envied. Male after male wanted her and she denied no one. That was what last night was like.

That's two orgasms. Came again when flautist (female) stuck her tongue along oboe player's (male) penis, which was stuck in my very female hole. Actually, by that point, I didn't feel as if it were a hole exactly but an entity swallowing up pleasure and men's dicks. Fourth orgasm happened when small bite was taken on breast while a heavy hand pushed my clit deep to my bone. Fifth, someone was inside me. Etc. Maybe not eighty-two but my super-cunt is worn out now and yet I am still yearning for more. Some button has been pushed and I think it will be a long time before it gets turned off.

Love this city. I feel so beautiful – yes, full of beauty. Full, full . . . seeping in fact.

Chapter Eight

July 6

Whew. Sal is trying to kill me. My left hand is dying from playing so many notes and my right hand can't hold a pencil at this point. Up bow staccato no less. Twelve minutes' worth. Bastard! Want to talk to him but he seems so drawn into himself that I can't – feel like taking a stick to his hermit crab's shell and poking. Not up to it after the other nights. Gave cunt a rest last night. Read a bit of Joyce – really! Made me hungry, horny, and depressed. Too many funerals, and unrequited lust – and too much food in that book: burnt rashers, beer, potatoes, crumbs of tea cakes on little boys' lips . . .

So, last night was it for a bit. Praise be! We're scheduled for another two weeks in Paris, no performances. Free, free, free. Good call on management's part. The shows in Germany had been back to back and made for gruntling among the disgruntled. Began with the bassoon section. Trish and Tony can't stand each other any more (funny, since they were two of the first WAAs to shack up together). He said she sways too much with the music and makes her bassoon sound like a farting bedpost. She said that at least she didn't smell like one. The quarters in the pit are rather cramped and make for short friendships. Being in each other's faces day after day (night after night . . .) – guess management thinks this an appropriate time to let the monkeys run in the zoo.

The musical fuck committee all smile now, knowingly, when we pass by one another. Ryan noticed and has been begging for the story. Tried not to spill the beans since the musical fuck vowed secrecy but . . .

Well, it was Ryan and who said I had to keep my acts from him? He was so impressed. Swore he'd never done anything quite like that. Doubt it but feel liberated somehow. A risk-taker, an adventurer, an orgy queen is born.

Which reminds me, for the first days of the break, Kristine and I have decided to take a little trip into the French countryside. Wonder if Kristine doesn't have a few of her own waiters she's trying to escape.

July 7

Kristine is not only a dominatrix but has a great fixation on horses. Great fun if one is sixteen but I think the diva's fascination is downright unhealthy. Secretly renamed her Catherine the Great.

At first, *moi* was amused by the diva when she showed up at hotel in a simple dress and a broad black hat. She looked every bit the French girl going out to the countryside in the summer.

'I have my *other* alter egos,' said Kristine to the look I gave her.

We boarded the train at Gare St Lazare and set out for Chantilly. A two-day tour, a two-day tour (cannot stop singing 'Gilligan's Island'!).

Could NOT stop thinking of Salvadore the whole trip out there. Watching the great green farms of the countryside, I heard Salvadore's lute music. I've never heard him play but I can imagine. Those beautiful, sensual hands caressing the instrument, bringing forth the deep and pure melodies of the Renaissance. Want him to hold me that way – I'll be his lute and he can strum and pluck to bring forth a vibrant song from deep within me.

Think Sal is used to hearing his music played not the way he heard it in his mind. Perhaps, the first time I played my solo it was perfect. Little pieces of his heart started drifting towards me. I imagine him playing a song for me now up through his heart and out to his fingers on the lute. Imagine he's certain I'll never hear it.

Welcome to the deranged mind of a rabid violist. Jesus – next I'll have us happily married and in a picket fence (I'll be the one speared atop it while Sal takes pot shots). I need to remember that, unfortunately, the creator must allow his creation to follow his own song. I mean, just because I imagine this doesn't mean ... Oh, I don't know what it means. Whatever!

Kristine noticed my wistful restlessness – how could she not, for I think I might've been jumping about and breathing out little moans. *Moi* is such a geek!

'All right,' said the diva, ten minutes into the trip, startling my reverie. Her left eyebrow was arched comically, her mouth a twitch. 'Spill it.'

I thought of half a dozen things at once. Was this a question about how I ended up on the Mission's bus or who I was sleeping with? Or did the dominatrix know something about the book? The musical fuck? Waiter & co.? (Come to think of it, I have been very busy!) The diva surprised me with her intuition (though I suspect Sal also confided something to her –

now wondering if K's little countryside outing isn't a ruse to get info out of me for him. Not past the Mission for that kind of plan. Tight little group).

'You have a thing for Sally, don't you?' The diva looked smug, her eyes glassy, two perfectly manicured red nails resting on her neck.

Was slow to respond. 'I like Sal but . . .'

'Well, who was the Merry Widow for? You went out that night with him then came back and borrowed . . .' She tried to get me to jump in and finish the rest of the sentence. An unfortunate habit I have that she seemed bent on exploiting.

'Oh. I see.' Understood she was grasping at straw, alfalfa, wheatgrass. Was not about to divulge the waiter story. It seemed rather sordid and mean to tell the tale under the circumstances.

'Well?' The eyebrow arched even higher. Even though it was country girl attire, you couldn't take the dominatrix out of it.

Was compelled to reply. 'Sally's cute. He's infinitely talented too. I just have a few things that need to get straightened out.'

'Like your back?' the diva snorted.

Not certain where that comment came from. Let it slide.

I returned to staring out the window. Trains, invariable, always make me think of sex. Perhaps because here/there is where IT all began. Lost virginity on first tour ever, eighteen years old and in Europe.

Q. What's the longest viola joke?
A. Harold in Italy

That was the running line on the tour. The principal violist could not play this very difficult piece. I ended up taking over and he was never going to let me forget about it. Awful! Wasn't my decision but that

102

didn't matter to the petty little scorekeeper. Any minor mistakes I made brought a very audible 'harrumph' from this most disagreeable of stand partners.

This new leadership position put me in touch with the conductor. Hadn't yet learned that sleeping with the man on the podium can be dangerous. Hadn't yet learned that the aching his piercing black eyes drove into me when he gave a cue to our section, hadn't imagined that the aching had its root in primal, biological lust. From my wise, near-middle-age present, I can now say that this man and his power over me was the beginning of my sexuality. I felt exposed in the solo and grossly scrutinised by my stand partner and peers. I was vulnerable and nubile and curious. It wasn't with lust I approached the man who directed us and whose every word we devoured but with an understanding that he could fill in some gaps. Didn't know what they were but knew he was the key.

I'd also been encased in baby fat at the time and unaware I was attractive at all.

The maestro's fingers on my throat. His lips on my neck . . .

He had his own car for our overnight travels. In there, the Spanish conductor took me (I think Rodrigez is Spanish – maybe he was from South America). Anyway, I lost everything all at once – clothes, first kiss, virginity. I had seen men's penises (or is the plural penii?) before but had never felt one or experienced the fullness they could provide. It's where I fell in love with the cock – though beet-head told me later I was brainwashed by men. Don't think so. I'm sorry she never experienced any tender lovemaking from a male of our species, but it does exist. This conductor, for example, showed me the utmost pleasures and with great concern for my well-being. I'm sure he got great pleasure out of deflowering a maiden – for if it

103

hadn't been clear I was a virgin, it was clear by the time I tried to give him a blow job. I just blew on his cock – I mean, why do they call it that anyway?

The first lips I ever felt on my clit were his and, at first, all I experienced was a hot sensation down there. But soon I could feel more intensely that I had a throbbing little organ down there that increased its pulsing. Can you believe it – I didn't exactly know I was coming. Sure, I'd been masturbating for a long time but it's different when someone else pushes you into that white space of a million exploding pieces of yourself inside.

'Chantilly, Chantilly,' came the announcement. The dominatrix was up and pushing past people so she could be first at the door. She looked back with disgust, seeing me let couple after couple pass by. I was in such a mood I didn't want to separate people. It seemed so rude. The diva managed to get a good trainload away from me. Figured she'd just have to wait.

Surprised I remember everything so well. That's what a train ride does to me. Everything becomes alive again – and new. Like I lost my virginity all over again and was full of a fresh new mystery. The smell of warm earth poured into me as I stood on the platform, letting waves of people pass me (and push me and curse at me too – apparently not everyone feels the way I do about trains). The diva came and dragged me down, looking a bit annoyed.

'What's come over you?' asked Kristine, not hiding her irritation.

Smirk, smirk, ha . . . come over. 'I love everything here. The smell, the sun, the people . . .'

'OK, we'll have time for that. Let's get a coffee and then walk around. Horse racing?'

I'd been thinking that the castle would have been better but didn't want to spoil the balance of the outing. Coffee sounded not only wonderful, but mandatory. And I certainly did not want to spend day off with a caffeine-deprived diva in bitch mode. I could smooth things over, Katie the mediator. The mellow one. Divas are bound to be high-strung, figured I from my worldly wisdom that I was in some way blessed with knowledge the diva was not. For example, I was not in a hurry for anything, for what is special comes to us. It was a Zen sort of thing. Diva struck me more as someone who would eat the Buddha for lunch if 'He' dared disturb one of her needs. And I was certainly less than a Buddha – yet, wise enough to know *that* at least.

Kristine brought two half-bowls of coffee and milk and some rolls to the table. Oh, how I savoured the smell. Yeast and coffee – eating and drinking them is always a let down. What does my body expect them to taste like? Both are intricately connected to our body parts down there, don't you think? Even a very clean ass has a bit of a coffee smell to it and the male scrotum always smells a bit like freshly baked bread. Or am I just remembering the conductor's privates? His is the smell which everyone else compares against – even if it's subconscious now. Sal, btw, smells a bit of the conductor. Maybe the warm yeasty smell means power and creativity.

'You're quite dreamy today.' Diva was trying a new way to get me to talk.

'People keep disturbing my sleep.' Amusement hung on the words. Let the diva interpret which way to push the phrase.

'People?' The eyebrow nearly made it to the hairline.

Oh, oh, ooooh – I just wanted to relax but realised this Chantilly trip was not a 'girl thing' (as the diva had explained to the boys) for bonding but for exposure. Kristine had a bit of the detective in her too. Ha

– she can't out-sleuth Katie the gumshoe. You're on, sister. Plus, I haven't been hitting all those high Es – so I do believe my brain is just a bit sharper. Not dulled by the vibrations and all. (I still hold a theory that sopranos and boxers have much in common from the certain injuries they deem OK to inflict upon their heads and the heads of others.)

I cut things short. 'Be frank, what are you asking me?' (In retrospect, a silly thing to say in France.)

The diva looked as if she'd swallowed her pet poodle's chew toy. She cleared her throat. 'Well,' she looked down and tightened the laces on her country dress, 'I think you and Sally would be perfect together. What do you think?'

Had a ready retort to this. 'Why is it that people can't help themselves from trying to put other people together? Do you really know any happy couples?'

The diva frowned. It was not becoming for her pink-cheeked and haughty face, which now creased in a way to make her look much older than her 30 years. Looked to me she was certain she knew a few but all she could recall at that moment were the unhappy ones.

'See what I mean? Please, Kristine, don't fix me up. I can take care of myself.'

Diva didn't like this challenge. 'But Sally is so wonderful. Look at those hands. And he's lonely.'

'Did he tell you that?'

'No.' Again the frown. Then a light passed into the diva's face. 'But I know he hasn't had a girlfriend in a long time.'

That you know of. I was privy to other knowledge.

'Could we talk about something else?' asked I in a flat tone.

The diva became all smiles. 'But of course.'

It was lovely to be out of Paris. No horns were honking. No one crowded near us with a Turkish cigar. I had some of those same feelings while going to the conservatory. Sometimes, I just had to get out of the overwhelming 'nature' of NYC. Perhaps that's how I came to live with Daniel. He promised so much fresh air. Stuffed shirt. Stop thinking about him, Katie – you were doing so well.

Anyway – we walked to the racetrack. I'm telling you, the diva knows how to gamble. I did not want to risk my money and made the minimum bets. But the diva enjoyed placing 100 francs down on each race and she usually came back with 130 or 140 francs.

'Come on, Katie. You can't really win unless you risk big.' The diva jumped up as her horse ran by, shouting, 'El Baroness'.

El Baroness won and Kristine was now at least 1,000 francs ahead. It was too much to sit back and watch her win so I decided to put 20 francs on a horse whose black tail struck me as graceful.

'Now, you have to have radical trust, Katie. Let go of the idea that you're going to lose.'

I did. Put out of my mind the potential loss of the money. It was making me think of other losses too for some reason. The shiny hair of Mother. Black, thick and straight. Not a hint of grey, always pulled back to never stray into her face as she weeded the strawberry plot or picked oranges from an overflowing tree. The first year of marriage to Daniel when things were truly perfect – except the orgasms. Maybe I'm the reason nothing worked right in the end. I lied from the beginning about that, in an effort to please him. Ouch, I really cannot write this. Ouch, ouch, ouch.

'Katie, are you focusing?' The diva transformed herself into a cheerleader. 'Focus. Your horse will win. Say, "Oui, Monsieur Bleu".'

'Oui, Monsieur Bleu.'

'Harder.' The diva was right in my face

'Monsieur Bleu.'

'Great. Now to the horse.'

Fuck off, thought I. Don't appreciate that kind of preachy, change-your-life tone. What was the diva trying to get at? It was as if she were selling magnetic furniture or something. To keep the peace, I half-heartedly shouted to my horse, which actually seemed to turn and look at me as it galloped on by.

Last.

The diva looked smug when she came back, counting her new winnings.

'If only you'd believe, Katie.'

It was all I could do to keep from hitting her. It wasn't like I was part of some cult. This was gambling and I lost, second-handedly contributing more to the diva's winnings.

Reassuring myself this was just a game, I said, 'Come on. I want to see the castle. Your treat.'

'Fair enough,' said the diva, putting down her arched brow.

Wouldn't you know it – the castle has a museum with glorious pictures and a stables with horses, donkeys, mules – and a lot of people who train them. Where did we go first?

'It'll only take a minute – I need to see my faves,' cooed the dominatrix.

I am stupid, stupid, stupid. What or who did I think I was travelling with – she's an adventurer, not an intellectual. I guess all those still pictures make her bored. Anyway, spent the rest of the day smelling the green tones of horse shit and watching Kristine converse in excited dialogues with the horse people. They all seem to know her. We even got to go to a special place in the stables – though, if you ask me, it still smelled like the same shit.

Then – you guessed it – dusk was upon us. Kristine urged me to hurry to the train station where we could still make it back to Paris.

No way, José. I came to see some goddamn pictures and that was what I was going to see, even if I had to sleep in the doorway of the castle to make it happen.

Dominatrix got all in a big huff and said, 'Look – we're not going to find a room here.'

To which I replied, 'What do you mean "we"?'

So, yes, she left after taking one last pat of all the horses' butts she could find on the way. Kristine, the equine lover to her death – I may be the one to kill her.

Future biographers ... you know the drill. If you find Kristine squashed under a two-ton stallion, I did not have anything to do with it.

So I wandered around Chantilly with my limited French trying to obtain a room. And I did! It's late now though, so I'll tell you more about it tomorrow. I scored big time – let's just say that.

Chapter Nine

July 8

I am on a fuck fest – that's for sure. Louis approached me at about eight o' clock last night and asked in pretty poor English if 'You sleep here or need to place anywhere?'

Oui, oui, oui. Gorgeous – the dark French with the blue eyes and a nice nose that nuzzles the clit but good. Anyway, I'm ahead of myself. When I explained I was a violist with Symphony X, his eyes lit up. 'Serik your friend?'

Apparently the three-legger frequently visits this region for some type of wine or oil or . . . who knows with the gourmand? Anyway, Louis is a master chef at the cooking school here and I was treated to a most amazing meal by the student chefs. I wish I knew what I was eating but all I can say is we didn't retire until very late. I was happily tipsy and full of fine tastes and Louis just looked like the perfect end to the evening. We hadn't spoken again about where I was sleeping. We both knew it would be with him.

I think he has a wife – who cares? I knew it was a

one-night stand. Not big on being the other woman but it was fun to feel I was part of a big secret. And he has a BIG secret. A delicious fit, if you know what I like. And he was French – aren't extramarital affairs smiled upon in that country? Have idea that wife is somewhere, banging away with the delivery guy, Guy. Makes me feel good, just thinking it.

I'm still sequestered in the guesthouse. Louis might come in any minute so if the writing breaks off, that's why. Anyway, he brought me to this little cottage which smelled (you guessed it) of lavender. And there were those famous lace doilies everywhere. In a nice way – I'm not big on the things, even if Elvis's popular song has me dancing around a bit inside. Seems every place I go triggers a song.

Louis laid me on the bed and undid my clothes somehow. I mean, I couldn't undo the skirt and blouse for the life of me. Luckily, I'd been inspired by Kristine and underneath my get-up was a lovely sheer lace bra and panty set which Louis seemed to admire, for he licked my nipples through the bra and breathed on my nether hair through the knickers. Very erotic. I felt like I was one of his food dishes he was testing before beginning the preparations. Making sure I was fresh enough for the sous chef. For the head chef. For the guests.

I passed, I passed. Like Charlie Tuna, kept saying to myself, 'Eat me, eat me.'

Louis prolonged my desire with a walnut-scented oil which he proceeded to rub over me with what seemed to be his cock. I assume that because his cock had the taste and smell when he fucked my face. Gently, mind you, but a face fuck, with balls slapping chin and penis going down throat. Then his lips were on mine and he was kissing me with a breath that smelled of walnuts, oranges and cinnamon, sucking my lower lip into his mouth. He caressed my eyes and

111

I think I did a very good job of responding with a sensitive sucking of his tongue and teasing of his lips. Had no idea I was that wet when he simply plunged in and slammed me.

Did I mention that I love a good hard fuck? Daniel sort of did that but he petered out – plus it was more like a bowel movement for him. Oh, how the Spider-woman episode has coloured my past. Anyway . . .

Louis thrust and thrust and I was feeling I might come with him when he flooded me with sperm. Then, the French wonder went down on me and sucked his own come out. Charlie Tuna got her wish and then some. His nose pressed into my clit and I came just from the newness of it all. Coming in Chantilly – I like that. Chantilly Lace and a come-smeared face . . . that's what I like. Cannot stop that happy melody from bouncing like uncased sausage about my neurons.

Saw the museum today to boot. Louis took time off, after feeding me chocolate croissants in bed at about 10 a.m. and – after a nice quickie of him entering me from behind while I swallowed the last bit of breakfast – took me to the Chateau, *sans* stable tour. Marvellous works of art are there – though there is one picture that really disturbed me. It was like the artist was trying hard to show off. One of those Velasquez-types, with paintings within paintings within paintings. Like, will the real artist stand up? What *is* the subject matter of a painting of paintings? That irks me.

Another problem lurked about in that every time I saw a naked or semi-naked man, I got the urge to fuck Louis. I saw him ogling the nude painted women and then leering at me. Btw, there were many more of that subject for him to look at than in my department. This is why women need to become painters, and fast. Anyway, God knows how many great works I missed but then Louis spoke to some important personnel there and, next thing I know, we're being whisked to what looked like a special collections room. Couldn't understand a word the man with a little goatee was saying ... thought he was attempting to explain the valuable this and that. Saw what looked like money exchange hands and then heard the door click behind, exiting goatee. Louis and I were alone among all these priceless works of art. The new thought that we could fuck right there and then had me anxious (we might be caught and I'd be exposed as a very different sort of art lover) but Louis seemed quite comfortable with it. He wasn't trying to control the heat seething out of his loins like I was trying to control my own. Was afraid this was getting way out of hand, that I couldn't stop this act even if it meant going to French Guiana.

Stripped off my skirt and shirt – yes, same skirt and shirt that smelled of horses, thanks to the dominatrix – at Louis' request. He then unrolled a canvas and showed to me a woman much like myself in body. Louis posed me on top of the table and pretended he was painting what he saw: the lovely naked Katie. Kept putting his thumbs together to make a half-box with his hands and then he proceeded to digest every corner of my body.

I felt beautiful! For the first time in my life – I saw myself as breathtaking. I know I'm not – I'm just a compact cute thing but in that room, among those rarities, I found myself feeling that I was every bit as precious. Louis, thank you Louis, for making me feel so. Funny, for so many years, I never wanted to be objectified but now I can understand the real sexiness of it. Of course, Louis did it right – I wasn't just an ass or a pair of boobs (love French men who think any-thing more than a handful is a waste). I was a goddess, accent on the last syllable to make it sound French. I was a thing to be admired, respected, worshipped – a Helen of Troy, a Renoir beauty without the ripples. A woman. Thank you, Louis.

113

With a large paintbrush, he 'painted' my body, starting with the face. The soft brush rushed over my eyes and lips, slowed down at my throat and then focused on my left breast. Louis looked to the painting and then to my breast, making me raise my left arm and then sighing contentedly – as if to look at me were the one thing he had always wanted to do in his life. The brush twirled on my nipple, it stiffening on cue. Louis stood back and again sighed. Brush moved down belly, down to bush, then legs. My skin purred when he began the brush up the calves and then pretended he was earnestly painting my ass.

'What colour?' I asked.

'Shh. Don't disturb the masterpiece I am creating.'

Sweet.

A final brush up the back and on the neck had me ready to surrender to anything he proposed.

We didn't fuck there. Instead, Louis took me to his school and to a class. An art class. I posed naked in front of twenty young men and women. Nothing to hide and it felt glorious to see that they were making my flesh come alive with their charcoal. Louis stood by watching and when only I could see, he touched himself through his pants. Glad I wasn't a man or I would have gotten an erection in front of the class. My nipples did stiffen but that could have been attributed to the cool breeze in the room. Began to think that maybe another reason that women are painted so much more often than men is that, in the nude, their physicalities are just a bit more predictable.

At first, the rather severe female instructor laid me out on my side with one leg slightly up and my head looking up over my shoulder. The students drew my backside and I felt utterly exposed as they did so. My inner lips were parted and, squirm as I might, they just wouldn't put themselves back together again. The moistness nestled up in its cave was enjoying a slight breeze. Held position for a long time, which didn't seem hard at first – just a few twitches here and there – but then thought I might die holding leg, looking over shoulder. Even fingernails began to have a sensation.

After an indeterminate but long time, I assure you, severe instructor with glinting glasses and pen in hair pulled me up and placed me on an even higher pedestal. Was asked to hold three lilies just so. Saw my pinkish skin and the darker pink of my nipple in contrast to the whiteness – saw that the class had switched from charcoal to coloured pastels. Caught my shade on a young boy's canvas. He blushed when our eyes met.

Couldn't move any more than that without a repositioning by the instructor. After perhaps three hours, lilies were beginning to wilt and shake, my knees were pink and Louis had gone home to wife, no doubt. He left instructions with one of the students to drive me back.

Clothes felt quite heavy and I took them off once inside the vehicle. Student swallowed hard, I think in an effort to pretend he was cool. Sure he was a virgin. I'm not a corrupter of youth. The blushing student and I only kissed in the car, but it felt deliciously illicit cheating on a cheating lover.

Must go. Louis is here. I can see him through the window. He's completely naked.

Chapter Ten

July 9

*B*ack on the train feeling amused, humiliated and slightly full of opprobrium. Depends how you look at it. Mother Nature spared me a very embarrassing moment by not having my menses gush all over the art studio while my nooks and crannies were being drawn. But she wasn't so completely kind. Timing Katie, it's all about timing (and misplaced goods. Ugh!).

Didn't know how to convey to Louis last night that period was starting. Was just beginning to spot. Thought I felt a bit puffy for art class but attributed extended tummy to wonderful meal night before and to Louis' huge cock stretching all inner regions. Anyway, I didn't feel fat, just full, like a ripe cantaloupe.

Make that a tomato. Gross! Anyway, was pretty sure Louis understood me. We were fooling around on bed and I asked him if he was OK with menstruating sex. He said 'Oui' so many times while caressing my ass that I thought he was going to use that as a solution. Was going down on him and thought, since

I really was only spotting, to pull out the tampon. That left me wondering where on earth to set it. On the side of the bed seemed convenient. Did I mention Louis had a poodle? A real big black curly dog that appeared fairly well behaved, given certain parameters. Woke blurry-eyed early in the morning, remembering that Louis and I had had a fantastic night, and that his large cock had massaged away my cramps and that I had better hurry over to the bidet, wash out the semen and insert a tampon so as not to spoil anyone's beautiful white-lace sheets. Chantilly Lace, blood all over the place.

Katie, stop it!

Forcing myself to tell this story so I won't obsess any more about it. Louis wasn't there – surmised he'd gone to the big house to be with wife but no . . . there he was, arguing with the poodle. Now what could they be arguing about, for it really seemed the dog had a bone to pick with his owner, growling incessantly. Louis saying over and over, 'Teeger, no! No, Teeger.' Finally, my early morning eyes fell into focus (it was 5.30 a.m. for Christsakes!). Poodle had a green string hanging out of its mouth and Louis was desperately trying to get the dog to give up his treat. Argh!

Slipped out without a word. Too embarrassed. I mean, what kind of gauche girl leaves her slightly used sanitary supplies on the side of the bed? Plus, fun is over. I need to get back before anyone worries about me. I'll see Serik and convey my good feelings and regrets through him to Louis.

I should at least give some final thanks to Louis. Send him two free tickets to the show.

No. I'll send him that underwear he so appreciated.

No. Wife might get package. Could send with Serik. No, Serik might get suspicious.

I know: do nothing. I'll be that beautiful, if neurotic, moment in his life which had a finality about it.

Sounds dreadful. Oh well. Maybe my problem is I don't finish anything, I just sort of drift away.

Hmm.

Oh well.

July 10

No, no, no. Picture here Ed Munch's *Scream* and you've got it. Did you know that estranged husbands still have rights? Like they can call the SX office and get an itinerary?

Who was inhabiting my hotel room when I returned but the double D Daniel: damned and defiant. Make that a triple D: deranged. First words out of hubby's mouth: 'I think we should have a baby.'

?!???!!!???!!??!!??!!!??

Second words: 'There sure are a lot of people who knock on your door all night long. Didn't get much sleep.'

Better you than me, buster. Guess W & co. didn't think the DO NOT DISTURB sign applied to them.

Bastard has managed to remain the same: cool and calm as the snake that he is. Unfortunately, the new chatty Katie really didn't know what to say. Besides, feeling a bit mental from period hormones and the flossing pooch episode – it's Daniel invading MY tour. I didn't expect to see him for a long time and, when I did, it was going to be on my terms.

I told him to leave but he wouldn't. Said we needed to talk. I said, 'Where's my journal?' He said he didn't have it. I said that if he didn't have it now, he used to have it. He said that I had no reason to get upset over a little book and if he *found* it, would I consider getting back together? Then we were back to our early arguments (was it 199 or 214?) which concerned the retelling of events in a way to make Daniel always come out the good guy and his beloved wife a total jerk.

But, I will have to congratulate myself here. I did not go in long for the argument. Just said, 'Are you trying to kill me with ennui?' That stunned him a bit. Not even sure the red-blooded American knew the word. Then came the sucker punch. Told him I was ordering room service to help sort this thing out. Called Leo instead. Asked if we had security because there was an intruder in my room.

Daniel hastily grabbed his bag and said, 'You'll pay for that, you little bitch.'

Make that 'bitch in heat' but not for you, old buddy. This D (and I mean divorce here) is going to cost him. I don't know how I can estimate pain and suffering but I'll manage. Daniel has absolutely ruined the peace and the anonymity of this tour.

I'm going to bed. This day has been way too much for me.

July 14

Storm the Bastille and *vive la France*!

Back with the Mission. Stayed out of the pussy action for a while. Today I'll be finishing up with the curse. Rather fuck a goldfish than have my period. Forget the 'commune-with-the-moon' crap of women's groups. The only good thing about a period is the feeling of lightness when the bloating and bleeding are over. Maybe that's why women live longer and are rarely philosophers – once a month, we're reminded we're part of the bloody earth.

Kristine and I are friends again. Rest of party chided me for not knowing that divas are notorious horse-lovers. How was I to know that high notes and hooves go hand in hand?

Salvadore seems to be bent on being very friendly yet distant with me. Wish I could explain better. He is so all-inclusive – as in, if all other people disappeared from the planet, he'd still be able to have meaningful conversations with himself. I do not agree with Kristine that he's lonely – just alone.

Serik says that of course he knows Louis. The pâté of Louis' family is the best in the entire world. Every time the three-legger is in the area, he goes to have a taste and a try at surmising what's in it. No luck – Louis won't even sell him the recipe.

Serik has a very silly, very skinny, very tall French girl who refers to him as 'My dear', every other word. I think they have a long-standing relationship (something must be long-standing there, given the basso's accoutrements). He mentioned that they get together at least every six weeks. I think it's serious. Oh well – why discourage Serik now with the tortures and regrets of ongoing relationships, like how they end up breaking one's heart (or in my case, my self-esteem and, temporarily, my career – think I'm doing a good job at self-therapy).

Means Serik is out of the sleeping picture. Too bad, for I have fantasised about that moustache in many places. But I don't want to be someone in the middle. Well, not psychologically anyway. It was OK with Louis since I never met the 'other' woman. Plus, that existed as a complete affair. It's finished but I know I'll be seeing Serik again and again.

Btw, Angelika is taking me to a sex club tonight. I'm supposed to go in drag too.

Heard through John that Slava and Wendy are doing the deed. Yuck! Heard that Ryan was nearly arrested for coming on to a cop – must have a thing for men in uniform. Dave has shacked up with nobody; just goes around taking photos without permission. Camera was confiscated at the Louvre. *Vive la France*!

Much, much later evening . . .

Drank lotsa wine and hope to stay awake to take off bandage. Can't. Wow. I will survive, hey, hey. Knock on the door. Get out of here, don't want you, little whore. Got all my life to live, all my love to give, I will survive. Yeah – Katie power! I think pillow's talking to me. Coming, my love.

July 15

Bastille Day quite a celebration – freedom in a whole new way.

Now, though, want to crawl into the deepest orchestra pit imaginable and then push the erase button. Not to be repeated! Feet hurt from Angelika lifting me up and then dropping me a hundred times. Headache beyond belief. Afraid if I sneeze, frontal lobe will come out through nasal passage. Things all a bit mixed up up there.

Yes, went as boy to the sex club with Angelika cross-dressed as herself. John helped with an ace bandage and we slicked the hair up under a hat. Colouring all my facial hair a deep brown and slouching a bit, I have to say, I (frighteningly) looked like a young boy. Put on some cool, lightly shaded purple glasses to hide my tiny crow's feet and *voilà*: Craig, Angelika's date.

Can't write more if I tried. I am fried, fried, fried. Drinking one too many Scotches to prove I was a man. Stupid, stupid, stupid. Plus, it's too painful to recall the lack of inhibition I managed to demonstrate for the well-wishers in the crowd. Not that painful. Need time to make sense of it. Period most definitely over. And super-cunt is utterly worn out.

July 16

Another free breakfast with John. Chided me for missing yesterday's. He didn't understand that I missed ALL of yesterday. The thought of leaving the room made me want to puke. Scotch and beer are off drinking list forever.

Still a bit worried that Daniel is out and about somewhere in Paris and the very idea is making me reckless. Like the cross-dressing thing. I mean, Daniel could figure a way for that to end up in the divorce papers. Don't know how, but he's somehow still yanking my chain. How dare he be here! John and I brainstormed a bit about a plot to get him to leave but nothing sounded right.

'Tell the police he raped you,' was John's first idea.

Not good. It says on the passport we're married to each other. Same stupid unusual last name.

'Tell him you have contracted a very deadly disease.'

No again. This time, it's my paranoid karma thing. Every time in my life when I've called in sick but, in fact, was not sick, I got sick immediately afterwards. So, reason I, if I say a deadly disease . . .

Neither of us were too inventive. Just pray that Daniel is gone.

Finally ready to write down for future biographers what happened at the sex club. With a few days passing, it doesn't seem so outrageous, so, well, embarrassing. Seems fun – like it did then. Just have to let go completely to accept the animal within.

We didn't go there until rather late. Of all things, the first person I lay eyes upon there was Slava. Only, he didn't look like Slava. His hair was slicked back and he had on a very snazzy suit. The French horn player who talked me into the musical fuck was on his arm. Not wanting to ruin my disguise, I urged Angelika in a different direction. Didn't know I'd chosen the 'queer room'. It was boys only. What can I say – fun to watch. Men kissing and groping each other. Sweaty men with huge biceps that they flexed while other men went down on them. Men whipping men, fucking men, staring at Angelika with a look of disgust or hatred – rarely amusement. My ass was grabbed many times though. Ha! (Though I'm not entirely sure who the laugh was on – surely my disguise was not that good.)

Anyway, Jelly (as Angelika has urged me to call her since we're friends) dragged me out of there. 'Not the place for either of us, sweetheart.'

Don't know how Jelly and I got separated but I decided it would be much better for me if I just ponied up to the bar and waited for her. But then came the drink buying. A big burly man with a beard, dressed from head to toe in leather, bought me a Scotch. No ice, just a half glass of poison. Didn't know I liked Scotch. Smooth. Strangely easy to drink. Like sipping a cooled-down pipe.

He came up and stood behind me. Not my type – one of those heavy breathers who think their sinus problems are a turn on. But then his buddy came and bought me a drink too. Still woozy from the first one, I thought I should wait but they insisted. I mean, like one put a hand on my neck (thank God he didn't knock the hat off) and the other tilted the glass to my lips. OK, so I'll drink. Then a third man showed up, said something to the other two who then left.

Now this guy was more like it. Looked like Mel Gibson in a muscle magazine. He went straight for my neck, sliding a tongue along an erogenous zone I didn't know existed. Goose pimples flowed all the way down to my calves. He bit my earlobe and whispered into it in French – you won't believe this – 'Je swee tray bone soosuz.'

Not knowing where to play my cards at this point and, basically, quite drunk, I kissed him. Figured that I could surmise how men kiss men from this experience. But, they kiss just as they would women. Perhaps a bit more aggressively, but I liked it. I was definitely being seduced. The Mel Gibson guy pulled me close to him and I could feel a very nice hard-on up against my hip. Wished I could've returned him the favour. Still didn't want to blow the charade, although, even drunk, I was beginning to question the morality of this. I mean, how would I feel if a woman, dressed as a man, seduced me into going to bed with him/her? Betrayed or amused? Or duped? Hard to say, but Mel was forcing my lower half to usurp any brain activity.

It was getting more and more difficult to manoeuvre so that he wouldn't grab my crotch or tits. Instead, I grabbed his crotch and let my fingers play with his balls though the denim. He liked that and closed his eyes a bit. The music was pounding so I'm not sure if he moaned or not, but his lips were open. Then he locked his eyes on mine, grabbed my ass and manoeuvred me in front of him to another room.

'Uh oh,' thought I. Now is the moment of truth. Great moments in a violist's life, like when she says, 'Uh . . . actually, I'm a girl.'

Tried to explain through charades by vehemently pointing to my chest and putting boobs there with cupped hands. Then, grabbed my crotch and immediately made the international middle finger slides in circle motion. Then left only the circle of index finger and thumb and pointed to my crotch. Mel was laughing, his grin gleaming and his eye leering. Somehow, I got the impression I conveyed I was a virgin.

He pushed me into what I would soon learn was the spanking room. Catcalls were hurled at us as we walked through the corridor of mostly men and a few women. For a fleeting moment, was convinced that Mel understood my sign language and that I now would get to witness some action without needing to partake.

I was half right.

Hands prodded and poked me until I was compelled to go forward to what looked like a scaffold. Was very sorry that I had drunk three Scotches and four beers or maybe the other way round. The alcohol made me a submissive and I went there like a good little dog. Big burly man who bought me the first Scotch grabbed my arms. Another man began spanking me through my jeans. I thought it rather funny and Mel seemed to think so too. The spanking man's big hand was larger than my ass. It hurt a bit, not much.

But, then the jeans came off and boxers were pulled down – John said you should cross-dress from head to toe to do it right. I struggled so that only my ass was visible. I mean, reasoned a very drunk *moi*, an ass is an ass, right? Girl or boy, it's still an ass and still does the same things, like get spanked.

Burly man's accomplice spanked once, twice, and then reached underneath to grab my . . .

Poor man did look confused. Burly man let go of my hands. I was so thrilled at shocking them that I took off my shirt, unbound my breasts and cupped them up for all to see. Hat still on, I scanned the room for admiring faces. Like seducing a priest – I mean, if these guys thought I was hot, I WAS HOT! But I caught only Jelly's eye. She grabbed me off the scaffold, laughing as she spanked my derrière before pulling my pants back up. Then we were dancing.

Being drunk does that to you – time comes in ground-up images with little connection. Pants were down, shirt was off, crowd was aghast and then, suddenly, I was dancing. Fully clothed with bouncing boobs – the bandage would get put back on MUCH later. I was the reverse image to Jelly in a way, who no one would ever mistake for a girl, no matter how sleek the velvet and how refined the lipstick. I was in drag from the neck up, facial hair still accented. But I was not a man, no doubt about it.

Jelly can rock. In those high-heels, teetering above the crowd, men were groping her everywhere. There seemed to be few women around and those that were consisted of the dyed-and-tied sort – sporting piercings and tattoos in places one might not expect them to be. Like a neck pierced with a snake tattoo growing through the hoop and coming up the chin to the lips, which sported another loop of steel. This snake women grabbed me, which made Angelika laugh but made me uncomfortable. I think I'm a prude at heart. Draw the line at the self-maimed. Don't get how that's supposed to be erotic. Like saying, 'I hurt myself, can hurt you too. Permanently.'

After a very backbreaking rendition of 'I Will Survive', I went to get some air. Still quite woozy. Left Angelika being picked up and put on the shoulders of the burly guy and his friend. WHATEVER.

And there was Slava, *sans* French horn player. I thought I heard him speaking English to someone – I mean, really good English with a clipped British accent. It was a weird thing, for he looked completely different just because an understandable version of our language seemed to be spewing from his lips. I mean, he looked hot and my cunt gushed forth its lubrication in encouragement.

Lasted one minute. He recognised me and moved forwards. Hadn't been him talking to anyone at all. 'Oh, Katie, you looks like man. You face. It dirty like man's.' There was Slava screaming in my ear over the music. 'But I am so lucky. At this six club and see you. Lisa here too. But if head weren't screwed, I lose her. Where she is?'

He began screaming for Lisa as if she were his baby on a detached railroad car. Tried to find my way back to Angelika but the pounding music, the throbbing lights and the wooziness of the alcohol were all conspiring against me. Then Mel was there again. Blocking the passageway. I smiled. He smiled. I moved left, he moved left. I moved right, he moved right.

Great. I thought there was going to be a fight and my wimpy viola fingers would be broken in the process and then I'd be sent home – only I couldn't go back to Polly's because she would have heard that I was impersonating a man and having my ass spanked and fucked by strangers in Paris and . . .

But Mel kissed me. More tenderly this time. I think he liked me. He took off my hat and ran his hand through my very stiff hair. He stopped that in an instant when one of his fingers found its way through some undried hair gel.

Quickly moved his sticky hand to under my shirt and to grabbing my breast. He twisted the nipple rather gently between his fingers and then kissed the erect thing through my shirt. Lovely. Someone screamed at us – I think the English equivalent of 'Get a room!' – but we paid no heed. I unbuttoned Mel's jeans and slid my hand in.

He was hot down there. I mean, not just a full-blown (well, not yet anyway) erection but physically hot. The balls were giving off steam. I massaged them the same way he played with my breast. He moved it right, then left and then squeezed hard. Did the same to his balls and Mel was grinning. Lovely white teeth and not a trace of that awful cigarette smell we Americans are so against in Europe. You'd think I was from California but – smoke-free is nice. In general.

Enough of the nicotine lowdown. On with the story. Mel led me to a hall with a series of rooms. He pushed me into one and laid me down on what looked like a massage table covered with a paper sheet. Got to hand it to the sex club: they're clean. Mel wheeled the table back and then disappeared. Suddenly, I heard a B flat – the sound of electricity – humming all around me. The beat of the techno music was very faint in the background. The feeling of bonelessness that comes with being drunk, like the floor was conspiring against me to not reveal its true depth. But I was hot.

Felt jeans pulled off, boxers discarded. Then a feeling of – what? Wood, metal, cardboard? – was on my back just above my ass. I turned around to see that I couldn't see my ass. I was the magician's assistant cut in two. My legs, out of sight and reach, kicked a bit, hoping to fend those off my exposed ass. Then I felt the table fold down on that side and my legs were on the ground. Like the art class but more interactive. I was being posed.

Mel appeared again, grinning so that his eyes were little Chinese happy slits. He pulled my shirt off and began massaging my back. I was comforted that he was with me. It made the unseeable exposure on the other side seem safer.

Then began a spanking in earnest. Hard, meaty hands which grabbed my ass and then swatted. Grabbed and swatted until I was stinging there. The whole time, Mel just kept rubbing my shoulders and neck in a hypnotic rhythm, which melded perfectly with what was going on behind the panel.

I felt fingers enter me and fuck and fuck while lips circled my labia and licked up toward my asshole. A bit embarrassing now but I loved it then. I mean, I don't think of myself as an ass-licker, if you know what I mean. Anyway, nicely oiled fingers in now oiled ass and in cunt – I think they were fingers. I felt hands on my hips and a cock entering and fucking hard. I slid back and forth on the massage table. Mel held me. It felt so good that tears sprung into my eyes. The man on the other side of the wall came and I felt the warm pool of his love juice slowly begin its gravitational descent. At one point, a buzzing vibrator was shoved up my pussy and another vibrating thing was placed on my clit. A very skinny third vibrator was inserted in my ass and was moved at an entirely different tempo from the one in my cunt. Had the effect of making me feel dissected – an experiment to see how independently my various erogenous zones operated.

Mel was still slowly massaging my shoulder blades. I couldn't stop myself. I was twitching and twitching with an orgasm. Orgasms. Felt like an animal having its tummy rubbed just so and the leg thumping without control. I was jumping back and forth from the sensations and then I began crying for them to stop. They wouldn't stop and I felt the wave of sleep upon me. Hard, like the black drape at a final curtain call.

I don't think it lasted long. I was turned over and then had a good view of where I was. Yes, indeed, it looked like my upper torso was growing out of the wall. I couldn't see anything going on on the other side. Mel solved that problem. He hit a switch and a TV screen came to life above my belly on the wall. This was bizarre, for it focused on my lower half. I had no idea I was so pink there, like half of a very ripe, hairy fig.

Now that I think about it, it was really like being bound by the wrists and watching all that was unfolding except, here there were no faces. Just the cocks.

Lots of men's asses and cocks. Mel put his in my mouth first – there was no action on the other side, though I had no idea how they communicated with each other. Maybe the wall was a two-way mirror. He came quickly in my mouth and I swallowed. He was delicious and I loved the smell of his cologne down there. Daniel might have gotten more action had he done this.

What am I doing thinking of Daniel!? Argh! Anyway, the cocks moved in.

I saw a thick, short cock with a ring at its base nudge its head into my drooling fig mouth. Ooo – to see and to feel and yet to have no control over the action. I loved it. Don't think I'd do it again but I loved it. The cock inched its way in and Mel massaged my breasts. Suddenly, the last inch of the cock was rammed up against the fig and all I could see was the intertwining of pubic hair. Then the cock pulled out again, all the way to the tip and then again, the long slow descent until the final thrust. Fantastic. But it didn't last long. Soon another cock appeared and this one pulled the first cock out of the way. This cock was fairly long but not as thick. Hands lifted my buttocks up and then long cock ploughed in. He was a hard fuck and I loved it too. He fucked and fucked, fast and furious, and came within a matter of minutes. I could feel his sperm pooling inside me and then I watched as it appeared on the cock of the third man humping me.

This man's cock was very, very large. At first, when I saw it approach the open fig, I was afraid. I'd never had anything that big in me, ever. I even thought it might be fake, like those nasty horse dildos Ryan told me he saw at the porno shop. But then he entered, slowly, and I knew this was 100 per cent man, not man-made. Serik's face flashed in my imagination but I felt sure it wasn't him.

He shoved into me so that the separating wall creaked and Mel had to put both hands on my shoulders to keep my body in place. The intense pre-coming fever raced through me as his cock hit up inside me hard. God knows, maybe he hit my cervix. After the initial penetration, a perfect rhythm was set where his huge cock felt as if it were fucking the other side of my clit. I came. Watching it on the screen and feeling myself filled up was overwhelming. But he didn't come. Just fucked and fucked and soon another orgasm coursed through me. It started as a light shudder – I don't think I was made to have all those orgasms in a single sitting – and then it crescendoed throughout my body until even my eyelashes were humming with pleasure. I felt the breaking up of myself – best way I can describe it. I was falling and being impaled and then falling and then light burst in my head. He still didn't come but pulled out. Now a beard was eating me.

I couldn't hear but it looked like it would've sounded like slurping. His hair and my hair meeting perfectly – his dark-brown beard and my dark-blonde pubes. I came again and was begging for them to stop. I really thought I might pee on someone, I was that close to total lack of body control.

They stopped and then I was sorry for my wish. It must be an axiom that the more sex you have, the more you need. Like affection really. Or backrubs. I NEEDED more and more and became afraid.

The wall was lifted up and I saw the other room. There were no men there, only the other half of the table mirroring the room Mel and I were in.

He kissed me sweetly and then began winding the bandage back over my boobs. Next, the hat went back in place. He seemed very serious about this and I wondered what rules were being followed or had been transgressed. But we didn't dress completely. He folded me over the table, poured something oily into his fingers and worked them into my quite fucked-out ass. He then followed suit with his cock. I was going to take it like a man, after all.

Mel came quickly – I was out of orgasms, not that I'd get one from the ass anyway. I then put on my boxers and the loose jeans – I was a homey in this drag – and stepped out into the corridor. A small group of men were standing around and they applauded. I ignored them but Mel hailed a 'Merci!' As I went out past the bar, I was very happy to be back in disguise. On a giant screen, over the bar, I could now see myself in repeat action. At first, I didn't like this and tried not to look so as to give myself away. Mel led me to a seat where three shots of Scotch were lined up – must have been some sort of initiation thing. We had an excellent view of the fig being stuffed by three Adams. Well, after the first Scotch, I began to think I didn't look all that bad. And Mel was kissing my neck.

Suddenly, Jelly appeared with Slava. She gave me a LONG sideways glance of a meaning which I couldn't determine. I found out later she was pleading with me for a way to break loose from the Slav. I was afraid she was referring to my porn movie debut and was admonishing me for ever going into the room with a bunch of strangers. That was before I knew Jelly better. Her stories of the night rivalled my own. But enough of her sex life.

We were out dancing again. Jelly was throwing me again. I was drinking Scotches again. I wretched once in the ladies' room. The line was shorter – the one bona fide miracle of the evening.

Then I was home to feel miserable for the next few days.

Chapter Eleven

July 17

I don't know what to say or do. I'm seriously thinking of leaving the tour. Daniel is following me everywhere. John says that D knew about the sex bar, though doubts he saw me there. Serik says that D was even talking to Louis. How does he know where I am, where I've been? He surely knows who or whom I've been with and that makes me nervous. I don't want all of his money but I'd like a little for putting my life on hold. Daniel could make this all very nasty in a connotation of the word I don't appreciate.

Saw Ryan. Says that I should let him follow D around, acting like he wants to seduce him. Not a bad idea. I'll have to give it more thought. Daniel is such a homophobe that maybe it would send him on his merry way. Did I say it before? L R!

The diva said that she would be happy to whip my husband into shape, take pictures of it and then blackmail his ass. I liked that idea a lot too. Encouraged Kristine to become good friends with Dave – he'd love to take the sleazy shots, I'm sure. Hmm . . . if Kristine got fixed up with Dave, it could really simplify my life. Except, despite her benevolently intentioned manipulating ways, I like the diva. I don't like Dave. Something about him is so off.

Salvadore did not comment much about Daniel. I got the feeling that Sal was hurt I'd gone to the sex club with John. Well, hurt is not the word. Nor is disappointed. Confused I think would sum it up. I'm a bit confused too. I didn't grow up in a Catholic school but am amazed that I am feeling little traces of guilt about that night.

NOT! No, really, I do feel guilty in the most bizarre way: like I shouldn't have been allowed to have that much pleasure when so many others in this world are deprived. I feel guilty to my former self. That leads me back to just being plain mad with Daniel. I mean, one does not have to have an entire building full of mostly gay men to have orgasms. One really skilled straight man could do the trick.

Oh – now I am feeling guilty. It was not all D's fault. I mean, I could have helped him – if he could have listened. How did I ever fall in love with him? And him me?

I'm wondering if the best solution would not be for me to just confront Daniel and get it over with. Ask what it is he really wants of me.

Here's the letter that was delivered to my hotel room:

Dear Katie,
You really are my dear Katie. Know that. When we promised until death do us part, I imagine that you then found me dear as well. Why ruin our happy union? I know I did a few wrong things but really, how do they compare to what you are doing now? But I forgive you, my dear. And I have a lot of patience. You are my wife

and I love you so. I'm waiting for you. Please reconsider.

Your loving husband, Daniel.

Ooo – now that I record this, it seems even a bit sweet. But I know this letter had its origins in artful deception. It's the beginning of the paper trail. The first piece of evidence so Daniel can now prove that he was the sweet one trying only to reconcile and I was the resisting bitch. Wonder how many copies of the letter were made.

Oh, Daniel, when is this anger to end? For I am still undeniably furious at you for being you. It's like being mad at a scorpion for having a stinger but I just can't help it. Please go away. Disappear. Crawl back to the swamp you came from and let me get on with my orgasmic life. I'm having too much fun to be bothered by your strange tactics.

July 19

I cannot wait for this break to be over. Just a few more days and then I can hide within the confines of the concerts again. Had the meeting with Daniel, arranged via the diva. She thinks he's cute. I told her to go for it – I am definitely not in love with him any more. Would love to see *those* pics. Daniel handcuffed with thirteen roman candles burning up his ass. Oh, I can only imagine with the diva.

Kristine arranged the meeting for Daniel and I in the café at the Ritz. She really loves those ex-pat places. And animal hides. Fine with me. Good reminder that my meeting with Daniel had nothing to do with love and Paris.

It's weird how Daniel looked smaller. An equally strange sensation to sit across the table from him and repeat to myself, 'He was your husband, he was your husband.' Love balloon has been deflated – could be cause of shrunken physique. Or perhaps diminished stature due to fact that I did not want to enter into any of our 'binding' arguments, where Daniel was the Master-deBator. In one of those epiphanic flashes, realised our marriage had been held together by a series of disagreements, those being our only real passion. When I stopped engaging, I stopped loving him.

Yuck! Ouch! Somebody call a therapist.

I'll try to record this as accurately as possible and please, future biographers, forgive my lapse. I was as broadsided by it as you'll be. Well, not now because I've told you . . . so don't say you weren't warned.

The Daniel and Katie Story: A Play in Acts or an Act in Plays

D: I've heard about your escapades around town.

K: And I heard that you've been following me. Pretty slimy, given *I* was the one *you* asked to leave.

D: That was a big mistake.

K: I'll say. Whose though? [No comment from D.] Why did you sleep with *her* in our house?

D: I was stupid.

K: That's a given. And why did you keep my diary?

[Here D's face looked as if it were going to collapse inward, beginning at the nostrils. I liked the look – for I'd only seen it once when he admitted to me, after his law partners chided him and threatened to kick him out of the practice if he didn't remedy his attitude, that he lost a case because of his arrogance.]

D: [After a very long minute in which said nostrils

slyly reconstructed themselves.] I have it. If I give it back, will you reconsider?

K: [I wanted my diary back so I lied.] Yes, I will certainly reconsider.

D: [Handing the diary over.] You know, I only read it to understand you better.

K: And do you?

D: I think so.

K: Well, what do you know better now?

D: [Looking quite agitated.] Um, well, our marriage made you unhappy.

K: You could have seen that in my face.

D: I wasn't looking hard enough.

K: Perhaps I wasn't showing enough [gag – painful to write this! – where was I going with that compassionate stance?!]

D: Katie, I have been thinking a lot about your needs. I think I can meet them better now.

K: For example . . .?

D: Here. [D hands me a brown-wrapped satchel.]

K: [Opens satchel to discover a chrome-plated vibrator . . . was amused, I admit.] Are you sure there isn't a law about these crossing international lines?

D: I think we're safe. Could say it was a massage tool. A marital aid. [Eyes hovering above a wink.]

K: Well, it is nice . . . [It really did look nice and this next was hard to say.] But I can't keep this.

D: Why not?

K: I don't want to put anything from you inside of me.

D: [Face red, eyes bulging, heart attack looming large.] You said you would reconsider. Are you lying now or were you lying then?

K: [Scorekeepers, this was a grand slam retort.] Either way, I won't be lying with you, buddy boy.

137

Thanks for the diary and stop having me followed.

I got up and proceeded to do my best storming out of the café. But I underestimated the powers of persuasion of Daniel. He grabbed my wrists and pulled me to the stairs. 'Go,' he commanded, pushing my ass up in front of his. I didn't want to be liking what I thought might be happening, but I was liking it. On the *premier étage* was the room. While Daniel fumbled with the key, I discreetly tucked the diary behind a potted palm, making a mental note to retrieve it later. I was not about to lose it again. The diary. I was fairly sure I'd already lost my mind.

Daniel opened the door and pulled me inside. What I saw next was enticing and disturbing. It was like base camp for Operation Get Katie. There were pictures of me everywhere. Pictures of me asleep on the plane, pictures of me with the Mission. Pictures of me in the orchestra. Pictures of Louis and I kissing. A photo of me in drag. But the fig pictures were what fascinated me. I stared at them, thinking, 'I'm breathtaking.' I don't even think I was being partial. Great picture: Ripe Fig Penetrated by Very Large Cock. Belongs in every living room.

I was wet. In the photo and in real time.

And worried. I mean, what did any of this mean? Daniel felt the ripple of confusion and did not waste a moment to take advantage. He was always one to fill a power vacuum.

'Come on, Katie. It could be our last time, if you want. A way of saying goodbye.' Said so sweetly, with honey breath, the serpent encouraging a wanting apple-eater.

For a moment, I wondered who would be taking a picture of us and how Daniel would use all this to his advantage. But his hands slid up my skirt, into my knickers, and the vibrator parted my lips.

Zing! The thing purred at an unnerving pace. My knees buckled and Daniel led me, with the buzzing phallus, to the bed. What was I doing? This was *not* the first step to make sure hubby goes away. Vibrator was completely inside and he bent me over the bed, my legs still on the ground. Clit was rubbing up against the bedspread in a most lovely way. I was amazed that this position reminded me of the sex club and I was even hotter. That axiom of the more sex you get, the more you need ... I couldn't help myself. Daniel moved the device in and out at a perfect speed, saying, 'This is what Katie likes. She likes it fast, furious, unexpected.' Whispering over in low tones, chanting, 'This is what Katie likes.' I was mesmerized. Even better, I was going to come. I was going to come for the first time with my husband. Sort of. He was the pilot of the thing, after all. And in Paris, no less.

The room spun gold, heard Daniel saying from far away, 'This is what Katie likes.' Clit moved into bed with pounding. Felt my insides open and then constrict and convulse. I screamed when I came. I even think some of my own moisture blew out. Was mad, I tell you. Insane with that orgasm. Like some being whose entire nervous system rests in her cunt. Tingles, sparks, fathomless joy and contractions broke upon me. It was more than a coming: it was biblical. The sort of orgasm one would wage a war for. I would've done it again and again, just like that, to hell with the consequences.

Then I felt Daniel's cock trying to enter my ass. Just like that. Six years of marriage and he refused anything remotely off the record and now here he was – the homophobe wanting to pierce my derrière.

I let him. To be frank, I would've let him do anything. If he'd been smart, he could've produced those blank tax papers and I would've signed. Delirious.

You can't tell from this diary that I'm *not* a big fan of anal – it's weird how I've been enjoying it on the tour. Maybe because it's always accompanied by something else ... like a chrome-plated vibrator on maximum speed. There D was, slicked up and shoving himself and vibrator in at the same time – a double D, so to speak. And then he pulled both out at the same time. In, out, in, out.

It took a while since everything was a bit overblown but, and not in the biblical sense, I had a second coming, with the help of a certain angle on the mattress. And then D came and he fell on my back in an uncomfortable way. I am grateful to him for that, because I was about to be in love again. I mean, my husband could give me an orgasm, and *that* kind of an orgasm – AMAZING!

But I realised it was for him, not me, that this whole thing happened. He wasn't intent on the orgasm for me and now that he came, he couldn't care less whether I was in the room or not. He wasn't waiting for me, it was just taking him a while. I mean, I understand the selfish fuck but then, people need to have some sort of closure afterwards. Even if it's just a little kiss. Something. D said, 'Nice ass.' That made me mad. I could tell he wasn't really new to butt-fucking but I didn't even want to imagine what might have been going on outside during our marriage. I bet Spiderwoman was just the one I caught. This was not Louis. This was not Paris. Or art. Or any wish that I be a woman. This was Daniel getting even. Daniel's objectifying of me made me enraged.

I put on my clothes and sweetly (no need to give him cause to argue) said, 'OK, that was our last time. It was nice but let's leave it at that, Daniel. Go back to New York now, please.'

140

He looked stunned and then, idiot, called me a slut. In a Serbian rage, I ripped all the pictures off the wall, tore them in half and screamed something about how stupid I was to ever trust him with anything. He'd be hearing from my lawyer and there would be a restraining order out ASAP.

Idiot. Me – I'm an idiot. How do I get an international restraining order? Now Daniel will never go back. He can dog me the entire tour from Paris to Antarctica. He'll have to leave eventually because of his practice but that could take weeks. ARGH!

At least I have my diary back. Jerk wrote comments in the margins. They contradict themselves – contrite and then conciliatory. Cantankerous and then cooing. The man is going mad. And he's trying to take me with him.

Pray that friends and I will come up with a plan. Feel like it's a long shot but I don't know of any other. Hey, wait, we'll be in Italy in two weeks. It's not personal, it's business. Heh heh.

No – future biographers, just a joke, OK? And a stereotypical one at that. Hmm . . . we are scheduled for Sicily on our second stop. There's jokes and then there's jokes . . . where one dies laughing.

July 20

I'm travelling in a private car to the next destination on our itinerary. Great way to throw Daniel off my tracks. Salvadore rented it and he and I are alone. Seems all the other Mission people over-extended their credit cards and couldn't rent one. Well, John could have but he thought rental prices outrageous in France. He'd be willing to take a train back to Germany and rent one for me there. Sweet but . . .

You ask, why not rent it yourself? Horror of horrors,

I don't have a credit card anymore. Daniel has cancelled it. Nice guy. And as always, great timing.

Sal insisted on paying for the car. Sweetheart! He said he needed a break from the bus, needed a bit more control in his destination conveyance. He's not a bad driver but the car ... HELP! The gear shift came off on a rather winding road and there Sal was, shifting a little metal stick, complaining that the piece of shit was going to break his nails – guitarists need those long nails to pick at their strings, I guess. (Very happy to learn that because I'd been entertaining the idea that Sal was a serious coke fiend.) Was desperately attempting to put the gear shift cover back on while S went between third and fourth gear. Third, fourth, third, fourth. Rather more violently than the situation demanded, if you ask me. I mean, it still worked. And we could've pulled over. Finally slipped stupid phallic thing back on so the man could have a greater grip ...

But it was nice to be alone with him. I like Salvadore. I mean, *really* like him. He has got to be the most interesting person I've ever known. The embodiment of creativity. And I was happy for the chance to kind of clear the air between the two of us.

Sal swore that he and I had only slept together once – and that one time had been enough for him. At first, the comment hurt but I saw him grinning – breaking out in a mock Elvis, 'You know what I like.' It was like he'd picked up on my Chantilly fascination.

Ooo, he IS cute. I'd really like to do IT again. But Sal's got that settled-down look in his eyes and I'm not quite ready for that. My cunt is ablaze with appetite and loving him would be more like a main course while I'm still on the appetisers.

So ... whom did I sleep with that odd night? I believe Sal, and seeing those nails recollect that I had not felt them during that mistaken tryst. Am reason-

142

ably disturbed. Par for the course, had to confess about other man to Sal because it seemed too strange to keep asking him if we'd only done the deed a single time. Sal suggested the waiters had snuck in. His wide-set eyes seemed to move even further apart, giving me the impression that was not the only idea he had as to my confusion. Didn't want to hear it. I'm afraid he knows too much already. Glad he still likes me.

We did not follow the normal bus route – it is a long way from Paris to Barcelona. Sal decided that seeing the back roads of Spain would be appealing. That's why I'm writing you now from a tavern in the middle of nowhere. Mr O'Brien (yes, it is Salvadore's last name – go figure) got so lost that we decided to wait until sun-up. I hope we're still in Spain and haven't somehow managed to get back into France again. I tried to help by pointing out the North Star and that's when Sal decided to call it a night. Rehearsal isn't scheduled until tomorrow night so we should be OK.

July 21

I've seen some LARGELY interesting things here. They're big all right. The big, the small, and the forest – and let's not forget the nuts.

Anyway, no we didn't sleep together – even if both of us are WAA. Well, we did SLEEP together but only in the literal sense. Sal thought he'd ordered a room with two beds but they thought he meant double bed so ... there we were. Also thought he'd ordered a room with a shower but no, we just got a sink. Toilets around the corner. Sal's own assessment of his Spanish is greatly inflated. Glad in a way. Sal was beginning to be a bit too perfect.

Now all of that might have been just fine except Sal had managed to drive us to a nudist retreat. And a great number of those people carried extra shadows, if you know what I mean. Maybe they weren't naked, just their outfits were covered in flesh folds. Anyway, the magnitude of our surroundings discouraged me at first from going to the showers. But then I started looking around. OK, so they were fat but, in a weird way, looked so much better than if they'd been covered in some clothing. It was a study in gravity really. This melting, rippling flesh all about, held from the earth by mere bones and muscles. Extra knees, elbows, chins, stomachs abounded. Some of the asses looked like sandstone shelves. Very sorry Louis' art class wasn't there to paint them. I was finding big to be very beautiful – if I let my mind free of 'shoulds' in terms of the human form.

There were mostly women whose bodies looked a bit like another species. What magnificent skin – I was beginning to feel silly in, one, my clothes and, two, my puny little frame. I mean, I was nothing next to these folks. Even six foot two Salvadore looked like he was emaciated. We were prison camp survivors here.

There was one enormous woman who reminded me of the Denny's dish, 'Moon Over My Hammies.' Her flesh pocketed and folded all the way down to her calves. It was crisply corpulent and made her look like a baby. Wondered if Sal would ever consider porking such a porker. He probably would. I bet he finds my body too insubstantial. It's so clear what I will look like when dead – I mean the skeleton. You know how sometimes you can so clearly see someone's skull that it makes them very unattractive? These people, for the most part, were naked but still retained an air of mystery as to the secret spots of their flesh. I felt cheap and a little tawdry. Just a little. One false move and you could see every one of my secret possessions. My little clam between the legs could certainly feel the evening breeze while the other women's seemed to be safely secreted away in extra folds.

Spied a skinny man wandering amidst the giants. He seemed to be enjoying the accidental flesh rubbings left upon him by those who forgot to look out for Lilliputians. This man was soon to became our companion.

When in Rome ... naked, we went to the dining room where everyone was handed a thoroughly bleached towel. Contemplated just putting it over my face in case anyone possibly recognised me, but then got it: all those fannies in one room, sitting down, sharing things we don't need to mention. Towel very welcome.

Began to suspect whole thing planned by Sal all along. Accused him but he swore he didn't know. I mean, think about it. A perfect date: take a girl to the nudist retreat and find out ahead of time what she's really made of. Any kind of hang-ups. Except ... we'd already slept together.

Well, that doesn't mean he wouldn't want to do some background check. I have a friend who asks her dates if they have any diseases *after* she sleeps with them. Some people offer spoons after the soup's been served – something Grandma used to say. I think that must have been a very nasty thing to do in Serbia, starving, watching the fire go out, as you wait for the blessed spoon. If you ask me, why not just drink from the bowl and blame your host for the rude manners.

Anyway, during our dinner of tofu-shaped quail eggs and other vegetarian dishes which were supposed to resemble *tapas*, the slight Lilliputian, who was balding in a charming way (sporting a little ponytail all the way to the middle of his back), joined us. He spoke English, a great relief to Salvadore's attempted Spanish ('más lechuga, por favor' was what

145

he considered a nice phrase for small talk with the gone-natives) and my attempted French (you already know what I can say in French – perhaps a good opening line in some situations . . .). If only people spoke ancient Greek, Sal's specialty, or Serbian. Alas, it will be a long time and a strange world if those become the means of international communication.

So, Jean-Phillipe put his towel between Sal and I and proceeded to explain where we were, what we were eating and other important things we must do while in the area. He noticed my case. (I've been carrying my instrument everywhere I go, just on the off chance it might be damaged or stolen and I'd be shit out of luck trying to replace it. Granted, I did feel silly having a viola case in the nudist dining room but . . . well, it wasn't such a big leap up from how I already felt.) Jean-Phillipe asked if I played *viola* NOT *violin*. This won him big points with me. He asked if we knew Serik.

Why does everyone, everywhere, know Serik?!

JP (he said to call him that), with laughing baby blue eyes, said that he was Serik's 'air dresser every time S was in Paris. I asked if Serik was 'airy, which prompted Sal to reach over and push my shoulder. We weren't going to be making fun of the Frenchman's accent. Ipp, ipp, urray!

It came out that JP was on 'oliday, with no specific plans for the month. We asked him to join us and he readily agreed. We'll all be packing into the car in a few moments.

It was lovely to sleep with Sal. We were both naked and just cuddled. Strange to say, sleeping like happy animals was, in some ways (and only some mind you) better than sex. Different anyway. Comforting, like the old married couple I always envisioned Daniel and I to become. Sal snores like a stuffed kitten. Cute. But he was up far too early by my standards. When I finally rubbed the sleep from my eyes, I could see that he had gotten himself breakfast (a coke and some egg/tofu thing), brought breakfast for me (tea and scones and jam – good boy!), written out the next numbers SX would play in Spain, and managed to cover the entire floor in socks, underwear and papers. Told you he was talented.

For just a moment, thought you, journal, were gone. Same old story born from well-founded paranoia. Meet a man, sleep with him, and then he reads your most private thoughts. Began to suspect Sal again of being Norton.

Then remembered I'd hidden journal under some pine-like needles on the floor of our room. Smells good and hasn't been disturbed.

Sal and JP have gone somewhere to get supplies for the last leg of our car trip. I am writing this entry after taking a walk in the woods. Love the Spanish green and the red soil. Was admiring a particularly bright yellow moth/butterfly thing when I heard the squealing. Was afraid I was about to become a casualty to the Wild Spanish Boar (don't know if there is such a thing but was convinced of it at the moment). I rested and allowed my eyes to roam the terrain searching out signs of cloven-hoofed beasts.

Well, instead it was Moon Over My Hammies being fucked by a man about JP's size. An intriguing picture. She had her enormous breasts consuming a tree while this small man thrust and thrust into the mounds of her flesh. His little hands on her ass made me giggle. It struck at my American sense of the proportion of things. Thank God his squeals were covering up my noises. Her ass quivered and everything shook all the way down to her ankles. Though first surprised, I grew by bits (mountains) to be intrigued, gazing with wonder and thinking, 'He likes it. It's like fucking a mountain.' She was probably wet all the time, moist from her own excess. A man could love the woman-ness of it, mystery in mystery within the folds. The beauty of it caught me off guard, given the anaemic notions American women carry about their own bodies.

Looked like he was riding a horse, plunging in and disappearing so that it seemed as if he were clothed and just riding her back. Her breasts slapped at the tree. He could've been fucking her ass for all I knew. Her pink cheeks grew pinker and his eyes rolled back. The couple became one breathing piece of piggyback and I was sure he found her exquisite given the guttural sighs foaming out of his mouth. Then a very large man showed up. He was more like an ex-football player than overweight. Small man came over My Hammies' back and then retreated. Large man began pounding into woman. I mean pounding so she was crying out and so I could feel the shaking where I stood. (Nice how easy it was, this exchange, with everyone naked already.) The tree swayed a bit. His hands dug into the meaty flesh of her ass and he fucked and fucked. I was still naked and thought, 'What the hell?' I played with myself while watching the cock disappear so entirely in the flesh. She shook and I wondered if she would be able to come like that. I closed my eyes, still hearing them panting and saying words I did not understand. Birds called over-head and I enjoyed the slight breeze dusting my wet cunt. Was pressing into myself, imagining I was large and men disappeared when they entered me. I con-sumed them. I was a canyon, a cavern. Closed my eyes and came.

Realised I wasn't in the movies with those nice sex scenes outdoors where not a bug stirs in the sky. 'Now what?' pressed down upon my goofy post-coming brain. I was drooling down my leg, and flies were catching the scent, as were mosquitoes. Oh, how nature loves a fuck. Ever notice that? Dogs perk up their noses and quail run in circles with humans copulating nearby. Thought deer would come out and follow me. Took a large leaf which looked rather soft, wiped my hand on my crotch and then on the leaf. Then saw the grass up ahead and figured I could just leave my trail behind there.

Was very nice with the grass brushing my nether-world and the drool cooling and drying. Little man startled me when I came upon him. You know what I mean. I didn't come on him, just stumbled upon him. We both turned bright red, each, I guess, knowing what the other had been doing. Oh well. Went back to the communal shower to rinse off.

At this moment, Salvadore is loading up the car. So sweet, putting my stuff in, helping JP with his. JP is still naked and it seems Sal is explaining to him that he would prefer it if everyone travelled with their clothes on. JP is shrugging, opening up a duffel bag, and throwing on jeans and a shirt.

Must admit, a day nude makes clothes seem heavy and ridiculous. It's hot, we're dying from sweating, but here I go to cover up my 'special' body parts with a skirt and blouse. Cannot do bra just yet – feels like a cage.

Oh . . . something has fallen from bag. Journal? No . . . duh. It's here and I'm writing in it to prove that existence. Oh – it's *Ulysses*. See Sal looking at it quizzically. Now he's smiling a self-contained, amused smile. I amuse him. Looks charmed. Putting it back in bag and coming this way. Gotta go – don't want him to know I have a journal.

Later . . .

Hpe you cn read writng. Hard to write in bouncing car. Boys are n frnt, bth looking at map. JP insists he knows who we are. Car stll moving. I afraid. Dad, if they find ths in wreckage, want to say I lve you. Polly gets all my divrce sttlement. Gve viola splinters to Dniel.

Chapter Twelve

*F*uck Dave Muller. Fuck him. Fuck you, Dave, you insidious creep, lech, little-boned scum. You aren't ever going to be fixed up with the diva. Not even to blackmail Daniel – that's how much I despise you. Fucking little camera prostitute.

There. Now, about the architecture of Barcelona which Dave will NOT ruin for me! WOW! I've never been here. Makes my blood sing. The Ramblas, the swirling weirdness of Gaudi and his cathedral, of which my room has a view – AND a balcony! Cannot believe we are staying at the Hotel Colon (you can already hear Sal's pronunciation of that one). This melding of cultures, piercing eyes out of dark skin. The white teeth, the clean grunge of everyone seems so familiar. Maybe this is really where my ancestors were from – but they got captured and somehow ended up in Serbia. What a beautiful city – can't wait to really see it in daylight. It glows pink and yellow now and smells of the fresh ocean and paella.

We arrived thirty minutes before the rehearsal

started. Sal jumped out of the car and ran ahead to Leo, who was set to copy the music ASAP. I think Sal put everything on a computer disk so it would only take a few minutes. Amazing. How much more would Bach have written had a version of the Encore software been around?

So grateful JP came with us. He even cut my 'air on the way down and it looks stunning! Quite the pro, given the winding road. Frankly (the joke is old I know – the first signs of tiredness: excessive stupid puns), we'd have never made it had I been doing the map reading. The 'aircutter really knows every trick to getting from here to there. Had JP park the car. I ran to see Ryan.

Ooo, such slippery eyes. He looked like he *ate* the Cheshire Cat.

'Hey babe, welcome back. Have a good break? Or should I ask, how many people did you help to have a good break?'

I hit him playfully on the arm and murmured, 'A few.'

'Bigger than a bread basket?'

'I hope not. Ouch!'

Then, Ryan dumped the news on me. Right there, with two minutes before the rehearsal started, with no time to seek revenge or cry or – well, what would you do?

'You need to take care of Dave. He's got pictures of what he says is you.'

Swallowed hard. Surely it wasn't the sex club. But then, how did estranged husband get those photos? Where the hell is my questioning, suspicious nature when it really matters? Like when I was back there, having an excellent time with chrome vibrator and estranged husband? Katie, stupid, stupid, stupid! What were you thinking? Have an orgasm – that'll show him . . .

'You've seen them?' I asked tentatively.

'Yeah. You're a babe in the raw.'

Fears confirmed. 'Who else saw them?'

'Mostly people who wouldn't be shocked. And Leo. He doesn't believe it's you.'

Then the music started and I had no recourse but to sit there worrying and fuming. It was one thing to have a fantastic fantasy fulfilled – quite another to have it mass distributed. Why was Dave doing this to me?

I forgot about it temporarily as Sal's music coursed through me. I could hear our car ride in the intro. Getting lost, gear shift episode, voluminous nudists, sleeping with me. So clear, as if he were just telling the story. It was our intimacy, our secret life. Inexplicable to anyone except ourselves. It touched me deeply for it was the kind of music I hear narrating my life when I'm alone. Music humming in accordance with my internal workings. Soul. Whatever.

Dave sauntered over – no, wait, I want to get this right – swaggered up to me after the rehearsal of intimate moments with Sal. 'Hey pink cheeks,' he called out, grinning so much it changed his ethnic identity. He carried a very stuffed manila envelope. Ryan was behind him and gave me a two-thumbs-up and an encouraging look, as if to say to me, 'You have balls: use them.'

But I floundered. All through the rehearsal I had played Don Quixote to Dave's demons and now the anger was spent, the war waged, and no battle won. My fury always comes in bursts with little lasting power. I wish I weren't such an ineffective human being.

Thankfully, it seemed that the Serbian anger was what Dave craved. When I replied in a monotone voice – 'Why would you have pictures of me?' – it shook him up. He had had his hand inside the envelope ready to expose them to my horror but stopped. The pictures didn't come out and Dave didn't answer.

I continued with what must have sounded like indifference but was really simply the other side of anger. 'What are you doing with those pictures, David? Are you trying to blackmail me? You're supposed to wait until I don't pay you off before you pass them around.' Then the tears came to my eyes. Dave made a step forward as if to comfort me. I stared at him, unable to stop the flow and not really caring to. Was embarrassed at the display but, through half sobs, did manage to get off a good parting line which am proud of: *Those pictures you carry around say much more about your meanness than they do about mine.*

Ryan assures me that Dave stood there, stunned. It was not the game he had bargained for. Pretending to be a buddy, Ryan took him out for beer. Of course to a gay club, though Dave was oblivious at first. Love Ryan! (L R!) Got Dave really buzzed, tried to take the pictures but Dave was too wise on that detail. Ryan did get out of him that Dave was at the club, was in fact a participant. Said he'd been hired by a well-paying individual (Daniel I am sure) to follow me around and then, he got the bonus: fulfilling a high-school dream. Ryan swears he socked him one right on those so-necessary trumpet-playing lips. 'Not too hard – couldn't break my hand over the asshole.'

L R, L R, L R!

I'm sick. I mean it. Dave's dick in me and there's photos of it. My face isn't there and I could always deny it – I couldn't care less what Leo or anyone else thinks. But there exists proof that I enjoyed having Dave's dong in my ding. What more could go wrong? Yuck, yuck, yuck!

God, it was fun though. I wish Dave hadn't ruined it. He could've gone without the confessional and I would have had a true anonymous fuck. Fuck you,

Dave Muller, you sick, twisted, poor excuse for protoplasm.

I don't even want to know which cock was his.

July 23

I think Dave's was the cock with the cock-ring. It makes sense that he would need to accessorise. And I didn't enjoy that cock so much . . . I think. I'll have to look at previous entries (oh God, the neurotic puns . . . stop it, stop it, stop it!). I bet he was the one spanking me so hard. He is still mad about high school. There should be anti-stalking, anti-Dave Muller laws. His behaviour . . . I wish it were a crime to be a jerk.

Wonder if Dave told Daniel of the special penetration – surely not part of the contract of stalking me. Sure the pics made their way to Daniel as a punishment to me. Wonder if JP kept hair clipping. Maybe I could pacify Dave with those strands of protein and he'd just stay out of my affairs from now on.

Btw, JP is doing Wendy, aka Cynthia. Or should I say, he's being done. His head rests perfectly on her breasts when both are standing. I fear for the Frenchman, though Serik says that he is quite capable of pulling a thing or two and don't worry too much. If she's really good, perhaps he'll present her with a merkin of his own hair. Bassoonist Trish is now hooked up with one of the musical fuck-sliders, trombonist Harry. Slava looks to be enamoured with the musical fuck French hornist. Serik is still with Ms Lithe (aka some impossible name with a lot of diphthongs, tripthongs and excessive French letters). Ted seems to be eyeing Kristine and me. I should sleep with the guy one more time for sentiment's sake. I think the concertmaster and Ryan are slowly working on something. Dave is . . . all alone. Ha!

Later . . .

Suppose Sal heard about pictures because he has written for Dave the most awful trumpet part imaginable. It sounds easy but is extremely difficult, which puts Dave on the moron level for those not in the know. Plus, he's the only instrument to hold over on any of the chords, so it looks like he's not paying attention. SX players got tired of Dave asking the conductor over and over, 'Can I check a note?'

Touches my heart to think S would do that for me – especially given what it concerns. Could still deny that that luscious, penetrated crotch is mine but I'm not a particularly good liar. And Ryan, still love Ryan, is probably not a good secret-keeper. Get the impression that he tells the tale and then defends my honour to the max.

In a weird way, this whole thing has gotten me thinking. It's nice that Dave and Daniel have given me something definite to hate. Had Daniel never been caught making the beast with two backs, I might still be married to a man who really doesn't love me or respect me. And had Dave not shown his creepy hand so soon, we might have gone to bed together. Now both have confirmed their hookworm tendencies to get in there and feed off of my intestines – sort of. My vulnerability and my sensuality exploited. Ugh. Thank God didn't sleep with Dave.

Ooo – except we have. Yuck! Does it count if only my lower half participated?

July 24

It was bound to happen. Just wish it could've come at a different time. Salvadore wrote another solo for me – actually about ten minutes of every show has become *Katie's Viola Playing*. The front stand had it. Benny and Jenny (really their names – though I should change them on principle) went on strike. They stood up and moved to the back of the section. Conductor yawned 'I'm not the composer' in answer to their complaints that they hadn't played one solo or duet this entire tour. Good for them – lucky stiff morons! Jealousy is so strange. Most of us don't want the solos, including B&J. But, hapless violist from the back getting them – well fuck that. The old youth symphony mentality rears its head and says, 'That's not fair.' As if music has ever been about impartiality or fairness.

Now Ryan and I sit in the front. Jenny has actually flown home to show her protest. Don't know her but good riddance. It's just a gig, for crying out loud. Benny sits by himself in the back, fuming. Can feel it on the back of my neck up front. Yes, I'm principal, and now Ryan has to turn MY pages and mark MY music. (He's doing a much better job of it than I ever did for him.) I think Benny supposed that he would be playing solos now but they've all been switched to me. Me, me, me!

Beet-juice hair girl (Valerie is her name) is directly behind me, nose-ring glinting. Don't know what to say to her. We had our moment a long time ago. Want to be nice, want her to like me, want her to pass my bowings back to the stands behind.

Really need to be careful now not to have a mutinous section. In those concerts where one of the violists' bows is going a different direction from the others' ... well, if it's a professional orchestra, it's most likely NOT a mistake. The other players simply did not like the bowing and decided to do it differently, come what may. Or the chain of command broke down, let's say at femme henna, and now the front stand's bowings are not being passed back. Third choice will not occur here, where front stand are idiots and decide to mark bowings secretly before the concert, making the entire section look bad.

All these worries and all I want to have is sex. More sex, more sex, more sex. Pictures are out, what can I do? Cry? I'm not getting any different looks than I got before – except younger lads now sit up and take notice when I'm in the vicinity. Hmm . . . should take advantage. Besides, the tour will be over soon and I'll go back to whatever mundane life falls my way. This is the sex of a lifetime. So, who's next?

Here are my priorities:

1. Salvadore again and again.
2. Ted one more time.
3. Slava is looking great, try him (I know he sometimes has greasy hair, but the bod! And he's got to be forty, which I find appealing too).
4. The other percussionist next to Slava – he is gorgeous, though about nineteen.
5. Serik, maybe.
6. Someone quite anonymous.
7. Anyone with charm (or at least good hands).

The Salvadore thing is awkward. We slept together twice now under different pretences and now he knows of the pictures. Will he sleep with such a one as the libidinous Katie?

Ryan's cocksuredness lessons are rubbing off on me for I'm sure the answer is yes. When, though, when? Ryan says that just by wanting a thing, not 'hoping' it will come to you, you get it. Most of the time.

July 25

The concert tonight was hysterical. 'Percussionist. Two thumbs?' I murmured to Ryan in a lull in the music.

'Maybe. Looks good.' He smiled. 'Greasy hair though.'

'I mean the other guy.'

'The little chickling? Aren't you the baby stealer!'

Then suddenly, we were in another of Salvadore's passages. A punk rock version of *Madame Butterfly*. Word had gotten down to the pit that Kristine planned to jump off the fake building of the set and on to a mattress on the other side. But, we were soon to learn, Angelika had substituted a trampoline instead – it was cheaper since the stage already had this prop. Oh, I yearned to see the diva kill herself for fun.

Kristine jumped off and the orchestra played weeping sad music which morphed into a medieval-sounding funeral piece. Sal's voice rose over the top of it and then there he was, at the precinium of the stage, black hood, dagger in hand. I was afraid. Where was the immorality in this play? Death conquers all? Was he out of love, full of a million regrets? Heart-wrenching music which comes from the deep recesses of our soul was out there that night, choking the orchestra and the audience, causing us all to view humanity and its fragility with a longing that is impossible to describe here. The loneliness hurt. Deeply.

Needless to say, it was quite a shock to the sombre moment when laughter twittered through the audience like Spanish champagne. Even with a broken heart, watering eyes and a longing to caress Sal in the most intimate way (not fucking exactly, if you know what I mean – more like a soul-merge thing), I was dying to know what was happening. Risked it and stood up in the rather deep pit. Could just make out the diva coming up over the top of the fake building. Kristine was looking worried. Up she came again. And again. And again. Could see the Spanish headlines now: The Diva Who Wouldn't Die.

'It's the trampoline,' I whispered to Ryan. 'And one of her boobs is out of the bustier.'

This prompted Ryan to stand up, but then the conductor suddenly turned to the violas. It was that Strauss thing again and it was all we could do to make sure the section came in correctly. Frenzied, gaudy, last night of pleasure music teetering on the precipice of eternal darkness. Our fingers flew, our bows whirled and we finished the evening exhausted. Henna-hair Valerie tapped me on the shoulder.

'Excellent job of leading.' She wasn't being sarcastic. Sweet.

When we exited the stage, I caught a glimpse of fluorescent white hair on the floor. Had something happened to Sal? My heart pounded, my ears rung. Convinced self it was a seizure. He had had a heart attack. The Mission had eaten a certain seafood bisque that day which the diva pronounced as being 'hearty'.

'Yeah, as in it gives me a hearty tack,' replied Sal laconically.

Convinced as I have always been (and there is not one shred of evidence to back this up) that we are capable of seeing our own deaths hours before they actually occur, I walked with a dreadful foreboding to the body. His music so touched the deepest recesses of my soul, I thought it had taken every ounce of his strength to write it and now, here he was on the ground, curled up, in pain, dying.

Of laughter. A snicker was what I heard. Millions of snickers upon one another. Sal was balled up on the ground laughing and the dominatrix was attempting to apply a whip, not too playfully, to Angelika.

'Cheap bastard,' she screamed in between flicks of

the leather. 'Cheap, cheap miser!' Serik was doing a half-assed job of restraining her, laughing so much that not a sound issued forth from that lovely moustached mouth. Tears streamed down his face, then he looked at Sal on the floor and fell down beside him. They rolled back and forth like little pill-bugs with Angelika running between them on her eight-inch platforms, in an attempt to avoid the diva's blows.

'John!' screeched the diva, knowing that calling Angelika by his real name was the grossest form of insult when the transvestite was dressed to kill, 'you will pay for this. It was MY death scene. Mine! Cheap bastard.' She was now throwing all of her detachable accessories at him – and there were many. Huge earrings, stilettoe shoes, rings with nasty barbs, and a silver motorcycle-chain necklace all pelted the trannie.

I intervened. I hugged the diva, shushed her and pulled her bustier over her boob. 'You still died heroically,' I said to pacify her.

'Yeah, like a hero, you just kept getting up and fighting again,' giggled Angelika.

Idiot. Important to know when to keep the mouth shut. The diva chased him out into the street and I fell down next to the boys, laughing and laughing.

Stomach still hurts.

Later, much later . . .

Can check one of the priorities off the list. Ted came to the door tonight. He was laughing and grinning and saying, 'Wasn't that the funniest concert you've ever done?' Have to admit, it rates there with the 1812 Squawking Overture.

I looked at him and said, 'For old time's sake?'

He said, 'Well, I'd call it an evening up of the score but . . . whichever helps us get into bed.'

Ted is nice looking and he speaks out of the side of his mouth, like some Clint Eastwood character. If he weren't good looking, this little affectation would be annoying. I realised I haven't described him at all and I should, for posterity. Blue eyes and everything else about him is long and skinny – beside his you know what. Nose is skinny, hands perfect with skinny fingers for violin playing, legs able to contort and bend into all sorts of positions. He's one of those knees and elbow guys, which doesn't suit me for the long run. Must be biological – I like having a big man who could protect me in the next holocaust. Or viola section seating changes. Those powerful shoulders being another reason I must have fallen in love with Daniel. FORGET DANIEL! Anyway, Ted kissed my eyes and led me to the bed. Suddenly, I was inspired by Kristine. I said, 'No, Ted. Now it's my turn. Want you to have a memorable last time.'

There were no handcuffs so I took some old strings out of my case and bound Ted's hands together through the headboard. I love Spanish hotels with all the wrought iron. This would never have worked even in the nicest of American places. The G string was especially thick but pliable enough to keep Ted my hostage. Not that he was resisting.

Took off my clothes and then rubbed my breasts over his smooth face. Knowing he had shaven prior to visiting me made him even dearer. 'Kiss my nipples darling,' I instructed. 'Kiss them like you would kiss my clit.'

Ted did a fantastic job of complying. Around the tongue went a nipple, then he flicked it back and forth and sucked slightly. Around and then flicking. I pushed my two breasts as close to each other as they could get and he flicked his tongue back and forth between the two. I bent my head down to join his tongue and soon both our tongues were mingling and playing with my nipples. I didn't know my boobs were so flexible or even big enough to do so. Must be, dread of dreads, getting to be THAT time again. Stay away from canine haunts, at least.

So, I kissed Ted's neck up to his earlobe and then down to the place where his neck and collar bone meet. I love that indentation on men. OK, I even loved it on Valerie. Unbuttoned Ted's shirt and began sucking his nipples. His hands jerked on the G strings. 'You don't like it?' I asked.

'I love it. No one has ever restrained me before.'

I find that hard to believe, but then again, here's a man who doesn't like oral sex. Except he was beginning to with me. I do NOT want to know Ted's sexual background – like his uncle used to force him to endure monkey pettings or something. Would not have helped our lovely, and last, sexual encounter. Strange that I call my time with Ted 'sex' and that time with Sal 'making love', *n'est pas*?

I teased his nipples like he had played with mine and then I began to suck them in earnest. The harder I sucked, the louder were Ted's moans. I reached down to his jeans and touched his cock. It was swollen and pressing hard against his underwear and the denim. I thought to tease him longer and left his clothing on.

'Now suck my clit as if it were my nipples.'

He pulled the clit out between his teeth and sucked hard. I didn't think I could take it, I was twitching and feeling a bit like I might involuntarily kick him. 'Suck it like it was your shaft, your head.'

This was better, the intensity pushed back a bit. He still sucked but now the tongue slithered along the base of the little clit and then up to the tip. Around and up. I sat on his face, making it difficult for him to breathe, but I didn't care. Keep sucking, Ted. I'm going to come on you.

He swirled his tongue into my hole, plunging it in and out. I moved up and down as if fucking his tongue. But I needed him back on the clit to come and said so. That buttery tongue moved to the clit again, pausing just when I was about to climax and then starting again. The way I can give head to make it really intense. Confirmed with Ryan that yes, indeed, it was a very good game plan for giving the other party one hell of an orgasm. Push close to the brink and then retreat. Brink and retreat.

Ted licked and sucked, up and down just like my clit was the little cock it was. Blood rushed there, cunt lips swelling, feeling slippery, swollen, heavy, heavy, pounding. Then that sheet of colour fell upon me and I knew I was about to come, had to come, would kill someone who interfered.

Ted did not stop this time but sucked at a perfectly increased speed. Yellow and orange flashed before my eyes and I closed them to let the final burst, the quake, move itself from my head to my clit. Shaking, shaking and then the brilliant white of the orgasm where I felt I was breaking up into the stars.

Finally to breathe again. For both Ted and I hadn't done so in nearly a minute. Our chests heaved in unison. After catching my breath, I eased down to Ted's jeans. I pulled them off and began licking his member through his underwear. Ted thrashed a bit, I think it wasn't play-acting, but the G strings tightened on him. Old strings really are good in emergencies.

'I'm not ready for this, you know,' he whimpered softly.

'It looks to me like you're ready for some action, Teddy boy. Some action now.' I pulled his underwear off and put his entire penis in my mouth and down my throat before he could protest. Pulled out and said, 'I'm going to suck you like you sucked my clit. So, it's like I'm going down on myself, not you.'

It was one of those epiphanic moments where I knew that was exactly the way to help Ted. And to help me, for I do like giving head. It's sweet to see grown men moan, to feel their soft balls up on your chin, to know that they would do anything for you at that moment . . . and later for the chance of repeating the action. To know that even if you were an old hag, if you'd gotten to that point in the courtship, they'd find you beautiful. And because I, frankly, like swollen things that burst in my mouth. With groans and sighs attached.

I twirled Ted's mushroom cap in and around my tongue, looking at his face to discern where his pleasure points were. I thought he might not really know himself so I tried to imagine how he moved himself when he was inside me. He pushed up hard when he was fucking me and so I applied a lot of tongue pressure to that area under his head. Ted twitched and moaned and I knew that I had something. Parsing out the sex act, I then thought that he would really like to be licked how he licked my clit. Keeping the pressure on that area, I moved round and round his shaft, following my tongue with my hand. Like a corkscrew. Ted was writhing, moaning a bit too loudly for comfort – I was a bit afraid there might be some rule against fellatio in that mostly Catholic country. He thrust his hips up and up. He was fucking my face and then the cock stretched its last little bit and I felt the pumping that comes right before the sperm release.

Poor Ted. He must not have had sex since we were last together, for he flooded my mouth. It tasted salty, like liquid caviar. Nice.

Tears were streaming from Ted's eyes and, for a moment, I was so worried that I'd done something horrible. I kissed his face, starting with the eyes. But he wouldn't kiss my lips. I guess just getting head was such a tremendous breakthrough that tasting his own semen on my breath would have been overkill.

I cut the strings before his hands turned blue. I think even the diva wouldn't have gone that far. He immediately began massaging them, as any good string player would his most viable organ.

'Thank you,' sighed Ted in a reverential tone. 'That was the most amazing thing that has ever happened to me.'

And that's how Ted and I have become friends. Isn't it strange? Neither of us wanted sex together after that. Then ... and I'm pretty sure forever. But I felt in my heart that he was going to be one of my best buddies from that night forth. And I had finally helped a human being. I didn't send extra money to starving children or join a human rights organisation to stop torture in prison or to keep our planet green. No, I, Katie the wonder violist, helped one man learn to appreciate oral sex.

Well, if we all were involved in such worthy causes, wouldn't the world be a better place?

Chapter Thirteen

July 26, morning

I am *not* making it to breakfast. After Ted left, I intended to go to sleep. Still haven't caught up from that 'restful' night next to the naked kitten. About the nudist retreat – I've been kidding myself. The entire night next to Sal, I dreamed about just reaching over and taking him. He would not have resisted but it didn't seem like the thing we were destined to do. When I am around Sal, I begin to think of fate and destiny and all that kind of pre-determined crap that would make any Calvinist proud. So, it was not a very peaceful night for me, though I am sure Sal slept well. I should know. I watched him for three of those four hours before succumbing to dreamland.

So, last night, as my head hit the pillow, I heard guitar music under the balcony. I got it wrong. Sal is not a Renaissance guitarist, he's just a renaissance guy. He plays classical guitar and Spanish guitar and the lute. Tonight he was playing Flamenco under my window. The words went like this:

I'm a nice fella and I love her pundella
Más lechuga, por favor
Maś lechuga, por favor
If my honey doesn't get it, she'll snore . . . señor. Olé!

The entire hotel was leaning out of the balcony. One woman threw all the flowers she must have collected on the Ramblas and showered them upon Sal. Sneezing and sneezing, he ran away. But not until he put one red rose in his teeth and gave a salute. Woman on balcony turned her lined face to me. 'I thought it was the custom,' she said in an East Texas twang. Ooo, why is being idolised so difficult? Wanted to tell her the show was for me but then she looked so happy, I just couldn't.

Besides, maybe it was for her. I have no exclusive right to all of Sal's songs.

Later . . .

Kristine is really getting on my nerves. I am not good at being told what my schedule is every five minutes. I think I'm going to avoid her for a while, until I can just get my bearings. If you're not careful, the diva will plan your entire life, including bathroom time. Exhausted.

Conclusion came about thus. Met up with her and Serik. They were dipping bread in their café leches and looking to be quite jolly for ten in the morning. Serik seemed happier now that Ms Lithe has been safely stored away back in France. She is too fussy for him, I think.

The entire breakfast I kept thinking, 'It's now or never' in terms of making a move on Serik. When the diva and I went to powder our noses – she's got very oily skin just like me, except on her, the zits never

168

appear ... bitch – told her that I was going to make a move on Serik.

'Why would you do that?' asked with an undertone of great distress. Sometimes, when people speak that way, it reminds me of bad meat really spiced up.

'Because he is the three-legger. Why wouldn't I?' I'm just bad meat, forget the horseradish.

The diva was clearly twisted from some internal knot. Painful to watch. She pretended to change the subject.

All smiles, she asked, 'How was the trip with Salvadore?'

Ah ha. She's jealous or intent to fix me up with Sal or something. OK, not such a great 'ah ha' but, well, fuck you. I'm not the queen of 'whodunit' ... obviously.

I was careful with my wording. I do not trust the diva anymore. She's devious and certainly has her own agenda. I'm sure it's a soprano thing, but that's still no excuse for getting me embroiled in it.

Hmm ... in it or embroiled with it?

Anyway, told her that the drive and overnight stay were a very *natural* experience. Let her make of that what she will. She didn't seem surprised. Of course, she pressed for details but I annoyed her by saying, 'Come on. Serik is waiting.'

There are days that are the opposite of *carpe diem* – they seize us. The sunshine, the sound of boats docking and fish being hauled in, the lonesome cry of seagulls, the smell of coffee and yeasty bread and a hint of a spicy, vanilla-type cologne on the gorgeous man next to you ...

Yes he was. Bronzed from the sun, little flecks of silver in his dark hair catching the light in a most flattering manner, moustache waxed up over very full and red lips. His black eyes were fixated on mine and I felt the heat of electricity that was passing back and forth between us. My hand, I didn't want it to but it began to travel to his crotch of its own accord. Wasn't the only one with physical insanity. I saw his own huge hand moving towards my chest. Hands fluttering upon the iron table making shadows of butterflies in love. Moving into each other, closer, closer, his cinnamony scent wafting over me along with that warm coffee, morning breath. I had to touch his crotch; we had to touch. I needed to confirm that all was true and right with the world. I think he felt the same reaching for the little handful of my chest. You could hear our breathing, the waiters stood by confused, and we moved in for the touch.

There was the shadow and then the presence. You guessed it, Ms Horsey herself. 'Come on. Let's go shopping.'

Serik and I sighed. Every attempt today that we made to touch or hug or just look at each other was thwarted by the diva. At one point, she even shoved a plate of paella in my face, the steam causing my eyes to water and my nose to run. When things cleared, I saw Serik looking at a beautiful small Spanish teenager in high white shorts and a backless shirt. Involuntarily looked to see if she gave him a rise.

Yes. Jesus, doesn't take much to move that mountain.

Diva looked smug, following Serik's eyes and pleased he stopped staring dreamily at me. She was mistaken, for at the very next corner, when a cart with horses stole her attention away, Serik and I kissed.

Mmm! Like being hugged with a mouth. His big hands cupped my cheeks and I greedily rubbed my pelvis up against a greatly impeded boner. Or an impeded great boner.

'Lovely,' said the Human Vibrator in that deep voice which resonated all the way down to my crotch. I felt my legs move apart, my underworld widening thinking that he would soon be in me. I put my arms around his very substantial body and purred.

But carts and horses can't keep a diva down for long. There she was, with her arm around me, swatting Serik's butt and saying, 'We must hurry if we're going to make the tram.'

Tram?

Did I ever mention how afraid I am of heights? Especially man-made ones.

Serik and she went it alone as I wandered the streets of Barcelona with a dull throb of dissatisfaction between my legs, watching the beautiful simplicity of its inhabitants dodge tourists and go about their fishing, their drinking, their talking, and their loving. Very quiet is the loving, done mostly with eyes or around corners. Not like in the US where we need to show everything all at once. And then we don't even know why we did that. In a way, it was like the way Serik was making eyes at me. Not machismo, just real appreciation of the woman and her sex. Ooo, the diva. She had persuaded us all to let the day seize us.

Btw, Serik really looks like he belongs here. In a strange way, so do I. But the colour of his skin, the texture of his hair, those deep black eyes. And the way he moves without ever hustling. It's hedonistic serenity. He could suck on the right olives and grapes for hours and not need more. That's nice for a woman – a man who could eat all night the tastier things of a bounty.

Later . . .

Well, it's the bullfight without any spirituality. Daniel found me, again. I am embarrassed to write this but . . . I began crying about the pictures. I said, 'How could you have me followed around, taking pictures

171

of me? Why would that bring me back? I thought you loved me.'

The attorney practised what they first must learn in law school: deny everything. I cried and cried – I don't even know why, for I'm not really angry any more or sad or anything. Must have been some latent female biological thing that I instinctively knew would get to the bullying male.

It sort of worked. 'I am ashamed at how I've hurt you, sweet Katie.' He moved in, arms opening, waiting for me to step into the embrace and then he'd swoop me back to America where we'd live unhappily for ever after.

Liked that he said, 'I am ashamed.' Nothing accusatory, no extra meanings, no special clauses to pull out. He said, 'I am ashamed that I've hurt you.' Not 'that you've been hurt' but '*I've* hurt *you*.' I have been waiting six years to hear that, to hear Daniel just once admit that *he*, not the forces of humanity and/or the universe, had been the acting agent in another person's pain. It was almost enough to go back with him but then I thought:

What does Daniel really want from me?

I mean, think about it, Katie. What on earth does your presence do for him? It's a goddamn foil for his existence, that's what I am. He needs me around so he can feel really good about himself. How he can lie behind my back, how he makes more money than I do, how all those little clerks in the office kowtow to him while I am kowtowing to conductors and principal players and all that. That's what came to me then.

Carefully, so very carefully, I told Daniel that we were finished. There was no confusion in my voice and the seriousness of my tone registered on his face.

We'll see if it worked. He went away very sad, promising to call Dave off. Daniel even admitted that he had been paying Dave to take the pictures. Have to hand it to the big D – that took a lot of courage. He actually admitted to a minor crime. I mean, the man never even admits that he takes the soap from hotels. Once I even caught him with a hotel robe – he wasn't so lucky then, as it showed up as a nice $150 charge on the credit card.

Anyway, I pray that Daniel has really left Barcelona and the tour for good. Am afraid that I will sleep with him again just out of habit. So used to letting his will supersede my own. Must be a special brainwashing of his. Can't imagine at all what he still sees in me. I don't have long legs, I can't play that stupid lawyer glamour date thing, don't relish doting on him – though God knows I tried. For me, I guess I still see all that potential love that went awry.

Barf bag, barf bag. Somebody slap me. He cheated on you, Katie dear. What more do you need?

There is nothing to regret here. Nothing.

Chapter Fourteen

July 29

Can water be the colour of heaven in a baby's eye? That is where I was, floating in a cradle of a hand, seeing the water reflect in his own eyes. Waves crashing in the distance, the smell of salt and of life all about us, knowing that birds saw what men could not. There are moments in this world when everything is perfect, when one aches from joy and the greatest gratitude. When sky and sea and love melt together and you feel yourself expand out into nothing and everything.

Unfortunately, with such wonder all about, it's difficult to keep the running commentary to a minimum. Think Sal vastly annoyed with my keen observations, which threatened to destroy the tranquillity and grandeur of the moment.

In brief – Serik took us to Menorca. We left Barcelona at midnight and, by morning, we were there. Landed in Port of Ciutadella and there Serik's family met us with their own yacht to take the Mission, *avec* JP, to Cala en Bosc Son Saura. Oh, Katie, do not forget these names or places, for it is as if the universe smiled with utmost glee upon them and my heart wished to leap into each setting and absolve myself into nothing but pureness and light.

The magic was lost momentarily as we carried bag after bag off the boat and into the jeep Serik's family dropped off to take us to their villa. Sal complaining he might just bust a nail, Kristine upset she was sweating, John and JP trying to figure out how to hide the few bottles they had drunk on the way over, and me with viola on back, which kept swinging around to do a special clang with the heavy wine carriers in both of my arms. Serik has brought just about every exotic alcoholic beverage there is, especially a Catalonian wine called 'cavos' or something like that. Wasn't particularly fond of it (seemed exceptionally heavy) as it did remind me a bit of a cave, slightly mouldy and sweet. Or was that their liqueur?

But after everything, this was nothing, maybe even penance for the beauty we were about to see. Btw, everybody on the entire island knows Serik, which should not be surprising at this point. EVERYBODY EVERYWHERE KNOWS SERIK. As we rounded the drive, rose petals flew from the bushes and colourfully dressed men and women began chanting 'El Basso, El Basso'. Our Vibrator is their local hero – the boy who got off the island, made a name for himself, and always comes back.

The first day, we just all lay around the beach without clothing, trying to let the sun into every crevice it had previously been denied access. That's what I was trying to do, anyway. Sal seemed to be trying to avoid one really awful sunburn. He's so sensitive, and kept adjusting the umbrella over and over so as not to fry. Now that I think of it, the diva was doing the same. She needs that white skin, I guess, though she looks more Mediterranean than any of us. John, Serik and I baked ourselves to a delicious golden brown, then jumped in the water where Sal had taken up new living quarters, face and shoulders swathed in SPF 40, the sunscreen specially formulated for those who sleep in coffins during the day.

I know that being nude is not a big thing in Europe but I still could not help feeling I was posing the entire time. Very conscious of sucking stomach in, which has extended greatly due to the Mission's gluttony. And I was checking the boys out. Thought they'd be doing the same to me. Like to make a good impression.

Must tell Ryan. Serik deserves his rep! Frankly, it looks too big. I don't think I'd ever be the same after having him in me. Does seem Ms Lithe walks like she's been horseback riding after giving birth to a twenty-pound toad. But the intrigue. My nasty little cunt kept watering, just in case Serik and I got together. Had to press legs together to keep the scent at bay. So while lying out, the inside of my thighs remained quite pale and I began to look like a zebra hybrid. Was afraid the soft sand would stick to my wetness and make my lower half resemble a sea anemone. Forced myself to stop ogling Serik in order to keep my netherworld from drooling with anticipation (or was it fear?).

When we'd all finally rested, the sun was going down and there was a banquet being held in our honour. If they only knew I was a violist. I mean, banquets are for the stars. When was there ever a banquet for the violists in a pit orchestra? Or for hairdressers, for that matter? But JP seemed quite used to it. Perhaps he's a stylist for the stars. I know that people here are lining up for his shears. Not entirely sure he's only cutting hair though. He's sexy, funny and, most importantly, he's a French guy who doesn't smoke.

Salvadore had left early to write a little piece for all

of us. Bastard gave me four measures of impromptu, which I blew completely: *A Tribute to the People of Menorca, Ain't One a Dorka*. Something like that. But with a Spanish flair so not a single member of the audience was offended. In fact, Serik's father gave Salvadore another guitar, saying that it once belonged to another Salvadore: Dali. Didn't look like it was melting. Don't think Sal completely bought the story, though he was graciousness itself, making the rather tattered instrument sing fairly well despite its hums and twangs.

Anyway, fish and rice with pine nuts and sweet stuffed figs and God knows what else we ate. Kept trying to stop the gorging, thinking I would be naked the next day and not looking the better for it. As I was eating dessert, I decided that if I got into the water immediately, nobody would notice that I looked like I'd consumed a beach ball.

On the walk back, Sal and I heard rustling in the shrubbery and a very distinct 'oui' called out in utter ecstasy. I went to spy and Sal walked away from me with an alarmed expression on his face, apple cheeks moving towards the ears and all.

I was right! It was the hairdresser having a fabulous time with a very buxom brown-haired beauty. She was on her knees in the sand, her long hair brushing the ground. He had his two hands on her and was slamming into her in a way I most certainly approved of. Moonlight bounced off his shimmering cock which, now that I saw it erect, was quite large. I know, I know: size doesn't matter. Well, it does if you are having a one-time fling, doesn't it? So JP was a grower. And hairy too. It's true, you know, what they say about the virility of hairy men – I'm learning that on this tour.

They moved to their next sandy-bottomed position and the brunette grabbed JP and literally lifted him on to her. It was then I realised she was a good head taller than he. His head dove in to stay between her breasts. He must have loved it. They were so large I doubt he could hear anything any more. Can't say I quite got how the angle worked but it seemed that it was she who set the tempo.

And set it well, I might say, for I soon saw the telltale signs of his orgasm slipping down her leg. She released him and he fell to the sand and they both giggled. After a brief interlude of kissing, she began grinding her pelvis against his in a way I thought must have felt nice to her. It seemed to alarm the French man a bit. But he soon got what was going on and even added a hand somewhere down there. I think she came after that. It sounded like it anyway. Sounded like a trapped guinea pig, chortling and then squealing in questionable delight.

I moved on. Sal was nowhere in sight as I sauntered back to my room in the villa, wet with desire.

The next day was a repeat of the first, *sans* Kristine and Serik. He took her to comb the island for spices to bring back to New York. John and JP spent a little time with us but then found a scooter to rent and were off on a trek around Menorca. Now there's a pair. Fairly certain JP's not of that persuasion, despite the career choice, but am sure he could give Angelika's wig a much-needed makeover.

The sky was perfect and Salvadore's hair matched the clouds, as if they'd grown from his own thoughts. His green eyes were a shimmering blue near the water. We walked in the narrow lagoon, up through reeds and small pines providing shade. Sal looked eternal and ageless. He could have been twenty or fifty. Fact is, I still do not know his age. His shoulders rippled and it was the first time I noticed that he had a body like those Greek statues. Not beauty but an ideal beauty. Godlike. For such a soft-spoken, dry wit, he had power. It was layered under much gentleness but this was a very powerful man.

I kept those ideas to myself. Even my observations of our surrounding beauty were at a bare minimum in the beginning. Then I felt that hand. It just reached under the warm water and cupped me between the legs. Sal looked into my eyes, almost imploringly, like he was begging me to understand what he was doing. Or to know that it was important.

He lifted me up so that we could kiss. I was sitting on that great palm like it was a saddle and kissing him in a very intimate way. 'Katie, you are so special,' Sal whispered into my ear. Was quite shocked. Didn't know what to say. The hand lowered me and moved a thumb in at the same time.

Oh, that was divine. A thick thumb in the warm water, being cradled by a hand that was the size of my ass. Thumb went slowly in and out as Sal looked into my eyes. He kissed my forehead and then bent down to kiss me again on the lips. Then his mouth was upon my breasts and that's when I noticed I was filled with the 'in-love' fire. And I was in love with a god. Here in the waters of the Mediterranean Sea, where thousands of years ago Zeus could have been doing this to Athena – one of those gods anyway ... could never get those gods quite right but the feeling was of utter timelessness.

A strange thing was happening to me, as if my very soul were being plucked by the finger inside me. Sal's gaze made me internally squirm but then he stopped. I got afraid, I guess from the intensity, the religious overtones being with him evoked – and started speaking. Babbling really, with a sort of falsetto blessing about the whole island – did it all without seeming to breathe and was working myself into quite a dizzy spell. Saying how lovely it was, how beautiful everything was, how bright the sun, how warm the breeze, how nice the people, blah blah. Sal pulled that thumb out, kissed my cheeks and bid me to swim with him. I think he figured I couldn't chat while swimming. And I couldn't. Not much of a swimmer, unless I've got one of those little cheater boards in front of me. I more resemble dog than mermaid when it comes to water – I am sure there's an easier way but I just refuse to put my face in. God knows what's in the water. I mean, where do fish and birds poop? As Sal kept swimming far ahead and then circling back for me, I got the idea that it would be easier if I just grabbed his legs and let him lead me around.

Who would've known that Sal's greatest fear is shark attacks? Must have thought I was a very big fish and jerked around, nearly pounding me. Then he saw his mistake and cradled my head. 'Oh, Katie, you have no idea who you are.'

Now, what was I to make of that? But his big hands were holding my head and body, floating me back to shore. The hand on my breast now was more no-nonsense, like a doctor's. I ached to have him in me and could see I would have to make the first move. Before we got too close to shore, I squirmed around and attempted to reach down to Sal's cock. A wave hit me in the back of the head and I sputtered. I grabbed lower and lower and finally got to him. He was rigid – so I figured it wasn't really as if he were so indifferent to my charms.

'Sal,' I whispered, 'please be inside me, out here, under this blue, blue sky.'

'If that is what you wish, Katie, I'll be more than happy to oblige,' he said, while looking at me. He wrapped my legs around his back and treaded water for us both. The hot sun, the cool breeze and the secret we were sharing under the water. I could hear Sal enter me again and again because the water was acting like some audio conduit. Like breaking gently through rubber again and again. His hands were cupped on my ass, pulling the cheeks slightly apart so that I felt the water enter me everywhere. It seemed Sal was the water and I was Sal and the communion so perfect and so real I did not even let out a single gasp when his thumb stroked my button and I came. A brief ball of fire and then I felt so weak. Sal still treaded water for both of us.

His eyes fluttered back and I felt the warmth flood into me and then out of me again. Sal looked exhausted and I was afraid he would not be able to make it back to shore. I put my arm under him and began swimming my best dog paddle. When I'd gone all of three feet, realised I could easily stand up. There on the bank were the diva and Serik, she with a huge grin on her face and he looking rather hound-doggish. Think Kristine must have revelled in telling him some bad news. Or perhaps he's really in love with her. Or maybe the other way round and now she's finally over it. Maybe they saw us. Water is crystal clear.

Sal and I did not acknowledge what happened in the water by even holding hands. He glanced at me for a moment and I glanced at the diva and at him and he gave a slight nod. Maybe he was thinking the same thing about her and Serik. Who knows, for we didn't get to talk again. I've been trying to interpret that enigmatic nod ever since.

Maybe he was just trying to hide a sneeze.

We parted ways for the siesta. Walking back to the villa, I again spied JP with whom I thought was the brunette. No, this time it was a raven-haired buxom woman. Then, duh, it dawned on me: he dyed her hair. And not just on her head either. There's trust. They were in the shrubbery again (guys, get a room!) and he was munching on his new creation. She had her back up against the bark of a low tree and was moaning softly while he ate. I thought, 'Hey, that's the way to do it. Now, if you could only see that she wants your finger.' As if on cue, he inserted a finger and her eyes rolled back in her head. Here came the stifled guinea pig sounds and then a chortle. JP was still sucking when she pushed his head away. I knew what she meant; sometimes it is just too much pressure on the clit after orgasm. I guess some men are convinced that we women MUST have multiple orgasms and they could suck your clit clean off . . . so I've read. I get too sensitive down there.

She began going down on him, but I felt the siesta clock turning in me – I've gotten quite used to the napping – and had to head on down the road to my bed. Thought I saw JP look my direction but was mistaken.

Another banquet that night, over at another house on another part of the island. Dancing until dawn, sleeping on the beach and then it was time to go back. I felt like a little kid who is getting her pacifier cut up right in front of her. I couldn't leave. I almost left the tour right there but John said, 'Come on, be realistic. How are you going to make a living playing the viola on this island?' Good point, but I could manage something. Maybe I'd work for Serik's parents. They seemed to love me. I'm sure Serik would help – he was pleased at my good impression.

A now buxom blonde came to the dock with JP to bid us adieu. They kissed passionately in front of us in a way that had me longing to do the same with someone. His hand rested innocently on her left tit and her hand was grabbing his little handful of an ass as hard as she could. Wonder if she got the same thorough dye job as before. Like I said, there's trust for you.

'That was quite fun. Thank you, Serik, for inviting me.' JP cast those baby blues upon the three-legger. Realising that we hadn't yet done the same, we all pitched in our exclamations of appreciation. Then JP took off his clothes and went horizontal on the boat deck. Again, we all followed suit. Or no suit. Hee hee. Sal and Kristine, as per course, slathered themselves with SPF 40. Vampires!

Back in Barcelona now and Sal has still not acknowledged what happened. Fuck him. I'm not mad but, you know, it *was* a very special moment.

Kristine is coming over soon for some girl talk. I might just tell her of my latest sexploits.

Later . . .

New Word: ferrule.
Example: the diva's approach to sex strikes me as a toolmaster placing a ferrule upon each and every shaft she sees which needs reinforcement.

Kristine: diva, dominatrix, baroness, lover of horses.

Matchmaker. Oh she is so good but the little feline got out of the bag after our fifth glass of sherry. Ooo, Spanish sherry is DIVINE! We were drinking one that was like the finest juice of raisins ever given to God to ferment further.

Anyway, I am, for one, sorry she told me. I do not like feeling set up. In any way by any one – unless it pertains to gigs. Sometimes. But that is different. Even remember another friend trying to help in that regard, telling a certain concert organiser that I was a great player who just didn't do well at auditions. Like I told Dave, with friends like that, who needs enemas? Thanks for pointing out your own fears – what I should have said to 'helpful' friend. Auditioning IS part of it all and I do just fine – just find it a bit boring and unmusical. Like being fixed-up. I mean, people find each other for their own reasons not for other people's reasons. Then you are just a fish swimming

183

around in someone else's aquarium. And you can be sure, they are ALL watching.

Anyway, the evening did start well, I confess. The diva began by explaining her last time in Italy a few months ago. One of her beaus sent for her in a limousine. Not so typical in Rome. A very dark limo with dark leather inside. He'd instructed her to wear only a coat and she obliged. Hell, she had lots of time to kill before her next show: *Bridges Over Babylon County*.

Inside, he pulled off her coat and made her sit on the quite buffed leather. The driver drove like a good Italian and she was soon slipping and sliding all over the car. He tied her hands in front to 'help'. Then one of the windows was rolled down. The diva did not want her adoring fans to see her in such a compromised position so she squirmed every way she could to not be seen as the car spiralled about town. There was a breast flung out the window, the next time an ass's cheek. Her beau kept applauding each time she seemed to avoid exposing her face. Lipstick prints marked all the other windows. He had his prick out of his pants and sometimes she was simply thrown upon it, and then off it. 'Like the nastiest of carnival rides,' explained the diva to me.

At some point, she bumped her head and became quite disorientated, not knowing if indeed she were sitting on the ceiling of the car or on the floor. Her breasts were hanging out the window and a young Italian boy came over and began sucking them. Only in Italy. Then the driver tore the nipples out of the warm mouth as he sped again around St Peters, the G-force being so great as to send the couple hurtling back into the very back seats.

When the car came to a complete halt, the driver got out and came into the back. There he bent the diva over his knee and her beau began spanking. And spanking. And spanking. Then the driver went back to his unqualified task of moving her around via racecar methods while the beau laughed and applauded. She did not wish to keep her sore rump to the leather any more and let her body bounce freely with her ass in the air. Often, she landed upon the stiff pole protruding from the beau's silk suit trousers.

They came to a monastery and there she was instructed to put her coat on again. Kristine thought, 'Oh no, not again.' She says that many think she wants to have sex with the clergy, given the immorality acts she portrays with the Mission on stage. Not quite. Kristine admits that she does harbour a certain fantasy about forcing certain members to do things with their members but 'it is only a fantasy, those things don't work out, you know,' says the diva.

In this pursuit with beau, she was to be the ultimate temptation to a group of seminary students. That Kristine liked. To tease and then NOT to fulfil was more to her taste with certain types of males – and females.

So she was led up to the altar and the young men were led in and seated row after row. A perfect crowd, though smaller than the ones she was used to. And she had never been naked before so many. But, she promised me, it was more than OK. Sort of heightened her performing arts.

There were two massive candlesticks nearby and it gave Kristine the idea to do a very bad bump and grind. The beau disrobed her, as she knew he would, and she began singing a *Gloria in Excelsis Deo* that any short-on-cash singer knows regardless of faith. Thank God, for all the music jobs he/she/it provides. She began slowly weaving the melody into a strip act, sliding up and down the silver candlestick and then making sort of crucifix poses, after she ran her hands up her body. I imagine the walls echoed with her melodious and powerful voice. I've seen her do it before – if her initial voice can reverberate, she'll add another voice to the echo and so forth. If it's really echoey, an entire chorus might be heard for a few moments. And she has that glass-shattering diva quality that should be used in Alpine regions to locate lost skiers. According to her, she reached the highest notes when she turned around and inserted a candle in herself from behind. Like a very good porno queen. But not before she'd lit it with the other candle that burns forever up on the altar. 'I wanted them to always think that that stick had been in a woman when the males up there at Mass in their robes light it and pass it around.'

Filling the church up to its great Roman arches with voice and the scent of woman and melted wax, she sauntered by the rows, thrusting her ass in their faces, fondling herself, putting a finger in herself (and waving it under certain virginal noses) and, in general, forcing a good many of the lads to put their Bibles quite firmly down in their laps.

She saw a priest come in, wondered if she ought not stop. He looked familiar, though, so she decided he was part of the ruse. The ruse to get a rise out of the guys. But he did not look amused at the ruse. Red faced, big beanie cap. Dressed to kill in red. Beau nowhere to be seen, all young men looking down.

It was one of those holiness himself members. 'Jesus Christ,' thought Kristine. Btw, she likes that her name means *filled with Christ*. Made it seem rather appropriate to be in there teasing. Thought, well, why not? In a mad dash to get out of there (she had spied a choir robe and decided to grab it if beau wasn't going to show up again), she kissed the stunned priest and did her best to give him a three-fingered blessing.

Great story, isn't it? With anyone else, I would doubt the entire thing, but I've seen the flowers thrown to the diva, the love letters, the men following her city after city, and have heard of her friendship with a certain Cardinal she refuses to name. So, with this fate dominator, it doesn't surprise me that she finally admitted she has been trying to get Sal and I together since the beginning of this trip. 'From the moment I saw you, I knew you were just what he needed. The problem was convincing you that he was just what you needed.'

'Did you stop to ask either of us?' I asked incredulously.

'Why?' She didn't seem the least perturbed. 'Or should I say, why not? – that's my motto.' Oh the diva, the ballseyness of it all. The not-so-hidden agenda. Wish I didn't like her so much. 'You do like him, don't you?' she added.

'Of course. Who doesn't like Sal?'

'But you really like him. One can see that.'

Fine, glad I'm so transparent. Things with Sal feel special, not something to air out with a fun-loving but dominating female. It seemed to me that if I told her about our encounter, it would cheapen it somehow. Like doing your utmost to describe music with words – the only thing that really describes music is music. So, after a few more evasions of the diva's questions, I sent her on her way, suspicious that Sal had more a part in this than meets the eye. That nudist place, for example. NOBODY seemed to have a working credit card but everyone seemed to have money for all sorts of other things. And it was their idea I travel in a car.

I'm thinking of asking Ted for a favour, which may solve this.

Chapter Fifteen

August 3

I cried leaving Spain. Don't know why, but it sang to
my heart, that city of Barcelona. Menorca is where I
discovered another soul. Travelling this way makes
one flippant – no, better, unattached. Whether it's
people or places, you start to view them all as
postcards. Memories stored as they are really happening so in the end, you weren't there at all while you
were there but more there when you are comfortably
at home thinking about the good times.

Don't ask me to repeat that one.

After a short flight, we arrived in Rome. The show
this evening has been entitled *Bananas for the Romanas*,
Kristine supposedly wearing a monkey suit for a good
portion of the show. Whatever. We played most of
Sal's music, which sounds a bit like Jacques Brell,
Wagner and Gregorian chants all rolled into one.
There's gongs with violins, sax and harp together.
Violas, of course, have centre stage, playing what
sounds like very insane monkey-grind music. When
will I ever see a show?

Told Ryan I saw IT.

'Bigger than a bread box?' he began quizzing.

'About the same size.'

'Don't suppose it got into the oven?'

'No, you bastard,' I said. 'This kitchen ain't equipped for that style of cooking.'

'Maybe I am.'

Sometimes I worry about Ryan.

About Serik – nothing to worry about there. His picture should be next to the definition of cocksuredness. He's the 'well-hung' man in any tarot deck.

Between rests, Ryan mentioned again that he was still up for giving me pointers. At first I thought he was referring to my section-leading skills but then I understood what he was up to. Agreed. Will report on it tonight.

Our Romans love the act. Hoots and hollers plus a rain of roses fell upon the stage and into the pit.

Last stand/formerly first stand guy went home from Barcelona. Threatened to sue. Who though? Sal? Me? SX? Now Ryan and I are collecting his principal pay which is ⅓ over scale. Hot dog!

Later . . .

Shit, shit, shit. Absolute disaster. New word is old word: humiliated. Sal surprised me with a visit shortly after dinner, right after I had attacked my face. I couldn't resist, I just needed to know that every single one of my pores was unclogged. I mean, it is hot and Rome is dirty and my face looked like a filthy flesh orange peel in desperate need of blackhead removal. With a red face resembling something that looked more like an encounter with a beehive than an attempt at beauty, I opened the door, expecting the maid or someone.

'Katie, are you sick?'

There were those fantastic eyes mocking my war-torn face.

'No, just a little washing.' I tried my best to make a type of worried Greta Garbo pose so as to hide the extent of my zit picking. What a disgusting habit. The posing.

'Why are you wrapping your hands around your face? You're sick, aren't you?' The ever-observant Sal leaned closer into me. I turned away.

Whispering over the Greta Garbo shoulder, I asked Sal if he could come back a little later, thinking that, thank God, I wasn't in the process of bleaching my facial hairs. Vanity, vanity, vanity. Why am I embarrassed to be a higher primate?

Sal left, a bit dejectedly. I think he wanted to talk about our time together and so do I, for it was lovely. But I want to turn to him with a radiant face, the kind of face that he'll write music for for the rest of his life and say, 'It was one of the most heavenly days I've ever had.'

No, no, no . . . that won't do with Sal. He's too great for such clichés. I want to wow him with the most fantastic Joycean dialogue to thrust us into the arms of the poets. I want to dazzle, to shine – and not in some lunar-faced way.

Later . . .

Life is beginning to feel like a pointless run on the hamster wheel.

Ryan came over and I mean that in every sense of the word. It was lovely, until I remembered, when I heard the catch of the door, that I had told Sal to come back. Why didn't I lock the door?

The old cucumber thing started and I showed Ryan what I knew, sliding my tongue down, sliding the hand up after it in a spiral motion.

190

'You know, I never do the same thing with the same guy – so unmusical, wouldn't you say?'

'That's right. Jesus, with more women like you, we prostitutes would be out of business.'

Let the word 'prostitute' hang in the air. Ryan worries me sometimes. Flicked tongue on the 'underside' of the cucumber, following it by a thumb.

'That's excellent, Katie. Just the way men like it. But what about the pressure?'

Told him I didn't feel under any pressure.

'I mean, it's important where to squeeze and where not to.'

Somehow, in the course of our enthusiasm, Ryan took off his pants and I practised on him. He said I didn't need much help and I slid my tongue and mouth up and down his shaft while my viola fingers swirled up and over the head and back down again. Ryan was quite hard and quite encouraging.

He told me to dig my knuckles up under his scrotum while sucking. Stimulates the prostate. Didn't know that. Was pleased that Ryan was bucking around like a frisky bull.

'Katie, it's superb. You sweet cocksucker,' Ryan repeated over and over between gasps as my mouth engulfed him.

His scrotum was tightening and he smelled hotter there, like bread out in the sun. I increased the tempo and the tension on both hands – digging the little naughty knees of my fingers further up behind his balls. Paused for one moment, licked his balls, and then engulfed his humming cock. A vein on the right of the cock was pulsing and I licked it before setting back to putting my hand next to my lips making what must have felt like a very long, wet mouth canal.

Up and down I went, harder and faster and harder and faster.

He came in my mouth.

'Your husband was an idiot for leaving you,' said my stand partner in between pants.

L R!

That's when I noticed the flash of white and the quick green of an eye.

Sal.

Ryan said to not bother explaining. Only gay men could possibly understand how what we were doing was something purely educational. I'd give myself an F right now for 'Fuck-up'.

Well, not completely. I am sure this little 'lesson' could come in handy some day. At a complete loss what to say to Sal.

August 4

SX has got a few days off again. I love this gig! We're treated well wherever we go. We're only doing one more show in Rome. Salvadore is probably working on the music right now. I told him there was to be no impromptu parts for me but he only grinned. Want to talk to him about our fun in the lagoon but don't know really what I want to say. I want more, am not ready for only that but could be soon. Just want to say, 'Wait for me, Sal. I'm almost there.'

Where, Katie, where? I mean, what's the rush? Since I'll be sexually attractive till the day I'll die (that's pussy-assuredness talking), why choose just one man? Just know I need to pile all that experience I did not get before my marriage. I want a bit of everything – though am getting more certain some of the things I really like. I don't think Sal will wait. I have not seen him ogling another woman. He doesn't even ogle me, exactly. It's that intense stare which makes me feel scrutinised and greatly appreciated at the same time.

Sal's way of looking at you and through you and beyond all at the same time.

I want him though – perhaps I'm like a horse (no Kristine, STAY AWAY!) . . . If you chase it, it will run away never to be yours. Only when you push it away will you really be the master.

Therapist!

OK, that's not quite it. Thinking, thinking. I just like Sal. His integrity, his honesty, his creativity, his wit, his body, HIM.

Btw, Ted happily agreed to my request. Almost too happily, for it involves the diva.

Dave seems to have disappeared off the face of the earth, which gives me the creeps more than if he were out in plain sight.

New checklist:

1. Get Sal to absolutely idolise me THEN bed me.
2. Sex with a few more strangers.
3. Sex with Slava . . .? Hmm, not sure why I wrote that. He intrigues me.

August 5

Here's my idea regarding Dave and Daniel. If Daniel shows up again or if Dave asks on his behalf, the Mission has been instructed to use any means available to ridicule them out of existence. (That is a bit extreme, isn't it? Just want the pair to GO AWAY!) Said that these two might very well become the subject of the next immorality play – except here, 'sin' is *not* going to win. Ted is keeping an eye out as well, and John has gone so far as to get Leo involved 'for the sake of an orchestra player's sanity.' Says Leo agrees. Ryan has also recruited Slava to keep watch because

Dave seems to talk to Slava a lot. The two seem to have some camera thing going.

Rome has me giddy with its fountains – so far I've counted fifty-five in the vicinity of our hotel. Serik keeps coming back with so many jugs of homemade wine that I'm beginning to believe the red liquid too flows out of the mouths of bearded men and seraphs. Each bottle we empty reappears like magic, full again.

Shameful, we even brought wine to breakfast (at 10, praise be to Italy). And consumed bread, olive oil, figs, peccorino cheese, espresso and a good two jugs of simple red refreshment over a two-hour period.

Can't talk any other Mission people into this, but Rome has me in the mood for wandering. It's all old news to them and they are setting about exploring their favourite haunts while I am attempting to discover what mine are. Hard to admit I've joined the frantic camera crowd for everywhere I go, it's more like a picture than real life and I keep snapping away, hoping to glimpse the image at a later time and then convince myself that what I saw was real: the smooth-skinned girl with witchlike eyes pinning up an entire basket of fine white linen; the old man kissing his equally old friend on the street and handing him square bread and a jug of wine; the piercing blue sky which can be seen at times through the Roman pollution; crumbling fifteenth-century apartments; menus written on walls hundreds of years ago. How can I really believe this?

Strange, wouldn't you say? That this familiar modern apparatus which captures our manipulations of sight – that it can make this beauty seem more tangible, more real. Perhaps it's the chance to put a border around this kaleidoscope of sights and scents. When we see a picture, why don't we say, with the same astonishment as when the situation is reversed, 'Fantastic. It's just like life'?

Boarded the wrong train, don't know, didn't care. Just wanted to ride somewhere away from the ceaseless honking cars. The conductor, after we got started, asked for my ticket. Couldn't find it. Looked everywhere in that stupid piece of leather I call a purse. Really, it's just a delayed trip to the trashcan. 'No problem,' smiled the conductor. 'For you, no problem. You're beautiful. It's free, see?'

By God, this tour is going to convince me that I am. He smiled and pushed me up into first class, where I watched tomatoes, bourganvillea and laundry go by with the same clarity of form. Things seem outlined in Italy – same feelings as when I was here so many years ago (BD, before Daniel). The land holds the people, the architecture reminds them of their greatness. It all seems underlined, like an epic movie. I feel that my actions are historical yet inconsequential. The sun continues to shine over the same old battlefields, temples, decayed and new homes. The women and men who walk among the gods and still see the dirt on the ground, smiles splitting faces like knives in melons. Oh, to live here and let the sun take me up under her wing. A fantastic place and a fantastic race.

Later . . .

God, am I sick of masturbating Italian men. Can't I just walk the back streets of Rome without watching flesh salamis stand at attention? And the exposing of themselves. Suppose somewhere, somehow, it must've worked just once for them. But please, not even offensive – just annoying. Like watching Hari Krishnas dance themselves into oblivion. For what? To prove they can really let go and behave like idiots? Maybe it's something in the Italian water. Don't think I look 100 per cent American (i.e. slut). Whatever. Just keep your whacking thoughts out of sight. I don't mind the *idea* that I am the cause of a man's touching himself but I draw the line when perfect strangers show me their innermost fantasies. Forcing me to see more museums.

Btw, why does Michelangelo's *David* have such a little weenie? Must be a grower.

Sweet. After hearing complaints of unwanted naked men sightings (this is not a nudist camp, after all!), Sal volunteered to walk with me this evening. I'm glad. He is the perfect accompaniment to my sensibilities at the moment. Understanding the wackiness (no, no pun intended) of the beauty surrounding us.

August 6

Walk lovely, tossing coins in fountains, exchanging confidences. Not too many, for mine as of late are not put in a context I could easily render into dialogue with a man I so greatly desire.

Learned from Sal that his parents are from Ireland, both schooled in Latin. Both artists. Mother a painter, father a granite sculptor. Father went blind from the rock chips in his eyes. They were good friends with the man who made melting clocks a part of our subconscious: Dali. Yes, Sal's namesake. Both parents died in an auto accident when he was sixteen. Lived on his own ever since.

When I said the normal, 'I'm sorry', Sal replied, 'Why? You didn't do anything. Besides, even though I loved them and still miss them, they were such powerful people. After they died, I realised how much influence they had had on me. Their death was a kind of freedom to my art.'

I nodded my head. 'A bit like a divorce but with longer-lasting consequences.' I regretted saying it, for I immediately understood how trite fell the words.

No, not trite. Just inappropriate. Irrelevant. A non sequiter.

An idiot.

Hollow sounded our feet on the old stones. An accordion moaned in the distance, horses came towards us. The moon was shining in Sal's hair and everything had sort of a *National Geographic* light to it. Buildings stood out as if bathed in a black light. The breeze was warm and seemed to swirl about my ankles and neck. It was strange hot/cold earthquake weather and everything around us seemed set on edge, anticipating the crash or repulsion of the two great plates miles and miles under our feet.

Suddenly, Sal pulled me into a little alleyway and we kissed. 'Sorry. I shouldn't have done that,' he said, after a hungry moment of tongue touching and lip nibbling.

'Why?' said my eyes. I'm sure he read the expression in them. Really, I ask any of you, why? Why not kiss me and take me right there and then? Instead, he grabbed my hand and said, 'Come on.'

We ran over the streets, twisting and winding, all leading back to Rome. There was the Trevi Fountain again. Sal jumped in, wetting his khakis to his nice ass and revealing to the world that he wore red briefs. His white shirt was wet too and clung to his arms in a way that made me want to lick it dry. I didn't, however. I did not even jump into the fountain. I only had one dress left. Rayon. It would take forever to dry and I would have nothing to wear for the rest of the trip. I keep losing my clothes in sexual encounters and have no money to replace them. Damn, poverty makes us cautious. And not very sexy.

Saddened by my dry land tactics, Sal climbed out. 'Didn't you see *La Dolce Vita*?' he asked.

'Yes, but when she gets in the fountain, it all dries

up. I didn't want you to experience a sudden emptiness.'

'That's my point, Katie. Not every time that you get all the way in does it vanish.'

Another Sal cryptogram.

Evening ended sweetly, with a rose planted behind my ear and a kiss on both of my cheeks. I really have done this courting thing all backwards with Sal. Sex first, then sleep, and now dating. Soon we'll be just meeting as if on a blind date.

Chapter Sixteen

August 7

*B*rr. Chilled to the depths of my soul. Got my wish. Wishes. And not exactly the best of them.

The catacombs. Went there alone since none of the Mission wanted to go. Musty smell of exploded grapes and dirt. Down and down below the city. Not the smell of death but the smell of no life. Nothing grows there, not even bacteria. Cool, damp, lifeless. A friar was leading us through the crypts and galleries but I got separated from the tour group. Wandering in a maze, got turned around and then utterly lost.

Hands grabbed me around the waist and pulled me into a dark corner. I could have screamed and someone would've helped. Didn't. Liked the suspense. Didn't feel in real danger. Hands pulled down my jeans. Heard zipper from behind open. Hands under my bra, on my breasts. A mouth in my hair. A mouth chewing my hair and kissing my head and shoving a cock in my very wet place. Kissing and pushing my legs further apart. Now in a little more. Now completely. Jeans stretched to their limit above knees. Felt weak. Heard snap of the condom. Then a swift reentering. Pounding hard, intense but soundless. I was soundless too. Just being fucked and fucked in the deep recesses of the city, surrounded by dirt and damp.

I turned to see my intruder but my head was pushed forward again with lips. Hands were on my ears rendering me deaf. Fucked and hearing nothing except an internal pumping and my heart trying to break free in this lifeless place. It became a dark sort of heaven, this anonymous lovemaking. I wanted to know who was in me but I also did not want to know. My fantasy again come to life. The penis without a face. Not rape, this was consensual. Biological. I couldn't help myself. I wanted this penis with no history, filling me. Unable to control that it must have me. Must possess me. Must release seed into *me*. Am I that much a slave to sex? When greatness is thrust upon me, I acknowledge it with a widening of legs and heart. Oh, thrust, pound, pummel, slam, drive, hammer, gorge, gouge, impale, skewer me upon that sweet thick cock.

Hard to explain, but the very idea of what was happening to me nearly pushed me over the edge. Touching myself lightly, I came like a voiceless animal, squeezing myself every way I could to keep from howling out. The cock still pumping in me, oblivious to the pleasure I just experienced. This cock just wanted to master the hole. That's its only mission. To fuck and to fill. To fill and to fuck. Biological. Animals, wild animals, fucking, copulating, frolicking, screwing, humping – whatever.

I feel the shudder first and then the warm flood. Then the rational came back, the wild animal gone. The coming and the odd moments afterwards where no one wants to see each other. I did not desire to see my loving assailant just then. I hesitated (a fateful pause, I tell you). What to do? Now the awkward moment. Should we face each other and say thanks?

No, I did not get to ponder this long. Didn't turn around when anonymous cock zipped back into pants and I heard another zipping and then the unmistakable sound of a camera shutter opening and closing. Two shots of my come-filled hole before I pulled my jeans up.

Angry, wanting to see, I turned around. Nothing but skulls faced me. Went racing through catacombs but gave up shortly. Who was I looking for anyway? I think this kind of thing, according to Kristine, happens often in Italy where men are always ready to fuck a beautiful woman. But to take a picture also? That seemed more a tourist thing. Maybe the guy thought I was Italian.

Anyway, chilled is how I feel. Great until the picture. It was so beautifully beastly and then the modern apparatus recording the act. And that part was NOT consensual. Guess I still didn't learn from the sex club. But who could resist? This won't happen to me when I go back to the States and put up that protective layer which makes me think that I can ward off unwanted attackers by emitting a certain vibe. I lose my willingness to abandon in the States. Just like I lost my inhibitions here.

Still feeling odd, I returned to my hotel room. No one else was around. But there was that nineteen-year-old drummer/midi player. Was going to have an experience where I was in control.

Asked Allan to meet me for dinner. After showering, put on a fishnet bodysuit I had purchased the day before. Crotchless. Nice. Put on my short, black, and only, dress over it, high-heels and was ready.

Went, on John's recommendation, to an inexpensive but exquisite little trattoria overlooking St Peter's. Jesus, Rome is a noisy city. Horns blaring everywhere,

201

people talking as loudly as is possible. Allan and I barely exchanged a word. He mentioned something about living in the new millennium and I think I instinctively tuned him out. Youth! Right now, I am not after men with great conversation skills. Obviously. (That's why you, Sal, need to wait – please wait. Though, wait. What exactly has Sal spoken to me of? Well, I'm sure he's a great conversationalist if I'd shut up. He did talk a bit the other night . . .)

Loud music, loud horns, loud conversation, bells ringing every fifteen minutes, cell phones exploding with urgent calls, waiters having vocal affairs with girls passing by. Couldn't hear any of Allan's twittering. Ate instead. Watched him suck at the pasta and thought something was familiar in that. The way he sipped his wine. It wasn't him but it reminded me of someone else. Who, who?

Decided that getting drunk with a near illegal might meliorate all sense of unfulfilment. His treacle began to turn me on. Slammed glass after glass of the musky-fruity wine down followed by three glasses of a lavender grappa. God, I got drunk. Silly, run naked in the fountain drunk. Didn't. Instead, youth and I went respectfully back to his hotel room where I ripped off his clothes and threw him on the bed.

The lioness. I licked his neck, devoured his lips. Sucked them into my mouth. Pulled off his tight T-shirt. Youth has a bod. A very nice bod!

Pulled off his pants. Nice, nice, nice. Felt a bit familiar, again in a hard-to-say way. Didn't think too much of it. Couldn't quite place why bells were going off in my head. Thought they were just left over from the earlier noise.

Sobering up slightly, I stood up and began an elaborate striptease for the youth. I watched his penis grow with each article I removed or caressed myself with. Shoes first, dress pulled down to reveal boob. Dress pulled up to reveal fishnet-stocking ass. Bra taken off under dress – sure that surprised the youth but you know I've had practice at that. Then, all at once, I slipped up on to Allan's crotch and sank down, still looking like I was fully dressed, *sans* shoes and bra. In he went, with a great look of surprise. Pulled dress over head to reveal the body stocking.

The youth pulled my nipples through the fishnet and pulled me down so he could lick. Lovely. Again, familiar. I humped and humped him but neither of us came.

Then he pulled out of me, rolled me on to my back and plunged in all the way to the base of his cock. You know what they say – drummers stick it deeper.

Allan thrust and thrust, my love juice spilling out on to the fishnet and the bedding and making everything a bit sticky. Despite having déjà vu, I liked him in me. It felt good, looking at a face and fucking. His eyes were rolled in the back of his head and he came in a cascade of sighs.

Youth! Exactly thirty minutes later, he was in again with slow deliberate thrusts and words of such utter gratitude poured from his lips, you'd have thought he was a virgin.

'Thank you, Katie. You are a sexual miracle.'

'What a fantastic woman. I've never had it so good.'

'I will do whatever you want, please just don't say stop.'

'I adore you. I worship you.'

Blah blah blah.

Oh, we did whatever I wanted, including inserting his toes inside me, and a very delicious, if inexperienced, tonguing of my clit. Then he was in me again, staring into my eyes.

'I think I love you.'

A bit too much, I confess. Couldn't respond – and I'd been putting off coming for so long, I then couldn't. Too much pressure, it seems. Like I had to come. I must come. I mean, seemed to the youth that orgasms came (get it) with love and he now loved me, after all.

Felt like I was betraying the youth. Fell asleep with Allan – wasn't feeling satisfied, as you can imagine. Sheepishly got up this morning, leaving Allan where he lay. The Mission was downstairs eating breakfast. All raised one arched eyebrow at the sight of me. Had forgotten to wash.

John broke the arched silence. 'Something tells me you aren't down here because of a free breakfast,' he giggled.

Well . . .

Told in vague tones there was a man in my room. Sal appeared to be keenly listening. Keep and kept examining my heart, trying to ascertain why his approval matters so much.

'Ah yes – the longest interval is between coming and going,' yawned Serik.

Shows what you know.

'That's not a young man but a young boy, you matronly corrupter of children,' Ryan whispered hoarsely as he walked by and winked.

Was wondering why Ryan would possibly be at breakfast. But a look he and John exchanged – subtle, but those slippery bedroom eyes told all – left little doubt.

'Want to hear about our air miles?' giggled John.

I'll be brief here – for, though not exciting, it does hold a certain charm for its future prospects. Sure I'll be happy later that I've recorded this.

John and Ryan's rules for amassing air miles, free lodging, etc.

1. Find the weakness of the establishment and exploit it. For example, our hotel doesn't frequently replace towels.
2. Order weakness repeatedly.
3. Make sure airline or hotel is a well-known international one with a good reputation to threaten.
4. Establish your good international reputation.
5. Let the free gifts pour in.

August 9

It's very early in the morning but I have much to tell. *I'm on to him.*

We played that silly game from Rome all the way to Villa San Giovanni, the sex or bad musical experiences game. The train compartment sat six and the Mission and I made five – JP has gone back to Paris. I'll really miss him. His *bon vivant* attitude changed us all into more relaxed good-time folks. Sadly, now the Slav made No. 6.

On his turn, began by telling of bad musical experiences inflicted upon him while playing in the BBB Mortuary Band in San Francisco.

'I, me, in general, we play, they drink.'

'Who drinks?' asked John.

'You have saying, no? Drinks like a sturgeon does our fearful leaderess.'

Well, it took quite a bit of prompting on John's part but we got the story out that Slava was sitting in the Irish pub across the street when in comes a harried blonde who asks him if he's still able to stand up. She's carrying a soprano saxophone and wildly gesticulating with it as if it were an arm extension. Slava demonstrates that he possesses upward motion and gets strapped into a gong and a very filthy captain's hat. Told to hit the gong when she gives him the sign (didn't ever tell him what that sign was). Slava was promised thirty bucks. ('Time means cash,' he told us, to emphasise the point.) According to the Slav, that was the beginning of his percussion career.

We were a bit confused because this was supposed to be about one bad musical experience, not a lifetime of them, but had to admit that John and Kristine's little board game was not exactly scientific.

Have to give some vent to the imagination here. You're in a bar, in comes a crazy woman best known as the mistress of death, who is in desperate need of a gong player for the Chinese funeral going on across the street. You're chosen because you happen to be wearing a black suit and have not consumed enough alcohol to get disqualified. From this great musical event, where drunken band members march down the street pulling on each other's coat-tails to point out the pretty girls on the sidewalk, followed by a Kentucky Derby portrait of the deceased propped up in a Cadillac convertible – you go on to become a percussionist in Symphony Xevertes. One must admit, that's quite a leap.

I was in San Francisco once, in North Beach, on Beach Blanket Babylon Street, and am sure I encountered the motley crew. They ruined my breakfast, in fact, attempting to play some half-jazz, half-Yanni tune at ten in the morning – where the gin shots organised for the enjoyment of the players' minds and the absolute annoyance of us sober coffee drinkers who might still be nursing last night's hangover without beginning work on today's. Point being, one doesn't start a career by being in the BBB Mortuary Band. It's sort of a dead end, right?

Not only that, what was striking me odd about Slava's story was that, while his English was filled with odd idioms and mispronunciations, he seemed to understand us perfectly. My experience with our Serbian relatives is that is not the way it really works. You usually can speak better if you understand everything well. More than that, when I finally pinned him down as to where he was from, he replied nervously, 'I, me, in general, I from Montenegro.'

Well, I *know* they speak Serbian there and I tried a few phrases on him of which he seemed to understand nothing. Even said, 'Fuck you, your mother is a whore.' I know that always got a rise out of my relatives – not to mention my parents who were forever sending me to my room when company came. The Slav smiled and pretended he understood but I *knew* he didn't. Tried to make those 'intelligent eyes' – the same action I've adopted when the Italians speak their rapid language to me and I don't understand a damn thing.

Suddenly, that flash of English I thought I heard from Slava at the sex club came back to me. My bullshit meter was running on high and I was determined to draw that sucker out. He was fitting the spy persona to a T (Btw, what does 'to a T' really mean?).

'Where in Montenegro did you say you are from?'

'I, me, in general, my family from small village. You know it? Has no communi . . . ga, ga, gation but very good it has forest.'

'Near the ocean?'

'No very in hills.'

'What's the name of it?' By this point, the Mission looked a bit perturbed. Outside our train window, beautiful Italy was flashing by and I was fixated on getting out of this language-handicapped man where he was from. Let it drop when he pretended for the fifth time not to quite understand me. How many 'in generals' can one hear without getting that the man refuses to be specific? Isn't that the downfall of all liars?

The game continued. Jelly landed on a sex square. Kristine asked the question, 'Have you ever fooled a man into thinking you were a woman?'

Sal snorted and added, 'Be specific: ever fooled a man who wasn't legally blind?'

'While I was in bartending school, and a lot younger than now, I started experimenting with crossdressing,' began Jelly when all the running commentaries had completed their course. 'At first, just on Halloween, that sort of thing.' He giggled. I love that about John, for it keeps him ageless and makes me trust him 100 per cent.

He continued. 'It was wigs at first, then high-heels. I think the make-up came last. It's hard to believe but I wasn't that hairy when I was twenty. When I applied the foundation, lipstick, blush, etc. – well, I was stunning.'

I'll skip the report on the running commentaries here, which mostly came from Serik about the way make-up really tricks men. The diva did not appreciate this, as one could see from the red glow behind her painted cheeks.

'I think it was in Boston, when I had just worked up my first lip-sync act. I hadn't gone blonde yet, honeys.' Jelly/John peered at us with those crossdressed eyes. He was still in jeans but the face had eyeliner and lipstick. 'I was hot.' Serik snickered and John added, 'Fuck you, unbelievers.

'Anyway, I was coming home on the metro when a rather ravenous-looking youth offered to carry my bag.'

'Was he holding a gun?' snickered Sal. I'm surprised the Mission still tells stories to one another, for it seems no one really listens. Oh wait – what am I thinking? The impetus behind these must have been the two new pieces of meat for their listening audience: Slava and Katie.

'Anyway,' John continued, rolling his eyes and looking annoyed with Sal, 'he walked me to the apartment. My apartment, you Perry Masons, and in we went.'

John looked around the room to silence the innuendoes that were expected after such a comment. Oh, we were all so good. Except Slava, who asked, 'Perry Mason was with you in apartment?'

Nice try, Slava, old boy. Good routine.

'So, after kissing, when it came time, the youth was quite surprised to discover that I was not his type. Beat me up pretty bad, come to think of it.'

Here, all of the Mission's little smirky faces dropped and they looked genuinely sorry for John. 'Bastard,' said the diva. 'Jerk,' echoed Serik. 'No good lowlifes grow up to be wife-beating baseball players,' chimed in Sal.

John looked nearly in tears. 'It was a bad experience, you know. Cost me a lot, for I only had catastrophic health insurance.'

Slava attempted in his poor imitation English, 'So, violence in America is violent.'

At this point, I just blurted out, 'So, Norton, what are you going to report here?'

The Mission turned to look at me with a collective 'Take-her-to-Bellevue' expression. I admit it, I was not being very clear. Very concise. Very sequiteur. How could I be?

Slava faltered and made a blunder, for if his English were so poor, he would not have said, 'Norton? Is who this Norton?'

Ah ha! Holmes finally rears her pretty blonde head! 'Did I say Norton was a person? Just an expression we use in upper-state New York for people impersonating others.'

Jelly looked hurt and I realised that she/he thought that was the reference. 'No, John. I mean the youth impersonating a nice guy.'

209

OK, it was lame but I did say it with the utmost sincerity. The Mission, more about moving forward than pondering the trivial details of life, let it pass.

August 10

My black bag was loaded in the storage bin on the boat along with everyone else's. Quite a few of us had the same type, colour, even wear and tear. Watched Slava hand his into Leo's hands and wondered if I might just affect an entire switch on my own.

Waters to Sicily were choppy. These gods do not want our immoral group coming to their traditional island. Asked another passenger why they didn't just build a bridge. I mean, it's not that far away. The man looked at me as if I were asking what flavour kitty litter he preferred. He answered in a haughty, you-ignorant-thing tone. 'It would have to be made of rubber.' Learned today that Sicily and the Italian boot are constantly moving towards and away from each other. A little creepy, if you ask me. Tried to imagine what I'd do when the earthquake, volcano or tidal wave rained hell down upon us. Would I attempt to outrun the lava or lay down and make a nice Pompeii-like pose for posterity?

The diva managed to wear the perfect outfit to make her look like a charming Mafioso's daughter. A long skirt, tight, and a thin tight blouse with a broad hat and closed-toed sandals. A little lipstick, a little rouge, a few bracelets and *voilà* – she was Sicilian. The men on the ship were falling all over themselves for her and I began to suspect that the Sicilian experience we were all about to have was due to the dominatrix's good name in that part of the world. Do bad men like to be told they are bad? Plus, in addition to French and Italian, the diva speaks a good smattering of the local dialect.

As a crowd gathered around her, I made my move. Opened each black bag, looking for the book. Found it on third try. Was tossed back and forth in bin space and did not want to know what the grimy liquid was which went rolling first left, then right, first north, then south. Cigarette butts rolled back and forth, a bottle cap, a tampon tube. Did, and do, not want to know. Took entire bag out.

Fatal error. Although I was carrying my own diary in a separate bag, I had forgotten that all my toiletries, underwear, and change of clothes resided in the bag I left for exchange. I should have just taken the book but feared could not as easily explain that possession.

So now have Norton's socks, dirty underwear, toothbrush, deodorant, all possessing an unmistakable odour, which smells so familiar, it's making me insane. I know this person. Could it really be the Slav? And why, why, why didn't I pay attention to whose bag went with whom? Too busy fucking. Too fucking busy. WHATEVER.

John told me that, no matter what, you want to be first off an Italian boat. 'Trust me.' Yes, as always, John was right. Like in the subways, there is a crowd that wants to get on the boat while the other crowd wants to get off. If you start shoving first, they tend to move out of the way. For a girl, John really can push. He even knocked over an old woman dressed all in black. Fists were shaken, thumbs bitten, Norton's black bag spat upon. But we parted the sea, leading the rest of the orchestra to the promised land. Promised indeed. A good many of them were not hearty sailors and had been puking their guts out in the various toilet areas. And I do mean areas. Want to think even less about the murk our bags had been floating about in.

Orchestra was quite disgruntled. No bus was there for the instruments or the bags. I don't think many minded the public transportation, but their possessions did. Our instruments had been jostled, tossed about, heaved up and down, for a long hour. After a long train trip.

Things got much worse before they got better. Leo had not charged his cell phone and, for once, had not called ahead to confirm our hotel rooms. We arrived, after a very hot forty-five-minute bus ride, to nowhere. After sitting on the side of the road, shading our instruments with our bodies and each silently wondering how much SX could be sued for the damage, watching the roadie van with all the stage equipment go by, waiting in the hot Sicilian sun for two hours, Leo was about to be lynched. Thank God he's a diplomat and short – no fun to bully the short ones. He solved the problem in a very creative way. SX was going to be broken up and housed in three different monasteries in the area.

Liked the idea, for the Mission got to get a convent more or less to ourselves. Seven spots, Slava and Ryan to join us. Why not?

It was dusk when we finally reached our final resting place. Very nice hotel, I must say, with a spectacular tiled bathroom and nearly enough room to move between toilet and bidet. 'Piss and a pedicure,' the diva calls it.

Later . . .

Kristine and I are roommates. Monastery lovely, part of a hill looking over a very dusky green valley. Simple foods, lots of wine (Catholics and the Serbian Orthodox Church have much in common on this point), nice firm beds. In short, clean and light.

Doesn't make any sense, some of this European

plumbing. I mean, in the States, when you use a restroom, you sort of know what to expect. You know that your feet will not be made to wade in amazing horrors. You know the toilet paper won't give you splinters. You know the water will cover up the mess you've made and, if you're really good, most of the time you can even sit down. In Germany, OK, everything is standard except that you have to look at what you did for a few moments before the water whooshes it away – but the TOILET PAPER: it is like recycled newspaper. And in France, they have holes in the ground in the public restrooms. You're punished if you didn't go to the bathroom before you left the house. I missed the Spanish toilets – never a bad one. But Italy . . . so nice in the hotels but same public holes as in France. Not very civilised in this regard. And what is it with the pink crêpe paper streamers? I do not want to wipe my ass with party supplies. Besides, I swear crotch is getting splinters. I'm stealing John's stolen toilet paper. I began wearing boots on the road to avoid what I may be stepping in. The boat from the Italian boot to Sicily a perfect example: I'd risk a bladder infection rather than use the fly-infested shit hole.

ANYWAY, it's late and I'm in the hotel about to read. I'll summarise as my hand hurts too much to write this all down. I had to carry 'my' luggage and viola about three-quarters of a mile. The Slav was the most angry, with all those little percussion cases filled with strange tingling things one could beat. Leo assured us all there would be compensation for this. Right. Compensation would be to lynch Leo's ass to atone for his forgetting to charge the old cell phone. Well, to be fair, he's done great up to this point. But that's what being in charge is all about – everyone remembers you when you fuck up.

Even Later . . .

It's REALLY late but I'm fairly certain I'm on to Norton. Am angry enough to make wild accusations and see where the pieces fall. A few of these entries will be recorded here in entirety. Good God – what have I done? And what has he been doing? One should never be forced in life to see another's rendition of your singular actions. I mean, I am acting peculiar all the way around. Stealing suitcases, being humped by anonymous men, running away from good money in the form of soon-to-be ex-husband, and coveting a god: Sal.

While I'm copying this, hope to figure out what soul would possibly find an interest in telling such fanciful half-versions of reality.

Chapter Seventeen

Introduction(?)

I regret that I have a life to give my country and that my country would so be goddamn selfish as to ask for it – nay – demand it.

That was my speech in high school. During the patriotic/idiotic times. Don't get me wrong. I love my country and all that rot but I am not of it. Being an only child government brat, flung here and there with my father's willy-nilly career, left me with a sense of first impressions of the world and not much else. No great childhood friends to visit once a year and recall our glory days, no siblings to haggle over old disputes, and now no living parents to remind me that I was once an obnoxious child with no manners.

Free is my calling card. I can pick up and go without so much as a care of who will water my dying plants. Thank God they're replaceable, unlike Fluffy. But, that's another story.

Call me Norton. Norton Norton. No matter what you sick little Freudians, Jungians or Vegetarians might infer from this book, it's not about me. For once. And it's not about you either.

I was asked to follow Orchestra XX (the name of the orchestra has been changed to protect the guilty and my publisher) on their whirlwind tour of 85 countries in two months with Jezzabelle, the singing monkey, headlining the whole operation. I was supposed to get into their minds and let the potential readers know what makes those instrumentalists tick. Shocking, I say. And you will too, later. Right now, I'm sure you're just skimming this because, as we all know, only the academics read introductions. They think the world's like them, infusing meaning into a few sly words that only another handful of sly, crafty individuals will be able to decode. Hence, all the 'secret' knowledge passed on in those tiny parts of books. The tiny parts of which the vast majority of us never dain to read. Hats off to you if you're still with me.

So, I could just write a bunch of crap here and mostly nobody would notice. That's mainly what I've done, starting with the little historical revelation of *Moi* and ending with an explanation of what I am doing. In case this is read though, I need to explain that the 'I', its infrequent appearance, the 'I' is me, Norton Norton. These stories are true, or as close to truth as musicians (or anyone else for that matter, save a few feral children) allow themselves to be. They were either told to me or experienced first-hand. And I might as well clear the air now and say that yes, I did sleep with the violinist. That is what makes her story all the more true. Cynthia, forgive me. How I wanted to help you. How did it come to be so awful?

That's the most startling discovery of all. For once in my life, I wanted to change, to help someone, to be all that I could be. Alas. What horrid news to learn that people simply have their own paths and no matter what sympathy, empathy, compassion one throws their way (and at considerable expense to oneself), it all winds up sucked up and blown out the end of a weed-eater. That, dear Cynthia, is why this book is not dedicated to you, but to the dear French hornist.

* * *

To save time (not to mention my right hand), let me be brief. In another fifty pages, Norton tells about Cynthia again, though it's not so interesting. He thinks she needs therapy; she thinks he needs a bigger weenie. Actually, that's my inference from the reading. He then tells that the French hornist is absolutely the most amazing woman he has ever partied with – with one exception. But he likes passion more when the other party knows it's him. I am disposed to write down the next entries since they may entail a lawsuit. Don't know if I prefer the truth or the fiction. Either way, do not like seeing *moi* played for such a dupe.

Katie, sex goddess (change names)

Unlike other tours, Katie could not anticipate how this one might play itself out. None of her immediate friends were going – they all had found better gigs. And she was not used to sitting in the front of any viola section but in the back, near the basses and nearly offstage. Many of her close friends were from that area: the back of the cello section, viola section or the basses. Nobody back there cared so much about orchestral politics . . . or even playing the music correctly. It was more a game of who could say the funniest thing and make the others laugh at inopportune moments. Katie was often the winner in these games, causing others to snort during slow movements of serious pieces and otherwise like her immensely.

Now, she would be the enemy. One of those up front making decisions that the rest of the section chose to ignore unless the conductor mentioned it.

To the unschooled, when a violinist's or violist's bow goes up when the rest of the section's bow is going down, it seems as if the player doesn't know where he or she is. In a professional orchestra, that is rarely the case. Often it's an act of mutiny, one way or another. Perhaps the principal player came up with the bowing the rehearsal before the concert, which is against the Musicians' Union rules. The rest of the section ignores the bowing at the concert, while the front stand obliviously plays what it assumes the rest of the section is also doing.

Another reason the bow would go down when it should go up is the chain of command is broken. The second stand of players, for many different reasons, refuses to pass the new bowing back to the stand behind them. This causes a domino effect which will last the entire concert series or tour. By the time the last stand realises they aren't bowing the same as the front stand it's too late. It's concert time and they haven't a pencil to mark the change. So they try to remember it to mark after the concert but then there's the champagne and the friends and the ride home and suddenly, it's the concert again and only then do they remember they haven't marked the part.

The last reason is the most complete example of ignoring your superior 'officer', the principal player. You simply play it your way because it's better. Later, if anyone even notices, you say, 'Really? I did? If it happens tonight, be a good sport and point it out, would you?' and then do it again – if there *are* any more concerts.

Now Katie was on the 'Them' team, vs the rest of the section 'Us'. It wasn't quite so bad because she wasn't the leader, only the co-pilot. Kind of a deputy orchestra position. It did mean an additional 30 per cent in pay though, and for that, she was extremely grateful.

Jezzabelle had been fired and a new group has arrived on the scene to take over the zoo. A quartet of defunct but talented derelicts who do not need the work. They think it fun to arouse our frigid audiences and then defile them. A drag queen, Gypsybelle (keep this name), a bass, Cocky (keep this name), a composer and guitarist, Jeremy (keep this name), a dominatrix diva, Kristine (change).

A Mission Impossible thought it was time that Katie have some impromptu fun that they could watch. It was

218

her birthday and a male stripper from Italy had been smuggled on the bus. When they got out on the highway, Gypsybelle turned on 'bump and grind' music. The dominatrix, not out of her garb yet, yelled, 'Come on out, boy!' as she cracked a whip on the bus's ceiling. I had been invited – or my little hidden camera at least had not been uninvited. Oh you prudes. Think I did something wrong? You and your little TV series on the private lives of the rich and famous can eat me. Later.

Out of the back 'bedroom' came a beautiful olive-skinned man dressed in a T-shirt and jeans. His abdomen was rippling, his arms like carefully laid stones in a river. The cupid lips, though, were what Katie most fixated on.

He began dancing to the music, gyrating around. He tussled Katie's hair as he went around her, then he whipped off his shirt and started massaging his chest with it. He stared meaningfully into Katie's eyes and though she knew it a con, she was enchanted.

The pants came off next and he stood before her, thrusting his thong-clad pelvis in her face. When he turned around with the muscled buttocks facing her, Katie couldn't resist. She spanked him, not so lightly. A word of semi-angry Italian escaped his lips but then Gypsybelle handed Katie a twenty-dollar bill.

'Put it in your teeth, babe, and then insert.'

Katie did so, inserting the bill into the front of the Italian's thong. His smile became warm and sparkling. It made her wet.

'Give me more money,' she yelled to the room. Kristine handed her a ten, Cocky a twenty. Katie then realised that Jeremy wasn't on the bus. She forgot it in a second while she stuffed more and more money into the very full thong.

'I think he's a grow-er, not a show-er,' said Gypsybelle with obvious delight. He had earlier explained the penis lingo to the uninformed in the bus. Growers were penises that might not look like much but could grow to lovely proportions. Showers, on the other hand, were up front already: what you saw is what you got.

Indeed, the Italian's penis was growing and Katie loved grazing her cheek on it as she stuffed more money in.

Some more words were exchanged between Gypsybelle and the Italian and then the Italian led Katie to the back 'room', closing the curtain behind them.

Katie wasn't sure what to make of this. She felt a bit like a beast in the zoo while all the zookeepers waited for her to mate with her favourite orangutan. Yet, the spontaneity of it delighted her and she was excited that others were just on the other side of the curtain.

The Italian kissed her. It wasn't a romantic kiss but something aggressive. He lightly bit her lower lip, which aroused Katie even more.

Then he pulled off her T-shirt in one gesture. It was disorientating. Katie would have preferred taking it off herself but now that she stood in front of him topless (she hadn't put on a bra), she felt the tingles begin at the base of her spine. She was on fire.

The bus lurched to the left and her bare chest was on his. The Italian put his hands lightly on her hair and Katie rubbed her breasts up and down his perfect form. Heaven, she thought. Hands were unbuttoning her jeans and she felt them come off. A finger went in her and she heard herself moan.

The Italian pushed her down on the bed, saying 'Belli-simo' which was about the only Italian word Katie knew. Then he was sucking on her pussy.

The tongue was warm and quite skilled. Katie knew this guy was a pro. He sucked and nibbled her pundella then reamed his tongue far in her hole. Katie's whole focus narrowed on to her cunt. It seemed she was one pulsing extension of the Italian's tongue. Before she came, the Italian stopped. He pulled off his thong and shoved a certain 'grower' into her.

Katie gasped. The man was huge, maybe even too huge. She forced herself to relax. There, it felt better with her legs down a bit. It felt much better. The fire was racing through her now and she felt the orgasm burbling up. But then the Italian came.

He kissed her, pulled out, pulled on his thong, and went out.

That wasn't very nice, thought a very frustrated Katie. What was she going to tell the Mission? That it wasn't accomplished?

Or maybe their mission had been accomplished. She was dying with frustration, willing to kill for a release. Was that the 'up the ante' they all so enthused about?

She resisted the urge to masturbate and fall asleep. Pulling on her jeans and shirt, she wandered out into the rest of the bus. It was coming to a stop. Gypsybelle was paying the Italian something. He then kissed the Italian lightly on the cheek and the man hopped off the bus.

Jeremy got on the bus. He had an electric guitar strapped on him.

'Katie, this song is for you.'

The guitar was plugged in to a small amp, the bus took off, and Jeremy began singing and playing.

Don't know much about stripping men
Don't know much about a hard-core gym
But I do know about insanity
And I know a lot about beauty

Katie, Katie, Katie, Katie
[right here Jeremy hit himself and made a record screech sound]

What I mean to say
You are beautiful any day
Since today is your birthday, if you are thirsty . . .
Have a beer on me.
[wild guitar riffs follow]

Katie was touched. A kooky song just for her.
'Listen, I'm going to do it.'

The mission murmured amongst itself.

'No,' Katie said. 'Really, I'm ready. Jeremy?'

He played a few guitar chords in the same progression as the song. Katie sauntered up to him and let her hands roam over his guitar-playing arms.

She sang, making it up.

> Don't know how to please a stripper
> Don't know much about tobacco dippers
> But I do know what I see
> That all of youse is my family
>
> Thank you for all the lovely gifts
> And thank you Jeremy for guitar riffs
> What I'm trying here to say
> I'm so glad you let me stay!

It broke into a group hug with Katie crying.

No, wait, that's not any good. Not a good ending.

Jeremy waxed his way to Katie and lightly kissed her ear. The camera did not catch the violist's expression but I imagine it to be joy. She loves Jeremy, even if she does not know it. Even her horrible ex-husband knows it. They met and both men knew the other was the enemy – like dogs sniffing each other's asses. Jeremy sang a song for Katie alone in her ear – a song of existence, a song of love, a song of everlasting happiness which made her eyes swell with joy and happy expectation. He sang while the others went to the front of the bus and drew the curtain in a semblance of privacy. They whispered happy thoughts for the couple, they wished them peace, prosperity and eternal orgasmic bliss. They talked to the bus driver about the weather, bad musical experiences, and what wines would best go with that evening's meal. In short, they were fully engaged in the moment.

You see, Jeremy knew that Katie was the special person for him. THE ONE. Even if she did not know it. I thought she might be my special one but no, she was his. The way he spoke of her was never a way I could, only here with words can I convey that she deserves to be satisfied always. She is a most giving lover and so willing to open up in a cosmic way . . .

I hear strains of Yanni coming over the PA. We're breaking up, we're breaking.

And now back to the New Age News with Jonathon, where nothing changes because everything is always changing. He sits stewing in the confusion like a non-enlightened Buddha with a hard-on and a tummyache.

Me too brother. Me too.

And here's the last entry I'll record. You'll see why.

The Orgy

The world is a stage to strut upon with walls and doors separating our various actions and even upon death, with the gathering of so many, we find we still don't know each other. A person's beauty may work from the outside inwards or we may discover a most succulent fruit hidden under false dry leaves. What would drive an unnamed string player to allow herself, sporting false whiskers and a flattened chest, to be dragged to and fro in one of the sleaziest and sexiest clubs in all of Paris? To trust five total strangers to tamper with her lower half while she remains, so to speak, behind bars? And what of those five men, what guided them there to perform in this ritual? Those men, several who swear they mainly are interested in others of their sex. Who have day jobs driving taxis, playing trumpet, teaching swimming, managing a lingerie firm, writing for a British tabloid? Who did not know this woman came in drag and fooled a great many before, as they say in the States, 'her ass was grass'.

No, she didn't die but I nearly did witnessing and participating in one of the most outrageous moments of my life. No longer can I hear music without reflecting that those conduits of melody also open themselves up in many other ways too.

You see, it was, at first, just a beautiful ass. Curious, we loiterers went inside at the insistence of a man who looked like he had just stepped out of an action film. Out of the wall, like a trophy from exotic safari, was the ass with smooth legs running down to the ground. It writhed a bit, this ass, and the legs kicked out at us but, somehow, the impression was given that this was a willing ass. It even scooted backwards a bit for our viewing pleasure. The photographer of the tour was there, snapping every picture saying, 'I've got you now, you little hot bitch.' Did the little hot bitch know her ass image now resided in reverse on 35mm film? That a video was being made with its main character being her ass and the juicy peach of her crotch? I haven't had the occasion of asking the owner of the ass but intend to at the right moment. I've known the ass under other circumstances as well, though the ass, both times, didn't know me. Figure that riddle out, you little Mensa punks.

The lumberjack guy swatted the ass on the thick part right above the leg connection. It quivered like firm jello pudding. The dim lights in the room caught the fine blonde down on the ass and the legs. Lumberjack stripped, photographer stripped, skinny man with skinny moustache stripped, confused-looking Asian man stripped, and I stripped.

We each swatted the now pink and shaking ass, each man trying to one-up the other in terms of how hard the blow. Our cocks were standing out stiffly. The photographer was about to shoot a picture of mine when I hit him hard on the head. He backed down, we animals. A lion den with one lioness ass to keep us satisfied.

The swatting ceased and next came a box of tools into our room. Bright Christmas-coloured dildos with ornaments, butt plugs, cock-rings. I took the ring. Skinny guy with moustache took the red and purple dildo, lumberjack a lime green dildo, confused man a butt plug, and photographer another cock-ring. Armed, we set to work.

There was oil too and some was poured on to and into that lovely ass. We all rubbed the ass as if it were the sacred urn of Mount Venus. Come to think of it . . .

Confused man first put butt plug in cunt but decided it better belonged in butt. He twisted and pushed until the lovely ass became accessorised. In went red/purple dildo in the other hole to be shared, then the lime green – a very merry effect. One of the dildos vibrated like a lawnmower and the lumberjack shut it off. After the thrusting of the instruments, and the application of vibrations and fingers to the little man in the boat, came the time for the flesh-coloured ones. I went first and plunged into ecstasy, moist, juicy, resistant bliss. Pounded and pounded until I spilled into her. Ass stuck itself out more, as if sorry, when I exited. Then skinny guy with moustache began slurping me out of her. That wilted my already spent cock down to a cocktail sausage. Ass seemed to love it though, wiggling enticingly, undulating hips, tipping upwards so sperm leaked into his mouth. Wonder if she felt the moustache tickling her blonde beard?

Oh, we had fun with more fucking, more dildos, more spanking. The trophy was turned over then and suddenly our wall became a two-way mirror. Sort of. There were 'windows' to see through to the other half of the trophy. There she was, happily sucking off the action hero. He looked up and winked at us, then gave an OK sign – which in Brazil means to kiss my ass. We weren't in Brazil. The mouth going down his shaft had been painted, so a fake moustache was there. But she was a girl. Glorious boobs flattening just right on her torso.

As soon as the movie star finished and she swallowed (good girl), her eyes seemed to peer out at us in amazement. Yet, we were all fairly sure she couldn't see. I went first, slamming into her red-pink juicy fruit so that the ass hit up against the wall. The other men held the legs and I thrust and thrust until the few droplets I had left spilled out. Quickly, lumberjack climbed aboard and fucked the super-cunt. It only seemed to open up more and more and wider and wider. My previous experiences with multiple uses had a woman's cunt go dry after about the third round. And this was only the third round with *some* of the same men. Twenty fuckings so far and yet, it clamped and oozed for more. Watched through mirror as other man massaged those breasts and kissed that painted mouth area. Watched as his hands pushed her shoulders against our thrusting. We were all yelling by now in various tongues. It was like a legitimised rape, I guess, for I cannot fathom the man who would get pleasure fucking a girl without her permission. Or paying for it even. If she's not willing, not able, or doesn't give of her own free will, how does one even sustain a hard cock for the time? But it wasn't rape. This ass quivered and swallowed us greedily. The mismatched mouth of false whiskers smiled impishly and the eyes were great pools of desire. No. This trophy hunted herself.

This orgy had us all stiff. Yes, the lumberjack thrust and thrust and then he came and when he pulled out, come dribbled with him. The men pretended not to enjoy watching the others fuck their prize trophy. Each of us wore a mask of detached amusement – as if we were all watching a porno film, not making one. I had no doubt that that is what was happening. No one's face would appear but our cocks, asses and the glorious twat would surely make the silver screen.

The photographer had an enormous cock, which sort of explains his personality. He really relished opening the ass's legs wide, with our help, and then slamming himself in hard. I think ass was afraid at first but seemed to relish it as time moved on. It looked as if her insides pulled out a bit with his cock. They were glued together, with one of his hands firmly on her clit. She shuddered. He grinned and said, 'Gotcha'. Snapped a quick pic. Odd to me to erase the immediacy of the moment with a reminder that it was recorded.

Skinny man ate photographer's sperm out of the twat, twat at this point twitching at an alarming rate. None of us thought we could keep up with the hunger.

Oh twat, I've been in you before. Did you not recognise my feel with the cock-ring on? You are such a sensitive crotch, you must remember that night you slid into my bed, kissing and cooing. Your skin was hot, your breath cool. So graceful and pliable and now, I know, so insatiable. I'm glad we had each other for a night. Two.

Katie, I daresay, I'm half in love with you. Lisa is grand but you are twenty of her. So much sexuality in such a little body. We'll see how this all plays out, you deliciously nasty thing.

Now we know. Norton was at the sex club. So was John and so was Slava. And so was Dave. Norton tells the truth as well as lies. Fuck! Norton writes well and convincingly and there is not a person in the world who would disbelieve any of it, for most is true. I cannot give this book back, ever. I'll just wait until someone claims it missing. Even then, what will I say? Can't prevent this author from having those thoughts and writing them down. Could prevent the publication, though if the names were changed, who could really prove that any damage has been done to me? Plus, I'd have to fess up to the light-fingered-Louis routine of being in possession in the first place. Shit, shit, shit!

I'm going to practise that violist Zen thing and just wait to see what happens in the oompahs.

You wimpy fatalist.

Chapter Eighteen

August 11

*S*ent him a note. *Urgent. Meet me outside the nun's quarters before mid-morning prayer.*

How did he manage to continue in that vein? Got to hand it to him, quite an act.

'Katie, you summon me? I here on time you say. Just like famous saying, time means cash.'

Rolled eyes. 'Come on, Slava, or whatever your name is. Speak English or, I should say, talk normal.'

'But for me is talking normal. Ignorance ain't always bliss and your room wasn't built in a day. Like in universe, me here, you there.'

'OK, but we have the same universe.' He was slipperier than Daniel ever was in evading the bald truth.

'Yes, Katie. I think about that. What do you think about the bug bang?'

Hmm. What to answer? What to answer? Any way you looked at it, was one of those 'Have you stopped beating your wife?' questions. Ignored him. Nuns walked by, carrying oranges. They looked intently ahead, hearing some internal music.

Slava continued the ruse. 'The body sound is better in the mind sound.' Pause. Then more twittering of special made-to-mess-up synapses. 'Chance is only a joke of life. Cock ... it's the real thing. Famous saying, no? Remind me in our country, we say, to have a sheep in the bush ...'

STOP IT! STOP IT! STOP IT!

He did, with the look of a rather unsatisfied Venus flytrap. Grabbed the Slav by the belt loops and pulled him into one of the cell rooms.

Locked door and pulled off his pants all in one motion. Smelled him. Norton said he slept with me so I should recognise something.

Smell – yeasty, chocolatey but not any more familiar than the other scrotum areas I'd smelled.

Tasted his growing erection. Salty from the incredible heat. Nice cock ... the real thing. Speaking of teaching the world to sing, the Slav began humming a medieval chant, I think to cover up his fear of groaning aloud. Humming as I sucked him. Oh, how he expanded both vertically and horizontally.

Then the Slav surprised me by pulling my dress up over my head. I really should wear underwear but ... just too hot. Slava nestled nose up at top of mound and began a most delicious chewing. He hummed a bit more and the vibrations shook me into an orgasm. So very, very nice.

Slava went horizontal on the little twin bed and I climbed on top of the vertical part. Forgot to really think if he felt familiar. Was this a cock that had been in me before? It did feel like that. Yes it did. It felt like that so long ago night in Paris when I thought I was sleeping with Sal. Just like I suspected. Good work, Sherlock!

Slava began moaning, in rather good, crisp English, 'Yes, oh yes!' His sperm bounded into me, greeted by an astonishing receptivity. I mean, my body *wanted* him. Still saying 'Yes' as last dewdrop was squeezed up by my greedy hole.

Hmm. I've heard of lovers speaking in tongues but not getting *more* articulate. Pushed that thought out and let Slava's thumb work my clit until I came with a cry. He pulled me on to his chest and stroked my hair. Sweet. Said, 'Katie' a jillion times and there I was, again asleep in his arms.

August 12

Morning found me still in Slava's arms. Still no confession. Really great detective work, don't you agree? Talk about messing with the evidence.

'Early bird gets warm, no, Katie? I am a sucking for beautiful girl. You know, there are many people existing . . .'

Looked him straight in the eye and said, 'How long are you going to keep the act up?'

He looked back at me with those melanic eyes, white forehead wrinkled and said, 'As long as it takes for me to get my journal back from you.'

My turn to have drained face; my turn to feel at the end of an accusing finger. Then, couldn't help myself.

I laughed.

'Truth is,' continued Norton, not his real name either. Was sure he'd have told me at that moment, except I completely forgot to ask. Idiot. 'I didn't think one single person would buy the act. I planned to give it up after the first day but Dave said to try it a little longer.'

Dave?!

'Yes, he was to be my photographer. You know who is sponsoring Dave and me?'

'Mother Jones?' Had reverted to my sharp-edged sarcasm as a way to hide utter Dave disgust.

'Very funny. The Musicians' Union. They had heard of last year's abuses and decided to see for themselves. Symphony of Xevertes would be a great organisation to collect fines from. SX is *very* well off. It makes one sick when you think how much we're making versus how much they rake in from a single CD sold at the concert.'

'They are hawking CDs?' I'm telling you, my mind was opening to the horrors of being abused by a big corporation. Nobody had told us about that.

Slava continued. 'Hey, who do you think sponsors these concerts?'

'How the hell should I know? Calvin Klein?'

'Close. It's Devronix. Their "arts" section. Don't you think the dominatrix diva has expensive taste?' It was a rhetorical question. 'She's a dominatrix Devronix. Even Angelika has a few outfits, though her size is a tad bit more demanding on the clothier.'

'Sal? Serik?'

'Neither of them signed the same type of contract. I'm guessing they have other things they wish to protect and see cashing in on Devronix clothing is a means of selling out. You'll have to ask them.'

'But, except for the CD thing, there aren't any blatant abuses this time. That's not what you're writing about.'

Hadn't meant to give away that I'd been skimming, er, devouring Norton's writing.

'You read it?'

I nodded sheepishly.

'Well, then I'm sorry, Katie. I guess I'm just going to have to kill you.'

For a moment, a long moment at that, I did think he was capable. I mean, to fool everyone into buying his horrible accent and to play percussion not too poorly to boot – isn't that what psychotic killers do? Look like the guy next door and then, when they've gained your trust, they tie you up and eat you alive with little rat teeth?

Slava/Norton/Whoever laughed. 'Just give it back, Katie. And I'll return your toiletries. Have to admit, I did enjoy the Princess of Monaco's facial cleanser.'

A true bastard. The most expensive thing I own after the viola. I did the exchange. I mean, I did already write down the juiciest parts, and if he ever uses my name, like I said: I'll sue.

Got Slava to tell about Dave. Dave wasn't planning on going but then he saw my name on the roster and was intrigued. When Slava asked him to be photographer, meaning more money, he couldn't resist. To boot, Daniel hired him to photograph *me*. How could he not go?

'I don't like Dave. I don't trust him and I don't like him,' I opined in a snarling tone.

'Do you like me?'

'Yes, but I don't trust you.'

'But I am fun in bed. You'll give me that.'

'Yes, Slava, Norton, whatever, I will give you that.' *But not as fun as the person I thought you were.*

Btw, other percussionist? That weird vibe of familiarity? Slava/Norton's brother. Once the dam of confidences had been unleashed, S/N revealed everything except his name. I'll discover that in time. I vow right here never to be written about again. S/N swore that he was only writing for his own pleasure and that he'd only publish it after I died. Again, the shiver of danger thrilled through me but I fought off the urge to sleep again with the potential enemy.

I don't like being written about and read. I'm certainly not for the general public. Unless it's one of those movies made for TV about my hard and increasingly happy life and how I changed the course of mankind.

August 13

Understand now a thing or two about a thing or two.

I have not slept much on this trip and it's beginning to show. In the rehearsal, I messed up every single one of my solos. Even began the rehearsal tuning the wrong peg for the A string. Thought I was playing violin and would've tuned it up to an E, but the thing refused to stretch that far and broke with an awful crack on to the body of the instrument. Ryan laughed. Wish that had been the end of it. Besides having the new string stretch out of tune all the time, I'd forgotten my mute. Sal's new 'Glory to the Gods' piece requires a muted viola solo to begin. Put clothes peg on the bridge but then forgot about it and it snapped off when I hit my bow on the damn thing. Ryan's laughter distracted me further when a passage called for pizzicato and I did arco and then it called for arco and I did pizzicato. Not my fault. Goddamn stupid instrument. Should be like the piano with only one way to play it.

Sal looked displeased, which sent me into further mistakes. Valerie leaned forward and said, 'You should go home, Katie.' Hoped she meant back to the cell I was sharing with Kristine and not a plane trip home. It wasn't a long walk and, after the rehearsal, I skipped the bus and nearly ran back to avoid falling face-first asleep on the side of the road.

Barely made it back and into the nuns' kitchen. In the violet blue of early evening, all I could think about after a simple meal of bread, cheese, wine and fruit was to lie down and succumb to the nothingness that was falling upon me. It was their meditation hour. I crept back to the cell so as not to interfere with any of the nuns' wishes which might at the moment be swirling around me on their way to heaven. My body

233

felt warm with the anticipated rest. Already my feet were slow, my head murky, my thoughts half-dreams.

Reached the cell and thought I heard muffled sobs from within. Afraid I hadn't the energy to console if the diva were weeping. What would she possibly need consoling from anyway? No, not sobs, my clearing head was beginning to grasp. No, not wind in the trees. No, not a cat's oppressed hunger or a child's finger broken in the park. More like a marathon swimmer's breath out of water on the final lap: low, desperate, seeking relief.

Pushed the squeakless door open and peered in. It was the diva all right. Recognised the toe-ring. A skinny man knelt at her feet, his head resting in her crotch. She clawed his back a bit, red lines like lace from her fingernails forming intricate patterns from his spine to his neck. They had been at this a while, for one of the lines showed traces of a fine trickle of now dried blood. Her groans seemed strange to me. Kept thinking, 'That's not how I am, is it?'

Watched for what seemed ten minutes and then her legs went straight out and she made a sound as if a dagger went right through her heart. I pulled my head back around the corner, thinking that was the end of it but then I heard his moans. Familiar moans. Couldn't help myself. Looked in again. I mean, I had an excuse. This *was* my room too.

There sat Ted on the edge of the bed, kissing the diva and playing with himself. Oh, there she goes. She's going down on him. He is not grimacing. No, he smiles in utter ecstasy. Watched while the diva put her head in his lap. Watched while she picked up his cock and kissed the underside of it. Put the entire thing down her throat and then jutted her chin out just so. Kept thinking, 'That's not how I do it.' She pulled it all the way out, looking up at Ted who was raining smiles and good wishes upon her. Then the skinny cock disappeared down her throat again. Ted beamed in bliss, his skinny fingers knotted in her black hair. What looked like tears were falling off his chin.

Was getting rather mad. I mean, I trained the guy. It's not fair that he should enjoy it so soon with another. So, I walked in. I mean, I backed up twenty feet and made as much noise as I could, coming down the hall. Tried to sound as if I were drunk so they could blame the alcohol on my 'mistaken' vision, if need arise.

Could see from the 'caught' expression on their faces that I did indeed surprise them and needn't have bothered with all the noise. Ted had most assuredly not come. His face was ashen, his breathing shallow. The diva looked guilty, though why I could not begin to guess.

'Oops. Guess I'll come back in a few minutes. So sorry, I need to sleep.' I really would have slept somewhere else but that wasn't an option. Considered Ryan's room. No, he would make me laugh with the retelling of today's antics. Serik? Too tempting. Sal? Not sure he'd accept me. Besides, he needs his sleep too. Not Slava. I need sleep. Mind you, this all passed through my head in a few seconds. No, was determined to sleep in my assigned bed alone.

After an awkward moment where I felt one of them was going to invite me to join in – who knows what I might have done if I weren't semi-delirious – Kristine volunteered to go with Ted to his monastery down the road. Thank God for Catholic countries. It was supposed to be all men but the diva said she knew a way in. All kisses was she as the two departed. Fairly sure Ted revealed my silly little plan to her about finding out if the car trip was really Sal's idea. Oh, it does not matter now. Really. We made the trip. Who cares under what guise?

Chapter Nineteen

August 14

*H*as it been clearly established here that I hate Dave Muller? I just want to emphasise that point again for future biographers. I've lost my dictionary or I would attempt to find a really special word for how I view him with the utmost antipathy. It's harmful to me, really. This feeling. But tell me, how could you forgive the following story? L R for bringing it to my attention. Head hurts in the telling so I'll make this short. My lower half is now featured on a web site. Not my face, thank God, but the fig is there for anybody to pull up and whack off to.

So desperate, I've even contemplated engaging Daniel to help me with the lawsuit. I mean, what else can I do? Feel sick. Low down, under the heart sick. Millions of men, men I'll never know, are pretending to know me. I'm being hit on and not even feeling it. And what about my intellect? My heart? Am I just some useful image of a happy hole?

Well . . . OK, it's not that bad. But the bastard didn't

ask. And it's Dave Muller, for Godsakes. Yuck, yuck, yuck!

August 15

Left a message with Daniel to call Kristine's cell phone. I think he would know the right course of action with Dave. I mean, Daniel is trying very hard not to be malicious and I am going to give him the benefit of the doubt and take him at his word that he wants us to always remain friends.

Syracuse. Amazing. There's a perfect Greek temple right there and that is where our last concert is going to be. SX is part of the festival and Sal is the reason. He's recognised the world over as the one guy who can read ancient Greek music and write it down for modern players. Not that that is what he's doing for us – though the music is sure to have a seven/eight feel. Probably more influenced by retsina than history.

Sal told me, as we strolled near the ocean, speaking about the lagoon experience (at last), that this place is where the Greeks made lots of plays up about the phallus.

Who could resist – though wished Ryan were there to hear. Wait a minute . . . haven't told R re lagoon. Seemed too special to be sullied by our little exposé game. Does this mean that I view Sal as a step apart from that game? I'm afraid it does. No surprise here. Only to the bastard who might be reading this journal without permission.

So, it was quite peaceful, comfortable – NORMAL – to be speaking to Sal. He's one of those down-to-earth gods. He said that he knew I was special from the moment he met me and could also tell I was disturbed. Writhing with pent-up emotions and he knew I would just have to act upon them before I exploded. I thought all the sex I was having would make him uninterested in me but he said – no. He liked a woman who'd been around the block.

Then was in a weird space of wondering if that really meant he cared for me – I mean, aren't potential lovers/boyfriends supposed to be jealous?

'Did not say I wasn't jealous. But one cannot clip the wings. Ever. I just knew that we'd be together eventually.'

Does this explain the kiss and only the kiss? Had Sal attempted to 'own' me by force, it would never have had the effect as this gentleness, which took everything in my power to resist and keep on my merry way. I just left one very long-term relationship and am sure the one with Sal is going to take a very long time. This guy is too good to be true. I've still got my worries but I might just have found my man. He also said, when I told him about D's temporary theft, 'If I ever found your diary, I would never read it in a million years. I know you wouldn't do that to mine.'

Well . . .

Well . . .

Well. That's one little blunder I'll just keep to myself. Which reminds me – the 'exchange' with the Slav is tonight and I am a bit nervous. After all, I did take something on purpose and read it on purpose. But then again, I am not masquerading as someone else. So I'm like a thief without the ski mask and the Slav is just a ski mask.

Therapist!

Later . . .

Shit, shit, shit to the tenth degree cubed. HE's here again. Daniel. Explains why he didn't return the phone call. Never left Europe it seems. He came to our first show here, holding up a sign which said, in

Italian, KATIE, COME HOME. Kristine translated. I suspect that she translated the sign for Daniel in the first place, for how would he know Italian? Jesus, I'm paranoid. Why on earth would the diva do that? Tonight made me feel like I just got off the immigrant plane, with my relatives trying to coax me towards their home. Waving unplucked chickens and carrots with dirt clods hanging upon their tentacles to show hospitality.

Wish I could just find it funny. I mean, a cheating husband who wants his wife, whom he asked to leave. Wants her back so much, he travels around the world chasing after her. She even wants to trust soon-to-be ex-husband with helping her sue the guy who posted her photos on a porn site. Oh, I wish it were so romantic. I feel more like Daniel is upset the puppy ran away. I think even that vibrator, well, it was to prove a point – not to give me pleasure but to prove he could. Somehow, in the tour bliss, I thought D and I might become friends. Don't know how, since we were never friends before.

Kristine promises (eagerly, I noted) to help with what I hope will be the end of Daniel and not in a way that the police will be after us. Grateful to her, for I've got a few too many things on my plate at present and the gravy is mixing with the peas. A smorgasbord of thrills and anxieties.

August 16

I believe her. She's no reason to lie. Daniel and she are in touch but only for my sake. And he doesn't know that part. But I've discovered much more interesting things than the contact between my travelling companion and my unwanted company.

Dionysus was an awful man. Great with finding the

best engineer of acoustics but nasty not to leave any hint behind of the dangers. Well, this time, things did not fall apart, the centre did not drop out.

Kristine and I were in the ancient slave quarters back behind the Greek theatre. I decided to confess. It seemed like the journey was coming to an end and I had a very bad case of backwards homesickness. Realised I did not want to leave Sicily because I did not want to leave Sal.

(Argh! Can you believe I asked such a seventh-grade thing?) 'Do you think he likes me?'

Kristine burst out laughing but then checked herself when she saw my hot, oily face crumple. 'Oh, Sal likes you all right. Nobody has ever gotten so many solos. Even I.' Here she looked a little wounded. Maybe it was that glaring sun. We both felt as if we were melting.

'Oh,' was all I could reply.

'No ... oh, I see. I finally see. You *like* him, don't you?'

Nodded as vigorously as a wilting flower can.

'I wouldn't worry about him liking you. It's more about your loving him. You do, don't you?'

Again, the wilted-flower agreement. Frankly, at a loss to say why. Something the Discovery Channel could explain, no doubt. That our sperm and eggs love each other. Who can argue with biology? Or destiny? Or that I already knew he was a fantastic lover?

'But what about all those other men? I cannot imagine you being with just one guy.' Here the diva was back. I could see that she herself could not imagine being with one guy. Marriage for her would only come in the form of polyandry. Ted might last for a week.

Hey, wait. Who is talking of marriage here? I am certainly not up for that for a very long time.

Anyway, I told the diva that I could tell Sal was a special guy. Special for me. But I had been married most of my adult life and not very experienced before that and who could blame a girl for going around the block a few times? (I liked using the term Sal gave it.)

'Sister, you not only went around the block, you've done an entire state.'

Snorted along with Kristine. I mean, she is funny and she was right ... this time. 'I just wish Sal could wait. I wish he knew that it's not out of my system yet – and I cannot guarantee it ever will be until I get it out. Make sense?'

'It doesn't need to make sense to me. Just don't get Sally hurt, OK? Besides being a good friend, he knows how to make my voice shine. If you get him all depressed, it'll be back to the alto dungeon for me and you have no idea what that means to my vocal chords – not to mention my image.'

Wanted to tell her to start smoking cigars for I could not predict how things were going to pan out. One thing for sure, I am not ready to give up this new freedom. Not yet. It's on the precipice of becoming old but hasn't flown there yet.

More sex, more sex, more sex. Imagine Sal is enough for me, given his mind and those fabulous hands. Just need to see.

So, when Sal came up to me after this evening's performance and asked me to go sit at the top of the marble terraces, I was a bit shocked. Complied – for I do love to obey strange orders.

The night was working its way to the cooler side of the earth and I began to feel chilled. And stupid, sitting up there alone, in the same dress I've worn since Rome (where have all my other dresses disappeared to?) – waiting like a seventh grader at the flower-power dance. Like I said: stupid.

241

Sal was nowhere to be seen. Lights lit the stage in a most ethereal way and then I heard my name.

'Katie, I can wait. I can wait.'

Sal's voice was as audible from the slave's quarters as I suppose our voices must have been to him. Think again that the dominatrix diva was playing her cards. Remember an elbow pressed, a shoulder turned. The diva leading me through this small labyrinth to the isolated little rooms with no ceilings. How was I to know that this entire structure was built so that the rulers could hear what was going on at all times? Could then outplot the plotters. Quite clever, don't you agree?

But, I don't really care now. My heart felt so free from those words. He can wait. He can wait.

Happy, happy, happy day.

Chapter Twenty

O h, happiest of happy days. The diva is a genius
and the Mission is simply the best.

We've been performing in Syracuse – a most glorious place which I will have to rhapsodise upon
another time. At last, the orchestra can see what is
happening on stage. Wild. The Mission has concocted
a series of amoral dances varying from ones with an
ancient Greek feeling (in 7/8 time) to a thoroughly
modern heavy metal opera marathon. Serik is fantastic
in this multi-purpose tunic which he heaves just so in
order to change centuries. Ancient Greece is depicted
by a regal flowing; Rome looks a bit more debauched.
By the time we get past the very upright Victorian
period and into our twenty-first century, all dignity is
gone and the tunic is bunched about in such a way as
to resemble pants with the crotch at their knees.
Clever.

At about the early part of the nineteenth century
(the orchestra was playing little quartets with foresha-
dowings of a more repressed Victorian era to come),

243

Kristine chose a member of the audience to come on stage and participate: Daniel.

With a Beethovenesque minuet being executed, the diva led Daniel to the special 'dance' area on stage. There he was dressed as Icarus and given some pretty ugly-looking wax wings that John had found earlier in the day at the bazaar. Frankly, D looked outrageous and the audience howled. Daniel does not like being laughed at and didn't even crack a smile.

The strings played a vortex of notes, which was supposed to lift Icarus off the ground and send him closer to the sun. We played and played and Kristine coaxed D to jump up and fly. He half-heartedly attempted to defy gravity.

Of course, it didn't work. Then she whispered in D's ear what I can only imagine. The diva told me that she urged D to have radical trust. As a sort of stage-hand, Angelika came out dressed as her namesake: an angel. 'Grab on,' she shouted over her feathered shoulder. Daniel, wanting to get off the stage as quickly as possible, put his arms around the tall trannie and they began to fly. Well, Angelika did anyway. Daniel, the homophobe, was not really hanging on but hanging on to the dress (a special hint from Kristine no doubt) and when the wires pulled Angelika up, her dress was left behind in D's arms.

So clever. Didn't think I could continue playing from the laughter brewing inside. As the dress unravelled, it became a huge penis. So there was D, holding on to this huge phallus that was soaring off into the sky. Took a while for him to realise that he was left behind. DICK FOR A DAY – the headlines will appropriately read. Suppose that when you're that close to an eleven-foot phallus, it's hard to discern what exactly is the pillar you are so attached to.

Trying to ascertain what he was left holding on stage, Daniel began to climb up the thing. He tore off his wings, and began an ascent up the papier mâché thing. It was not strong enough to support him and Icarus once again fell to the earth. The more angry D got, the more the audience laughed. Red-faced, D was led offstage by Serik, who had his tunic wrapped around his middle and was pretending to be a football player just come from the lockers.

Had I only known that public humiliation was the key to getting Daniel far, far away. Well, it was fun to watch anyway. I stopped playing from laughing so hard and Ryan had to cover (you guessed it) my solo. Not only had Sal written that, but he had given Dave a ten-minute succession of rapid triplets which left the 'photographer' puckered like a soon-to-be-prune in the Sicilian sun.

I looked in vain for Sal as Daniel was still standing on the stage with the penis swaying in the breeze, not knowing where to set it down. The lawyer was probably thinking he'd have to be careful not to damage any instruments and also to leave himself a good way to sue. Finally, he let the penis fall offstage and into the dirt. He flipped us off. Yes, indeed. You showed us Daniel.

The Mission came out together, each dressed in a vivid blue tunic, to sing a final chorus in Greek. Serik told me later that it was a retelling of the ancient traditions once held in that very spot. A time when flying off the stage while holding on to a penis was not only normal, it was expected. Serik's voice represented the phallus, Angelika's the muse. Kristine and Sal were the 'chorus', commenting on what the other two were singing about. It was accappella and SX sat there, stunned with the great voices and gestures of this group. They painted a picture with their voices. When they finished, a final sound was heard, muffled as if in the distance. A lone drum beating off. I mean if you listened hard, that was what it was.

I'm sad. The final performance of this tour. Many are leaving the day after tomorrow. Goodbye, fuck-fest, goodbye, Valerie. Never did really talk to you. Oh well. Goodbye, Slava. Goodbye, Leo.

Goodbye, Dave.

August 19

You wouldn't believe that after such an episode as recorded here earlier, D would be willing to talk. But he was. And not as a foe. Daniel, of his own accord, has agreed to come to my aid. (Frankly, I think the fact that I said I didn't want a thing from him, even the furniture, influenced this new selfless act.)

As I said, Dave has published my crotch on a pornographic Internet site. Oh yes. The fig – penetrated by him – is the pic that gets at least a thousand hits a day. Serik checked it out for me – not without a little gleam in his eye to show that I was indeed exciting. Faces are not revealed and I doubt that anyone, save a select few, might ever recognise the owner of that impaled crotch. But still, I did not give permission and I understand that the reason it is posted is not a sign of respect or even admiration. It's revenge, pure and simple. A strange kind, bred over years in conscious or subconscious recollections of an earlier era – but nonetheless, revenge.

This is what irks me and this is what Daniel, God knows how, understands. Perhaps it's what he himself is capable of. Maybe he regrets putting the photographer on me in the first place. In that case, I feel that Daniel nearly redeems himself in my eye and I can truthfully put on the divorce papers as reason for the procedure: Irreconcilable Differences.

Before, I had considered that maybe, under reasons

for separation, I would have simply put on the public document: husband is a philandering asshole.

Now, justice is what I crave, and Daniel atoning for his sins by promising to begin the lawsuit against Dave is a step in the right direction. And a reminder to me that help can come to one in just about any form, even a soon-to-be ex-husband. Oh, yes, Daniel has given up on us ever being together again. He's met Wendy, aka Cynthia. (JP ditched her after a few days.) I think the two are perfectly suited. There's even talk that she is going back with him to New York.

Well, best of luck to the happy pair. They both have no souls and the hearts they have rest in the smallest of cages. I imagine the sex to be great, not genuine. I can say now that I know the difference and have a pity for those who do not. I hinted I'm ready to forgive Daniel but am not so eager to forget the wrongs he did to my sexual self-esteem (what Slava once called self-steam – perhaps a better term).

Now that SX is coming to a close, I wonder what I've learned. Not sure that is even the right question. Do emotions have a timeline? Am I supposed to be entirely over the hurt of Daniel before I embark upon what may be the hurt of another?

Yes, this is about Sal. It has been about Sal all along. I sought him out after the last show, wanting to apologise that I missed the improvisation part he had given to me. Ryan told me that all it said was: 1st viola play for eight measures, key of D sharp minor. A shame I missed it, for now I do feel capable of playing things that are not written in black and white on the page. But who could look away from husband dumbfounded by giant prick?

The choice came and I didn't hesitate in the least. The tour is being extended to Ireland. Who would like to go?

And the winners are . . . me. Out of the entire orchestra. No joke. They had had it, being away from home, family, normal rooms. The Mission is going *sans* Angelika who has decided to go back to the Colorado and hang with his old flame, a man intensely concerned with the size of male anatomy and how to make his stand partner an instant best friend.

Ryan.

Yes, believe it. The two discovered they are as much in love with each other as they were in college. Want to work things out. Don't know who I'm more afraid for but it will be nice to visit them. One thing is for sure: that is not going to be a mundane relationship. Now I understand John's comment about Ryan, for he is a spendthrift and John has to be the queen of economy in all dragdom. I mean, he'd shit in a sausage casing and sell it back to the deli as bad meat.

Serik has gone back to Menorca and will meet up with us in a month. The diva is going to spend some more time in Sicily with Ted as her accomplice. She's gone with him to a resort outside Mount Iblei. Swears it is one of the most beautiful places on earth: once you pass the chemical factories, it's almonds and oranges all the way there. Slava is leaving the tour to go back to his magazine job. Said it's a major magazine and that I'm sure to recognise his writing and finally learn his real name. Thanked me for all the good times.

'Katie. You know, I meant it about being half in love with you.'

'I know. Which half?'

The Slav pointed to his crotch.

'Guess I need someone who is completely in love. But it was nice, Slava, aka Norton. It was really nice.'

We parted with a sweet brotherly kiss on the lips. Allan, his brother, on the other hand, would not take my handshake. He planted his lips firmly on mine and attempted to force his tongue through my unparted lips. Things got nasty when I didn't heed the thrust. Nasty. Just glared at me, turned sharply, and boarded the bus taking them to the airport.

Youth today.

August 29

I'd decided to stay an extra week in Syracuse. Enjoyed the peace in the convent, which made reflecting on my life easier. To tell the truth, spent about six hours doing that and then became quite bored with the melancholy torpor it left in my brain. How many times can you ask yourself if you're doing the right thing? I mean, you discover if you're really doing the right thing by doing it, right?

It took two days before Sal and I realised we were the only ones left in the monastery. Two more days before we were in each other's arms, murmuring sweet tidings to one another.

Ireland doesn't await us for another few weeks. Sicily so hot with desire. Travelled with Sal to a perfect establishment that sat on the edge of a perfectly intact Greek ampitheatre: Argrigento. Sunrise pierced the stage and then our balcony. Made love, of which shadows projected out from our nest into the hills, sighing with content and wonder. Made love at dawn behind corrugated pillar of Athena's temple. My knees were dusty and covered with fishnet-type lines from the temple floor stones. Feeling the air cool on Sal's cock before he thrust it into me from behind, hearing his breathing in this ancient, possibly quite sacred place, knowing we might be caught any minute ... well, it was the fastest orgasm I've ever had. Just imagining that the gods were standing all about us, witnessing this divine love, this glorious fucking – Sal came soon after me. I pulled back on that ever-increasingly dirty black dress and ran back up the hill after Sal to our room – our juices spilling out all the way.

I'm in love. Don't know if I've ever been before. Must be the nature of love – that it erases all who preceded. Still, astounding that every fibre in my being is alive in a way I never suspected possible. I swear, I can even hear Sicily as it moves away from the Italian boot and tries to form a completely independent continent of its own. I hear oranges ripening on the trees and can even imitate exactly the songs of certain birds that now answer me. Maybe Walt Disney was once in love – for my world now seems encrusted with magic. I want to talk to the trees, for I can't contain my spirit and happiness within the confines of this body alone. Seek Sal again and again for the release.

Sal touches me in a profound way – his hand on my cheek, his lips on my breasts. It seems a natural extension to our conversations. He has already admitted that he loves me. Admitted that he's afraid to say it too loudly, for I might bolt. Says he knew I was for him the minute he heard me play his music. Thought he was in love with me when we met on the bus. Admired my spunk, vivacity, and downright reckless way of living.

Don't know if I appreciate the reckless part. I've been careless, granted. But I am not a risk-taker with my heart. Oh, Sal is testing that one too.

After a week of pretending to be friends – without the slightest kiss – my lower half felt as if it might burst. Any conversation with Sal left my cunt longing to finish in exclamations what was started with mere words. Blood surged there and made it difficult to walk as we picked our way through the volcanic landscape of this beautiful island. We walked on the beach and watched the Joycean white-maned sea-horses gallop across the great ocean. We danced one night at a Greek settlement tavern where we drank ouzo and danced a rather odd dance with the owner, who clanged metal ashtrays together while his friends played the accordion. I played a fiddle that was offered and Sal a guitar and the owner danced his own teetering dance of mad liberty, inspired by the anise-tasting alcohol.

Oh, how my lower half throbbed thinking of this unrequited love it had formed for Sal. Sometimes he kissed my hair the way a father would a child's – which sent me into a rage of ecstasy. I did not want to be treated that way and yet, how I longed to return to our sweet night and day of unexpected, begged-for lovemaking. I had not forgotten that I had pleaded with him for that penetration in Menorca. Thought I'd imagined it had happened at all.

Sal even pretended to love another through all this. He spoke of Kristine in such tones that I thought he was bent on marrying her.

'She wears very provocative outfits, don't you think?' he asked me, glancing sideways with one green eye.

'Yes, Kristine has her own way of taking over a room,' I agreed.

'And any man in his right mind would want a woman like her.'

'So it seems.'

'She, so to speak, never hesitates to jump into any fountain, nor waits to make another jump at her bidding.' Both green eyes were upon me, piercing to the very core.

'I am not afraid to jump in, if that is what you're alluding to. I have more bravery in my heart than Kristine will ever have – though not that it matters.' Not sure that is true but I was indignant. To think of it, never in my life have I been refused what I desired. My fault lay in the object of that emotion, not in the carrying out of it.

'Oh, Katie. I know you have bravery. You're the prime example of an intrepid being. Outside. But what about inside? I hear you, you know.'

I knew exactly what he was alluding to but was uncomfortable to speak it. For as good as I had become at sex, I feared that I might not ever be good at intimacy. One could understand this from the way I'd thrown myself into performing in a way that I do not throw myself into with others. If I love a piece, it can course through me with an intensity I've seen in few other musicians. What my teacher loved about me at Julliard. I could be more intimate with my viola than I ever could with a human being.

Therapist!

Anyway, after some days, we kissed. So heavenly, this slow lip of Sal's. Hypnotising, as if he were speaking words to me with his tongue. Speaking my dreams to me and breathing into my soul. When he took me to bed, staring at me as he laid me down and gently caressed every inch of my skin with both eyes and fingers, I thought that the earth and the heavens smiled upon this pure, simple joy. So tender, I melted under his touch, like a lizard warms itself to the sun. I needed him to be around me just so I could continue to move.

When we came, me first, it flew through me like a huge sigh. The torture to that moment, the doubt, the jealousy of Kristine (oh, how foolish, I agree), the many men before Sal, seemed a brief second in the history of time and this orgasm – so longed for – a whole lifetime.

His orgasm, wrenched from the deepest place in his being, pounded through me with a penis seeming to gasp for air as it released its held back desire. Sal's moans were not like the moans from his sweet lips on those other occasions. These were without any restraint and with a boundless joy. He laughed after his orgasm, pulling me on top again so that I could look once more into those liquid orbs. I know – I'm so cliché. But they *were* liquid orbs.

'Oh, Katie. I am so happy you are here with me. I knew from the moment you played my music that you were going to be a very special person in my life. I just didn't know how special. Didn't dream it would be like this.' Here he thrust into me again, for he had grown while we looked into each other's eyes. I pulled up and pushed down on him, enjoying setting the pace of this. It wasn't long before sweet Sal came again and I fell over on our little Italian bed (they had put us in a room with two twin beds), exhausted and supremely satisfied.

Chapter Twenty-One

September 4

Alone again. Am I wise or the fool? Being careful by being reckless and now being reckless by being careful. Inside me, I feel like there's a trapped rat on a treadmill. Scurry, scurry.

Too intense. Like a honeymoon. Sal spoke once too often in a way that made me think we were fated to each other. Like we had to stay together for ever. I had already promised that once before to someone and look how it turned out. Those types of promises seem doomed in my life. Who says, as a species, we're supposed to be with one mate for ever anyway?

In Dublin now, wandering the streets I recognize from *Ulysses*. Should have read the book here. Would have saved myself a lot of time. Might have made sense. I am having own odyssey and it does not involve funerals and certainly not weddings. Involves a sort of belated coming of age. I mean, I am really in love this time and do not want to screw it up. That's why I ran away from him. Said goodbye to all my new friends (I really miss them! Got a postcard from

JP and another from John and Ryan) and left my lover back on a volcanic island with only this wish: Give me a week.

We were fucking six or seven times every day. My head is spinning still from the giddiness of it. Promises of 'I love you' and 'You're mine' poured from our lips. We stopped eating, continued consuming wine, ignored all communications except between ourselves (oh, that was world enough for me at the time). Like a perfect young love, full of wonder and lust – seeing the entire world expand in front of us and between our sheets. Drugged with happiness and satisfaction.

Too perfect. Felt inner-self drying up and merging with S's. I was becoming him. Don't know if he was becoming me but felt my will was his will and I would have jumped into the mouth of a crater had it pleased him. He wouldn't ask, I'm sure. But this insanity on my part. Only took one rearing of the head of the rational to make me run away to Dublin.

Not for long. Sal will be here in a week. Show starts in three. Vastly different type of show here. The immorality plays that he so loves for Europe are cast aside for sombre and mystical spectacles here. Sal craves now to not make his audience laugh as much as to make them weep. Suppose he's entitled. I mean, it is his island, after all. It's his party and he'll make you cry if he wants to – that sort of thing.

When Sal arrives, I think I'll know. I don't need much time but I do need to know that I am not leaping into something blindly. Already told Daniel it will be a long time before I return to the States. In a strange way, I'm doing in my thirties what I think should have happened in my twenties – though I wouldn't nearly be so grateful for it. It's this freedom to really be who I am. Not to ever squelch and squish my character. Musically, emotionally, sexually.

But not sure I know myself still. Or, should I say,

yet? Therein lies the rub. Perchance to dream, dear Katie.

September 14

S is here. I've never been happier. He doesn't care about forever. He cares about now. And now, I am with him in his lighthouse. That's right. Sal lives in an old lighthouse where he needs to be careful which rooms are lit at night so as not to disturb the ships passing. It's near James Joyce's turret, which he shared with the one crazy student who tried to shoot him. They say it was because he wasn't so faithful about paying the rent but who cares? Does history remember people for being unkempt or for being deadbeats? Btw, Sal is neither. But history remembers people like Sal for their art, the fecundity and the quality of it.

And I think history remembers great loves. Ours feels that way. Forgive the cliché, but when I'm with Sal, I feel the earth move. I jump in fountains and let their waters pour over my hot dusty head and I sing with joy.

I'll remember S as the one who taught me that a violist does not have to play by the book to make music.

Not that I am planning on turning Sal into a recollection anytime soon. I'm not stupid. I'm just profoundly in love. I'll accept each moment as it comes and if they string out into a lifetime of moments, so much the better. Not sure I'm up for living in Ireland for ever but not sure about living anywhere for ever. Important point is that it suits me now. With this bountiful heart, the States would seem so colourless, so void of green. And I am ripe. Lush.

Epilogue

September 30

*F*eel full of the lightest kind of happiness, skin flush
and tingling. Sal O'Brien. What a work of art!
Brimming over with life behind that dry humour.
More life than a horde of ants or a school playground.
More life than Daniel cubed. More life than Dave
diced.

But not more life than Katie – or at least, me with
him. Keep pondering Norton's writing on energy quo-
tients. How each person we come in contact with
either adds to us or takes away from our very being –
and not always of their own choice. A bit like the old
Serbian evil eye my grandmother warned me against.
'Don't you get enn da ray uff dat light from evil eye,
it knock you dead. Maybe cold, maybe miscarriage
but one way or nother, eet vill keel you.' Granny
believed one could possess this fated aperture and not
even realise that you were unknowingly causing great
harm to another just by your glance. Hmm – wonder
if that was what Dave thought about my eye, for I still
do not understand his motivations. Thankful that Dan-

iel is helping – uncomfortable with it, to be honest – but still thankful that the employer is unravelling his employee on my account. Maybe he really has changed his ways. We'll see when the divorce gets finalised.

Anyway, the point of this is that S adds to me and I feel so comfortable with him – more than comfortable, I just feel like I'm myself. And it's sexy. A very different kind of sexy but, with a lover who is so creative, one man is fine with me. Each lovemaking is magic. And I see no end in sight. He's vast. He contains multitudes and I could love him for a very long time. Didn't know this contact, this closeness is what I've been craving all my life.

Don't get me wrong. Not a single sex regret do I own regarding this fabulously liberating tour. Felt as if I finally claimed my body for myself and now, when I give it to S, it comes with a sort of independence. As if it, not even my brain but my body itself, *knows* that this man stands alone from all the others. That he is my happiness and I his. Disgusting stuff to write but, well, it's the truth. Sorry.

BLACK LACE NEW BOOKS

Published in June

SUMMER FEVER
Anna Ricci
£6.99

Lara Mcintyre has lusted after artist Jake Fitzgerald for almost two decades. As a warm, dazzling summer unfolds, she makes the journey back to her student summer-house where they first met, determined to satisfy her physical craving somehow. And then, ensconced in Old Beach House once more, she discovers her true sexual self – but not without complications.

Beautifully written story of extreme passion.

ISBN 0 352 33625 0

STRICTLY CONFIDENTIAL
Alison Tyler
£6.99

Carolyn Winters is a smooth-talking disc jockey at a hip LA radio station. Although known for her sexy banter over the airwaves, she leads a reclusive life, despite the urging of her flirtatious roommate, Dahlia. Carolyn grows dependent on living vicariously through Dahlia, eavesdropping and then covertly watching as her roommate's sexual behaviour becomes more and more bizarre. But then Dahlia is murdered, and Carolyn must overcome her fears in order to bring the killer to justice.

A tense dark thriller for those who like their erotica on the forbidden side.

ISBN 0 352 33624 2

CONTINUUM
Portia Da Costa
£6.99

Joanna Darrell is something in the city. When she takes a break from her high-powered job she is drawn into a continuum of strange experiences and bizarre coincidences. Like Alice in a decadent Wonderland, she enters a parallel world of perversity and unusual pleasure. She's attracted to fetishism and discipline and her new friends make sure she gets more than a taste of erotic punishment.

This is a reprint of one of our best-selling and kinkiest titles ever!

ISBN 0 352 33120 8

Published in July

SYMPHONY X
Jasmine Stone
£6.99

Katie is a viola player running away from her cheating husband. The tour of Symphony Xevertes not only takes her to Europe but also to the realm of deep sexual satisfaction. She is joined by a dominatrix diva and a bass singer whose voice is so low he's known as the Human Vibrator. After distractions like these, how will Katie be able to maintain her serious music career *and* allow herself to fall in love again?

Immensely funny journal of a sassy woman's sexual adventures.

ISBN 0 352 33629 3

OPENING ACTS
Suki Cunningham
£6.99

When London actress Holly Parker arrives in a remote Cornish village to begin rehearsing a new play, everyone there – from her landlord to her theatre director – seems to have an earthier attitude towards sex. Brought to a state of constant sexual arousal and confusion, Holly seeks guidance in the form of local therapist, Joshua Delaney. He is the one man who can't touch her – but he is the only one she truly desires. Will she be able to use her new-found sense of adventure to seduce him?

Wonderfully horny action in the Cornish countryside. Oooh arrgh!

ISBN 0 352 33630 7

THE SEVEN-YEAR LIST
Zoe le Verdier
£6.99

Julia is an ambitious young photographer who's about to marry her trustworthy but dull fiancé. Then an invitation to a college reunion arrives. Old rivalries, jealousies and flirtations are picked up where they were left off and sexual tensions run high. Soon Julia finds herself caught between two men but neither of them are her fiancé.

How will she explain herself to her friends? And what decisions will she make?

This is a Black Lace special reprint of a very popular title.

ISBN 0 352 33254 9

Published in August

MINX
Megan Blythe
£6.99

Spoilt Amy Pringle arrives at Lancaster Hall to pursue her engagement to Lord Fitzroy, eldest son of the Earl and heir to a fortune. The Earl is not impressed, and sets out to break her spirit. But the trouble for him is that she enjoys every one of his 'punishments' and creates havoc, provoking the stuffy Earl at every opportunity. The young Lord remains aloof, however, and, in order to win his affections, Amy sets about seducing his well-endowed but dim brother, Bubb. When she is discovered in bed with Bubb and a servant girl, how will father and son react?

**Immensely funny and well-written tale of lust among
decadent aristocrats.**

ISBN 0 352 33638 2

FULL STEAM AHEAD
Tabitha Flyte
£6.99

Sophie wants money, big money. After twelve years working as a croupier on the Caribbean cruise ships, she has devised a scheme that is her ticket to Freedomsville. But she can't do it alone; she has to encourage her colleagues to help her. Persuasion turns to seduction, which turns to blackmail. Then there are prying passengers, tropical storms and an angry, jealous girlfriend to contend with. And what happens when the lascivious Captain decides to stick his oar in, too?

**Full of gold-digging women, well-built men in uniform
and Machiavellian antics.**

ISBN 0 352 33637 4

A SECRET PLACE
Ella Broussard
£6.99

Maddie is a busy girl with a dream job: location scout for a film company. When she's double-booked to work on two features at once, she needs to manage her time very carefully. Luckily, there's no shortage of fit young men, in both film crews, who are willing to help. She also makes friends with the locals, including a horny young farmer and a particularly handy mechanic. The only person she's not getting on with is Hugh, the director of one of the movies. Is that because sexual tension between them has reached breaking point?

This story of lust during a long hot English summer is another Black Lace special reprint.

ISBN 0 352 33307 3

If you would like a complete list of plot summaries of Black Lace titles, or would like to receive information on other publications available, please send a stamped addressed envelope to:

Black Lace, Thames Wharf Studios,
Rainville Road, London W6 9HA

BLACK LACE BOOKLIST

Information is correct at time of printing. To avoid disappointment check availability before ordering. Go to www.blacklace-books.co.uk

All books are priced £5.99 unless another price is given.

Black Lace books with a contemporary setting

THE TOP OF HER GAME	Emma Holly ISBN 0 352 33337 5	☐
IN THE FLESH	Emma Holly ISBN 0 352 33498 3	☐
SHAMELESS	Stella Black ISBN 0 352 33485 1	☐
TONGUE IN CHEEK	Tabitha Flyte ISBN 0 352 33484 3	☐
FIRE AND ICE	Laura Hamilton ISBN 0 352 33486 X	☐
SAUCE FOR THE GOOSE	Mary Rose Maxwell ISBN 0 352 33492 4	☐
INTENSE BLUE	Lyn Wood ISBN 0 352 33496 7	☐
THE NAKED TRUTH	Natasha Rostova ISBN 0 352 33497 5	☐
A SPORTING CHANCE	Susie Raymond ISBN 0 352 33501 7	☐
TAKING LIBERTIES	Susie Raymond ISBN 0 352 33357 X	☐
A SCANDALOUS AFFAIR	Holly Graham ISBN 0 352 33523 8	☐
THE NAKED FLAME	Crystalle Valentino ISBN 0 352 33528 9	☐
CRASH COURSE	Juliet Hastings ISBN 0 352 33018 X	☐
ON THE EDGE	Laura Hamilton ISBN 0 352 33534 3	☐
LURED BY LUST	Tania Picarda ISBN 0 352 33533 5	☐

Black Lace books with an historical setting

Black Lace anthologies

Black Lace non-fiction

------------✂------------------------

Please send me the books I have ticked above.

Name ....

Address ....

....

....

.... Post Code ....

Send to: Cash Sales, Black Lace Books, Thames Wharf Studios, Rainville Road, London W6 9HA.

US customers: for prices and details of how to order books for delivery by mail, call 1-800-805-1083.

Please enclose a cheque or postal order, made payable to **Virgin Publishing Ltd**, to the value of the books you have ordered plus postage and packing costs as follows:

UK and BFPO – £1.00 for the first book, 50p for each subsequent book.

Overseas (including Republic of Ireland) – £2.00 for the first book, £1.00 for each subsequent book.

If you would prefer to pay by VISA, ACCESS/MASTER-CARD, DINERS CLUB, AMEX or SWITCH, please write your card number and expiry date here:

....

Please allow up to 28 days for delivery.

Signature ....

------------✂------------------------